THE BLOOD MOON

A Novel

David Neth

DN Publishing

The Blood Moon
Copyright © 2015 by David Neth
East Pembroke, NY
www.davidnethbooks.com

Subscribe to the author's newsletter for updates and exclusive content:
tinyurl.com/nkkxenq

Publisher: David Neth
Copyediting: Tammy Salyer of Inspired Ink Editing
Proofreading: Kiersten Deuel and Maria Garguilo
Cover Design: Jelena Gajic and Slobodan Cedic

ISBN 978-0-9905177-0-2
First edition

Follow the author at:
www.facebook.com/davidnethbooks
www.twitter.com/davidnethbooks
www.instagram.com/dneth13

To Ms. Early,
For planting the first publishing seed…

PROLOGUE

The sun rose as the small town of Salem, New York was waking up and shuffling off to work. The rain from the night before left the town glistening, capturing the light of the sunrise.

A puddle rippled and a woman's body emerged. Her bold green hair and eccentric clothing made her stand out in the traditional small town. Lifting her stiletto-booted foot up, she kicked in the door to a nearby house and made her way inside.

The woman's name was Toxanna, an evil witch who had declared a death sentence on the Bowen family. She stood just inside Danielle Bowen's front door. Danielle was the next victim on Toxanna's list, and she always outdid her victims.

Danielle's husband, Simon, was working on getting his restaurant started. He was spending today doing interviews for his future employees. Danielle, who was six months pregnant, was busy getting her future daughter's room ready for the new arrival. Blasting the radio and singing along upstairs, Danielle couldn't hear Toxanna enter.

In the living room, Toxanna glanced around at the decor. Everything was quiet and still, save for the music upstairs. The room was painted blue with white trim, and photos cluttered the walls and end tables. She focused on the photo in the center of the room featuring Danielle in an elaborate white wedding dress, smiling from ear to ear and hanging off Simon's arm. The newlyweds disgusted Toxanna, and she spit on the picture.

Toxanna's husband, Dragonox, appeared next to her in a flash of lightning. He immediately pulled out his wand and held it up, ready to use magic at any moment.

"Easy now. We'll find the witch." She spoke in a calm yet malicious tone.

Dragonox was a dark wizard. Toxanna was a witch. The only difference was that Dragonox needed help to focus his magic, and the wand provided that help. Toxanna, however, didn't need that assistance because she was a witch. She could focus her magic without any outside assistance. Her specialty was water magic, while Dragonox's was electricity.

Dragonox and Toxanna were some of the most sinister evils that roamed the universe. They were vicious and deadly and had vowed to kill every last Bowen since Pamela Bowen had attacked them in the 1930s. Dragonox and Toxanna kept their promise, slaughtering everyone somehow related to the Bowens since. The Bowens had put up a strong fight, but Dragonox and Toxanna eventually got every one of them. Now the only witches left in their crosshairs were Danielle Bowen, her husband, and their unborn baby.

Today, Toxanna was focusing on Danielle's baby. Danielle knew of her constant danger and usually kept to a crowd for protection. But spending every day at a grocery store or library was getting daunting, and she needed to get the baby's room ready. More for her sanity than productivity.

Danielle wasn't stupid. She placed all the standard protection charms and amulets in order to ensure her safety. The trouble with amulets was that they weren't always effective. If the wind blew it out of alignment or a stray cat thought it was a new toy to play with, the protection would be gone. Danielle's magic was experiencing the same ups and downs as her hormones, and so her charms weren't always effective. She should have made her husband place them, but she wanted to surprise him with the finished room. Not to mention, she wanted to save the lecture on why she needed to stay in crowded places.

Toxanna led her husband throughout the house searching for Danielle. She knew her enemy was home. The spell the witch had cast led her straight to Danielle's house. This was the first time in months that Danielle was alone, and Toxanna needed to act quickly.

As she slowly stalked throughout the house, she thought of her children. Zamball was already three years old. He was showing signs of magic, but it was obvious he was going to need a wand to channel it, just like his father. Devon, however, was Toxanna's stepson and only a few months older than Zamball. Devon was the result of one of Dragonox's trysts with his many lovers before Toxanna had enchanted him. Without an ounce of maternal instinct in her, Toxanna saw both Zamball and Devon as future warriors in her growing demonic empire.

Toxanna slowly crept up the stairs and around the corner into Danielle's workspace. There were old sheets on the floor and buckets of pink paint in the corner. Danielle was sitting on a stool stenciling in alphabet letters along the middle of the wall. Boxes of furniture that had yet to be assembled lined the opposite wall. The radio was perched on a step stool and covered in paint.

Danielle's black hair was pulled back into a ponytail, and she wore ripped jeans and an old T-shirt. Her round belly was prominent. She stood and placed a hand on her back, admiring her work.

When Dragonox joined Toxanna upstairs, one of the floorboards creaked.

Danielle spun around and saw her archenemies standing in the doorway. She was cornered.

Toxanna immediately held up her hands and shot water at Danielle's feet. The water then froze, and Danielle was stuck to the floor. She tried to use her power of cryokinesis, or ice manipulation, to unfreeze it, but it didn't respond the way it normally would, thanks to her pregnancy.

Toxanna couldn't help smiling. "Seems a little anticlimactic, after all these years. You slip up once, and it not only costs you your life, but your baby's as well."

Danielle wrapped one arm around her belly. "You're not going to touch my baby."

Dragonox lit a stick of sage and circled around Danielle, waving the incense in her face, muttering a charm to himself. Toxanna pulled out a candle, kneeled on the floor, and lit it.

Dragonox reached for Danielle's arm, but she swatted him away as best she could.

"Don't fight it," Toxanna urged as her husband pulled out a small knife and slide it across Danielle's arm, drawing blood. He handed the knife over to Toxanna, who tilted it and dripped some of Danielle's blood into the flame.

Reaching her hands out, palms facing Danielle, Toxanna recited:

The child you bear,
will be abandoned without care.
The spell that I weave,
will make me conceive!

A green light flashed between Toxanna's hands and Danielle's abdomen.

Within seconds, Danielle's large belly subsided, and she brought both hands to it. She was no longer pregnant.

Toxanna, however, was. Her stomach stuck out, and she suddenly felt weak in the knees.

Dragonox caught her with one hand and pointed his wand

at Danielle with the other. He shot a lightning bolt at her, but she created an ice shield. As soon as the lightning bolt hit the shield it shattered. Now without her baby, her powers were back to normal.

Danielle put up her hands and sent ice crystals flying toward Toxanna and Dragonox, but before the crystals could reach them, the evil pair disappeared in a flash of lightning.

With tears streaming down her cheeks, Danielle frantically ripped her cell phone out of her pocket and called her husband.

Before he even answered, she shouted, "Toxanna! Toxanna has our baby!"

"What!?" Danielle could hear the panic in his voice. He took a deep breath. "Danielle, calm down, we'll get her back. Stay there, I'll be home in ten minutes, max."

Danielle hung up the phone. She knelt down to work on her feet. They were freezing, but with her baby gone, Danielle felt numb. She couldn't use her cryokinesis to get rid of the ice blocks because her power only created the ice. Luckily, it was warm outside. The ice was already starting to melt. She put the lid back on the bucket of paint and then used the paint to break open the ice.

Prior to Toxanna's declaration of death upon the family, the Bowens weren't prominent or very powerful witches. The Bowens were the ones at the carnivals, giving out psychic predictions or performing "illusions" to entertain the crowds. However, that changed in 1932 when Pamela Bowen decided to take a stand and stop Toxanna from killing people who were severely suffering from the Great Depression. Since then, the Bowens had saved notebooks and scraps of papers with spells, enchantments, potions, and charms in order to maintain some sort of record of successes and failures with their magic.

Now that Danielle was free, she raced to her bedroom closet to retrieve her family's notes. She needed to find a way to return her baby, using white magic.

Danielle looked them over while she soaked her feet in lukewarm water.

When Simon got home, she was just drying off in the bathroom.

"Do you have the potion?" Simon asked. They were prepared with teleportation potions to go to Toxanna whenever she attacked. They never knew when they'd have to teleport. Since neither of them had a teleportation power, and Toxanna frequently moved her hideouts, the potions became a necessity.

"Got it!" Danielle had already gotten the potion from the kitchen cupboard with the rest of their potion stock. She jammed her feet into her shoes without bothering to put socks on. She gulped down half of the potion and gave the rest to Simon. After they both had some, they disappeared in a flash of white light.

* * *

When Danielle and Simon reappeared, they were next to a warehouse near Lake Champlain. This had been Toxanna's hideout for a few months now. She usually stayed in one place until one of her plans failed. Since Simon and Danielle were the strongest couple Toxanna had fought in the Bowen family, she was often moving her lair because Simon and Danielle had fended her off every time—until today.

Danielle entered and her husband was close behind. They made their way past the stacks of shipping supplies and found the center of the building.

In the middle of the floor, a hole of water shimmered through from the lake. Toxanna, Dragonox, and the rest of their cronies were gathered around.

All attention was on Danielle and Simon when they stormed in.

"Toxanna, give me my baby back!" Danielle was not about to lose her baby.

"I'm sorry, sugar, but you're not getting this baby back," Toxanna said. "You can see her in hell when she dies. This child is mine now." Toxanna stroked her round belly, smiling at Danielle.

"I'm not going to let you sacrifice my child for some twisted curse of yours." Danielle scowled.

"That wasn't my plan," Toxanna said. "I actually was thinking about raising her in the dark arts."

"Like hell you will!" Simon usually grew weary around Toxanna, but now he didn't care if he died trying to save his daughter.

"Dragonox, I'm feeling a bit tired. Get rid of these visitors so I can take a nap." When Toxanna spoke to her husband, she spoke in a seductive, evil tone.

The Blood Moon

Dragonox and the rest of the minions poised to attack Danielle and Simon.

Simon threw a potion in front of them that put up a force field to protect them against the attack.

Danielle conjured an ice sword and said, "If that bitch wants a fight, then it's a fight she'll get."

She took off toward the southern wall of the building and ran along the outer wall in pursuit of Toxanna. Meanwhile, Simon hurled potions at his enemies, fending off any more attackers from following his wife.

Danielle stopped a moment to catch her breath and saw that Toxanna was walking above her on a platform.

She found the ladder and climbed up to the platform, tracking Toxanna. Danielle couldn't believe how fast she was running without the baby, and she knew that Toxanna wasn't doing as well.

Finally, Danielle caught up with Toxanna at the end of the platform.

"Had enough?" she asked, letting out a deep breath with her words.

"I'm just getting started," Toxanna hissed.

Toxanna tried to conjure a ball of water, but the water didn't stick together. Instead, it dripped off her hand.

"That's one thing about being pregnant with a magical child. When your baby's gaining its magic, yours isn't as responsive." Danielle made a swift move to stab Toxanna but pulled back, worrying that if Toxanna died, her baby would too.

Dragonox suddenly appeared in front of Toxanna and started throwing lightning bolts at Danielle.

Danielle ducked them as best she could on the skinny platform. She fired ice crystals at Dragonox, but the ice bounced off the brute without inflicting any damage. As they sparred, she continued to walk backward on the platform until she was cornered. She conjured an ice sword and swung to slice open Dragonox's midsection, but he moved swiftly, knocking the blade out of her hand. With nowhere left to turn, Danielle ran through rhymes in her head to save her. In the meantime, Dragonox had picked up her ice sword and drove it into Danielle's stomach, turning it and watching the pain and horror cross her face.

Simon was a moment too late. He ran up to his wife, just as Dragonox pulled the sword out of Danielle. There wasn't anything he could've done.

Toxanna, who had walked up behind her husband, dropped her head back and cackled, "Haha! I've done it! That witch is out of the way, and there are only two left."

As the realization crossed Simon's mind, he grabbed the handrail of the platform for support as he grew weak in the knees. Dragonox took advantage of this and put his wand to Simon's neck. "Is there any particular poison you want injected?" he asked his wife.

Simon grabbed the wand, snapped it in half, and threw it off the side of the platform. He pulled out three potions and threw them at Dragonox.

Dragonox's skin started to boil, melting off his body, leaving his skin to drip from the platform. His body continued to burn until he was a shriveled mess.

Out of attacking potions, Simon lunged at Toxanna, punching her in the face and knocking her out. He knew he had to come up with a spell to get his baby back, but with her mother dead, there wasn't a womb for the baby to go. He was going to have to watch Toxanna closely and devise a plan to get the baby back once she was born.

In the meantime, he needed to get his wife's body back home. He picked Danielle up gently and drank a potion that returned them home.

CHAPTER ONE

Samantha rushed in the front door. She dropped her bag and called up the stairs to her sister.

"Kathy! Get the boys and the book and meet me in the kitchen," she yelled as she walked by the stairs and into the kitchen. Pulling her brown hair into a ponytail, she pulled up her sleeves and readied a pot of water on the stove to boil.

Kathy and the boys met her in the kitchen. Samantha's younger sister was a strikingly beautiful woman, someone who didn't need to do much to get attention from men. Not that it mattered much to Kathy, who was still married to Will.

"You guys ready to use your magic?" Samantha asked the boys.

"But, Mom, I don't have powers yet," Chris, the younger one, whined. He had always been the more adventurous between him and his brother. He held a large leather tome under his arm and placed it on the kitchen table.

Always ready to use his magic, Chris was more than a little discouraged that at fourteen years old, he hadn't developed any sign of his own active powers yet. Instead, he focused on the inherent magic that all witches had: the ability to cast spells.

That wasn't enough for Chris, though. Although he had become a great spellcaster and had a knack for coming up with quick and effective charms or spells, he didn't want to be one of those witches that relied on spells for every bit of magic. He was already quite jealous of the fact that his brother, Josh, had developed the power to control the wind. Granted, it was more of a short gust that he was able to produce, but Chris knew Josh was going to practice and perfect his craft until he grew stronger and his specialty enhanced.

"It'll happen soon enough, Chris," Samantha said, putting a hand on his shoulder. "I can sense it." Samantha had the power of the mind. What started off as simple persuasion evolved into mind manipulation. With some weaker-minded individuals, she was even able to completely erase their memory. It wasn't the flashiest specialty, but it certainly came in handy. Especially when she was able to reach into the minds of some of the lower-level demons and dark witches and control their powers to use against them. Sadly, the evils she faced nowadays were too strong-willed for that.

"What's up, Mom?" asked Josh. He was the leader, the responsible one, the one to think things over before rushing into an attack. Unfortunately, this also meant that he was a little more timid to attack. With his specialty focusing on the wind, he could develop that power into great things.

"Aunt Kathy had a vision," she said, opening the book and flipping through it. Kathy had the specialty of time. Her power had matured so that she was not only clairvoyant but could also stop time and travel through it. Her visions often led them to a new case.

Samantha pushed the book toward her sister. "I don't know exactly what I'm looking for." She turned her attention back to the pot of water, which had just started to boil.

Kathy skimmed through the pages of *The Art of Magic*, their leather-bound magic book, a tool that had been in their family for years through the various magical battles with all things sinister. "A man will be murdered by some creature with a giant sword for an arm. The creature has a lot of piercings and tattoos on his face. He…" She hesitated, not sure how descriptive to be with her nephews. "…uh…decapitates the man."

"Did you see when it is supposed to happen?" Samantha asked, throwing some essential potion elements into the pot. Her grandfather had taught her how to make potions. She had even dubbed herself The Potions Master.

Kathy nodded. "Luckily, there was a clock in my vision. It will be about one this afternoon." The hardest part about Kathy's visions was nailing down the correct time. Whenever a supernatural murder had occurred, there wasn't always a clock conveniently located so she could see.

THE BLOOD MOON

"Does this mean we don't have to go to school?" Chris was hopeful. He was always looking for an excuse to stay home. Especially if he was staying home to use magic.

"You're still going," Samantha said. "Just be prepared to leave early." She turned to her sister. "What am I putting in this potion?"

"I'll pick them up," Kathy offered.

"Thanks, but I'll pass," Samantha snapped. She decided to make a standard run-of-the-mill potion for a midlevel demon. She guessed by Kathy's description that this was what they were dealing with. They probably wouldn't even need the boys, but she wanted them as a buffer between her and her sister.

Kathy rolled her eyes and continued flipping through the book. She stopped and turned it to Samantha. "Here he is."

Samantha asked Josh to reach in the top cupboard for a spice for her, and she threw a dash in. "I'll have to pick up more rosemary when I take the boys to school."

"Sammy, we're going to have to talk about this sooner or later," Kathy pushed.

"Boys," Samantha said, turning to her sons, "why don't you brush your teeth and finish getting ready for school. I'll be ready in ten minutes."

Josh and Chris shuffled out of the kitchen. As the door swung shut, Samantha stared at her sister. "You need to be more careful."

"They need to know," Kathy insisted. "Yes, I screwed up. Of course I'm sorry, but I don't think hiding it from them is going to do them any good."

"They don't need to know that their aunt, their own flesh and blood, offered them up as sacrifices for her demonic marriage to a Dark Knight," Samantha spat. She had one hand on her hip and the other lying on the kitchen table.

"Don't tell them all the details, then. But don't you think they suspected something was up when I virtually disappeared for a few weeks, and then when I suddenly returned, you have a grudge against me?"

"They don't notice that." Samantha waved her hand and pretended to look at the book.

"You're not that good of an actress, Samantha. I'm not saying that you should make an excuse for me, but I think it's important that they know how easily and how deep you can slip into the darkness," Kathy reasoned. "I don't want them to hate me for what I did, but it is what it is."

Samantha stared at the book, not willing to look her sister in the eyes. She knew Kathy was right. The boys deserved to know. And it would be a great way to warn them about evil. But she didn't want to scar them. She already stayed up at night worrying that she was corrupting them by bringing them into battle with her. Ultimately, she knew it would do them well. Set them up for adulthood when they could have these years of experience and guidance to go off of.

Finally, she looked at her sister. "You stay here and make the potion, and I'll take them to school." She left before Kathy could respond.

The Blood Moon

* * *

Samantha had returned with a paper bag of herbs and spices to restock their potion ingredient supply.

"Hey, did you get my text about the sage and the juniper berries?" Kathy asked. She was hunched over the magic book, studying their latest enemy.

"Yeah," Samantha said curtly. She hauled the bag onto the kitchen table and removed items to put away.

"I can get those." Kathy pulled the bag to her.

"No, it's fine." Samantha tried to yank the bag away from her sister's grip, but it started to tear. "Fine. Did you finish the potion?"

"Mm-hmm," Kathy hummed as she reached on her tiptoes to the spice rack. They liked to keep the potion spices at the top of the cupboard just in case any of their mortal friends came over.

"I told the boys I'd pick them up at noon—" Samantha was cut off by a knock at the back door. She turned and saw that it was Will, Kathy's husband. The reason for their falling out.

"I swear, I didn't know he was coming. I told him to stay away from you and the boys," Kathy explained. She got up to answer the door anyway.

"Are you still seeing him?" Samantha seethed. After everything, Kathy still hadn't told Will that it was over. Samantha felt the pain of the betrayal all over again.

Before Kathy could answer, the door opened and Will

stepped through. A reasonably attractive man, he looked about five or so years older than Kathy. Definitely her type. Samantha wasn't sure of his actual age, since Dark Knights typically lived for hundreds of years. She was guessing he was at least fifty years older than he looked. It wouldn't surprise her if he was even older yet.

"What the hell are you doing here?" Samantha demanded. She had never wished for an attack specialty more than this moment.

"I heard that you were going to be attacked by one of the Queen's best men," Will explained. "I thought I'd drop by and offer my expertise."

"We don't work with evil, and we don't want word to spread that we do," snapped Samantha.

"Samantha!" Kathy warned as she glared at her sister.

"No, I get it," Will said, then added, "Well, not really…"

"That's a surprise," Samantha said sarcastically as she rolled her eyes. She stood with her arms crossed and stared him straight in the eyes.

Will groaned and threw his hands up in exasperation. "I don't understand why you're refusing help! Sure, you say I'm evil, but I'll be of help to you, so what does it matter?"

"Get out of my house!" Samantha screamed. "I don't want to see you near my sister, near my children, or near this house ever again!"

"Will, sweetie," Kathy said, trying to stop Will from getting mad. He ignored her as he glared at Samantha. In an even, menacing tone he warned, "You'd better change that attitude, because if you don't focus on the task at hand, then Garmond will destroy you."

"Garmond?" Kathy asked. "That's his name?" The book didn't mention a name.

"If you really want to help us, just give us his location," Samantha said, giving in to Will's presence. She knew Kathy had no idea where to find this guy. Her vision showed the inside of his office, not a lot to go on.

"I thought you wanted me to leave?"

"Leave or stay, I don't give a damn. But if you stay, you're going to help us."

"I'll help you in my own way, on my own terms," replied Will. "I'm not sure where he is, but I do know that he's not very well protected at the moment. We can find him."

"I want you to look me in the eye and tell me that you're not going to screw us like you have in the past," Samantha said. Will didn't say anything, so she added, "If you help, you follow our terms. Do you understand me?"

Will held Samantha's stare for a while before speaking up. "I will try to find out his plan of attack." He kissed Kathy on the cheek. "I'll see you later, baby," he said and walked out the back door.

"I don't understand why you just don't break up with him," Samantha snapped. "After all he put you and our family through. Kathy, this is serious."

Kathy bit her lip. "I know. But I can't help it, I love him. I just want to be with him."

Samantha was disgusted with her sister. "I can't even look at you. I really hope whatever spell he has on you gets broken soon." She grabbed her keys out of her purse and headed out the front door. "I'm going to pick up the boys. Finish that potion, and call me if anything happens."

* * *

As Samantha and the boys ascended the front steps to their doorway, they saw the front doors ripped off the hinges.

"Careful," Samantha warned as she led her children into the house. The furniture was thrown throughout the room, glass and fabric scattered everywhere.

Samantha used her power to sense if Kathy was in the house. If she concentrated enough, she could broaden the scope of her telepathic specialties to read any minds nearby. She breathed a sigh of relief when she recognized Kathy's thoughts.

"Kathy?" Samantha called throughout the house.

"Be quiet!" Kathy hushed, walking out of the kitchen. "He's knocked out in my bedroom."

"How did he end up in your bedroom?" Samantha asked. She put up her hand. "Never mind." That was a can of worms she didn't want to get into. "Are you okay?"

Kathy nodded. "Yeah, but he must've known what kind of potion we were making, and he threw it on the floor. So that's gone."

"Damn," Samantha breathed. "Okay, we need another plan. Maybe a spell or something. He seems midlevel, right?" She hated to ask Kathy to call Will for help, but she was running out of time to consider other options.

Kathy shrugged. "I thought so, but maybe somebody supercharged him or something. He was going for the kill, that's for sure."

There was a crash upstairs. They heard some murmurs, as if two people were talking.

"It's just Garmond up there, right?" Samantha asked her sister, staring at the ceiling.

"It was…" Kathy's voiced trailed off, wondering how long the second intruder had been in the house.

"Let's go get him!" Chris was exuberant as he headed for the stairs.

"I don't think so," responded Samantha, pulling on the back of Chris's shirt. "You boys stay back."

A tall man with piercings and tribal markings tattooed all over his face and arms strolled down the stairs. He smiled. His left arm was a sword from his elbow down to where his hand was supposed to be. He had two leathery black wings folded neatly on his back.

"That's Garmond?" Samantha asked no one in particular. Her heart beat a little faster as she realized she had no way of winning this battle.

Chris took a step back and squealed, "Mom, kill him!"

"Any ideas?" Samantha muttered to her sister. Despite her

anger toward her for everything with Will, they still made an impeccable team.

"Stabbing him doesn't work," Kathy said. "He'll just heal himself."

"So we need to do a quick kill," Josh said, "and make sure it sticks."

Will ran through the ruins of the front door. "Stand back!" He put out his hand and ushered Samantha, Kathy, and the boys back farther into the next room as he conjured a sword. As a Dark Knight, Will was able to conjure many useful battle implements, such as a sword or a shield. It also granted him eternal life, unless he was murdered. Dark Knights were often used as bodyguards and spies for demonic emperors. Will was currently a free agent, not committed to anyone's protection.

Garmond leaped from the stairs and moved to strike Will with his sword-arm. Will conjured a shield on his arm and blocked the attack. Samantha wasn't convinced that Garmond's attempt was as honest as it could have been. She wondered if Will was trying to play both sides still.

"Stupid knight!" Garmond shouted. "You will pay for your betrayal!"

His first lunge on Will having failed, Garmond turned on the others. Kathy dove out of the way, and Josh and Chris ran into the living room. Samantha was not about to run. Since she had no active powers, she made sure she was fit and skilled at fighting.

Jumping in the air, she threw her foot against Garmond's

chest, knocking him to the floor.

"Will, pass me the sword!" she called as she circled Garmond, who struggled to get up off the floor.

Will hesitated, but Kathy shouted at him, "Give her the sword!"

He tossed it in the air, and Samantha caught it one-handed and swung it in front of her. This was not her first time handling a weapon like this.

Kathy was not about to let her sister take on this demonic soldier by herself. She told Will to take care of the boys and ran to her sister's aid.

Samantha and Garmond sparred in the foyer as Kathy approached from behind. She jumped, grabbing ahold of the light fixture on the ceiling, and kicked Garmond in the back with both feet.

Garmond staggered but didn't fall. Instead he swung and missed Kathy's midsection, only tearing the front of her blouse.

"No!" Will hollered and ran to his wife.

"Will, it's fine," Kathy urged. "I'm all right." Kneeling beside her, Will blocked her view of the ongoing attack.

Swinging the sword in the air a few times, Samantha readied herself for another attack from Garmond. If he charged, she was ready. She saw out of the corner of her eye that Josh and Chris were hiding out in the next room. She almost wished Josh was more confident with his powers and could help her out, but she hated to ask. She didn't want to put her kids in danger.

"C'mon, give me what you've got." Samantha beckoned.

Garmond charged and she parried his attack, lifting her sword and using her free hand to push on the flat part of the blade against Garmond's. In a swift move, he knocked the sword out of her hand and it went sliding across the floor away from everyone.

Kathy struggled to get up, but Will pushed her back. "I'll take care of it."

Standing, Will turned to Garmond. "Hey!"

Garmond turned toward Will. Samantha moved to grab the sword, but Will conjured it into his hand. "Why don't you pick on someone who is a little more skilled at swordfighting, huh?"

Garmond sent another attack at Will, and they squared off. The room was silent save for the clanging swords.

Samantha and Kathy rushed to the boys.

"Do you think we can come up with a spell?" Kathy asked.

"I don't know; do you think you could freeze him so we could recreate the potion?" Samantha asked.

Kathy shook her head. "It wouldn't be enough time. My magic would wear off before the potion was done."

They heard furniture crashing as Will and Garmond made their way through the next room.

"Maybe we should just run?" Josh asked.

"No," Samantha said. "He came here for a reason." She looked at her sister. "I don't get it, your vision showed that he was killing someone else at this time. How did he end up here?"

Kathy shrugged. "I don't know! Maybe he got different orders? These things can change."

THE BLOOD MOON

There was a loud thud, and the four witches turned to see Garmond turn on them. Will was in the corner, lying still.

"Oh, Will!" Kathy cried, running to her husband's side.

"Boys, get to the kitchen and get upstairs," Samantha ordered. They ran to the kitchen as Samantha stepped out into view of Garmond.

Swinging his sword-arm, Garmond lunged at Samantha, who moved swiftly out of his way.

"You're going to get tuckered out eventually." Samantha smirked.

With his non-sword hand, Garmond grabbed Samantha's arm and swung her into the wall. To her surprise, he was very strong. Feeling warm liquid run down her nose, she reached for her forehead and saw that it came back bloody. She could already feel her lip swelling up, too.

In the time Samantha took to lick her wounds, Garmond was beside her once again, sending a powerful kick into her midsection. With the wind instantly knocked out of her, she fell to the floor gasping and clutching her side.

"Leave her alone!" Kathy warned, sending another kick toward the enemy. Before it had a chance to collide, Garmond grabbed her foot and twisted. As it crunched, Kathy shrieked in pain and crumpled to the floor.

Garmond turned back to Samantha and delivered another kick to her side. Samantha tried to lift herself, but when Garmond kicked her a third time, she began coughing up blood.

"What do you want?" she choked.

"Not so tough anymore, huh?" Garmond sneered, swinging his foot back to kick her again—but a brush of wind stopped him. He turned toward the kitchen and saw Josh with his arms out, palms open.

"I told you it wouldn't work!" Josh said to his brother.

Garmond walked slowly toward Josh but stopped when a vase crashed near his feet. He turned back and saw Samantha.

"Get the hell away from them. Run, boys!"

Will started to stir, and Kathy called to him, "Will, wake up! Samantha needs your help!" She still clutched her foot.

Garmond saw Will rising and lifted his sword-arm and drove it through Samantha's back. She gasped, collapsing on the floor.

Kathy shrieked as tears poured down her face. Josh and Chris stood frozen in the doorway to the kitchen.

"You killed her!" Chris shouted, his fists shaking. "You monster!" He shook with anger as Garmond screamed out in pain, and one of his wings shredded in a flash of flame.

"What was that?" Josh asked, looking at Chris.

Chris looked down at his hands. He threw them in Garmond's direction, and Garmond's other wing was blasted to bits.

Falling to his knees, Garmond pointed his sword-arm at Chris.

"No!" Will shouted, bringing down his sword on Garmond's sword-arm, severing it. Garmond screamed in pain.

"Chris, you have the power to kill him," Josh said. "Focus."

Chris took a deep breath and waved his hands in front of himself once more, obliterating Garmond.

The Blood Moon

Kathy gaped. "Whoa." Reality set in, and she crawled to her sister, desperately reaching for her wrist to check for a pulse. There was none. She grasped Samantha's hand and kissed the back of it, tears streaming.

Josh and Chris were at her side, both of them sobbing.

"Aunt Kathy, can't you go back in time and stop this?" Josh asked.

Kathy shook her head. "I don't have that kind of power, sweetie." She sniffled and slung her arms around both of her nephews, pulling them in.

They only had each other now.

Chapter Two

Tonight is the autumnal equinox," Chris told his brother as he carried their enormous magic book to the kitchen. "If we don't nail this imp by tonight, we're screwed."

"Why?" Josh asked, taking a seat on the stool at the counter.

"Because then he'll have our powers. I'm not too sure how it works, but I do know it's going to happen."

"How did you find all this out?"

Chris took out a pot from a cupboard underneath the stove and filled it with water. He set it on the stove and turned up the heat. "I went and asked a seer. She told me—"

"Wait a minute!" Josh snapped. "A seer? I thought we discussed this! They're con artists! How do you know she's not the one after our powers? Maybe she fed you a line so that you would be thrown off the trail?"

THE BLOOD MOON

"Yeah, but see, that's the point," Chris explained. "She knew about our powers and how strong we are. So that's why she knew not to mess with me."

"Or that's the reason she would mess with you." Josh threw up his hands in exasperation. "I can't believe you did that! Did you tell Aunt Kathy?" He knew the answer before Chris could even speak.

Chris bit his lip. "Not exactly. I told her all about the imp, though. Please don't tell her! She'll ground me, and then I'll have to stay home and miss all the action," he pleaded with his brother. "And I found a potion to destroy him." Chris gathered ingredients from around the kitchen. "And I don't care if you're with me or not, but I'm going after him."

"This is really stupid, Chris," Josh stated, folding his arms and glaring at his brother. Chris smiled, knowing he had him hooked. Josh sighed. "I can drive."

"With your new car?" Chris asked. "The imp lives in the bad part of town. We'll stick out like a sore thumb." He shook his head at Josh. "Maybe we should walk."

"That's not safe," Josh argued. "Unless you want to ask Aunt Kathy's opinion?"

"No!" Chris jumped. "I think we can manage."

* * *

Chris finished the potion and bottled four vials. Two for him and two for Josh.

"Let's go." He slipped on his khaki military jacket.

"Keys," Josh reminded himself out loud as he snatched them off the hook.

"I still think we should walk," Chris said, jamming his feet into his shoes. His beat-up old sneakers had seen better days.

"Just imagine how late it'll be by time we get there and come back." Josh knelt down to tie his shoes. "I'm willing to risk it with my car."

"All right." Chris sighed. "Ready?" He was already halfway out the door. Anxious, as always.

"Yeah," Josh said, following Chris to his new car. New, however, was not quite the word to describe it. Josh had saved and researched until he found a used car for himself. Although it wasn't brand new from the lot, it ran pretty well. "I told Aunt Kathy that we were going out. She's going to kill us if she finds out what we're doing."

They got in the car, and Chris directed Josh to the site where the seer had told him he would find the imp. They parked on the street a block away from the alley. When they got out, they crept around the corner into the narrow passage between the buildings.

"Careful," Josh warned. Imps were notoriously tiny and swift, sometimes undetectable when they were moving their fastest. The dampness in the air sent a shiver down Josh's back. He zipped up his battered hoodie. He wished he had a thicker jacket, but he wasn't going to risk ruining his new one.

As they meandered their way farther in between the buildings, the lighting grew darker. Chris looked up and saw that a few of the lights that were supposed to be illuminating the inner square were blown out. Shattered glass littered the ground.

"Be ready with your power," Josh cautioned.

Chris nodded.

A shadow in the corner began to stir. Josh tugged at the sleeve of Chris's jacket and pointed. The imp emerged, flying up in front of Josh's and Chris's faces. Lurching back, they swatted in the air to get the imp away from them.

"Blow it up!" Josh shouted, covering his face with one hand.

"He won't stay still!" Chris yelled. "You try something!"

Using both hands, Josh created a small tornado, sucking the imp into the cyclone. After spinning for a few minutes, the wind dissipated and the imp fell to the ground, disoriented and dizzy. It had wings and was very hairy. Its face radiated evil, and it had sharp fangs hanging out of its mouth.

Chris pulled out the potion and threw it at the imp. The imp screeched, then burst into flames. It writhed as it was consumed in a final flash of blue.

"Cool, and we still got three more potions," Chris cheered.

Josh glared at him. "Let's just get out of here, Chris."

"Not so fast!" said a voice from behind them.

Josh and Chris turned to see a woman with long brown hair walking toward them. She wore a brown shawl over her ripped and ragged clothes.

"You still owe me my payment, witch," she snarled at Chris.

"Is that the seer?" Josh asked. "What payment?"

"Well, I kind of promised her the imp as a slave, but now he's dead so you can't get him. Sorry." Chris raised his shoulders as he held out his hands, palms up.

"Then I guess you'll have to do." The seer stepped closer.

Waving his hand, Josh created a wind gust that stopped the woman in her tracks.

"Is that the best you've got?" the seer taunted. "It should come as no surprise that your brother is the most sought-after witch out of the two of you."

Josh looked at his brother. "Do something!"

"You don't really expect me to blow up a woman, do you?" asked Chris. Any time he had blown up a person before, it had been a demonic creature. This woman was more or less just like them.

"Well…" Josh hesitated. Chris had a point.

The seer produced a knife from inside her shawl. "I'm going to place my mark on you and bind you to my command."

"The story of my life." Chris threw his second potion at her, and it hit her shoulder. The potion blew up and left an open wound on her arm.

"Nice try," she said, dabbing the gash on her arm with the loose end of her shawl. "That won't stop me." She stepped toward Chris.

Josh and Chris backed up to keep their distance, but they butted up against the opposite wall of the square.

Trying his power again, Josh lifted both hands and blew the woman backward. Even though she fell to the ground, she was still blocking their only way out of the square. She leaped to her feet and lunged at Chris with the knife.

"Blow her up!" Josh ordered. He was starting to panic.

Chris braced himself and grabbed the woman's arms, pushing the hand grasping the knife away from him. His hands weren't free to use his power.

Josh jumped into the scuffle and pried the woman's arm off Chris. Letting go, she stood back and turned her attention on Josh. In a flash, she sliced through the sleeve of his hoodie, drawing blood.

Taking advantage of the moment, Chris waved his hands and sent the woman exploding in a burst of flames.

"You okay?" Chris asked.

Josh nodded. "C'mon, let's get out of here."

Chapter Three

"Sorry I'm late, Mr. Harper, but I was stuck in traffic," Mr. Parker, the school guidance counselor, explained. Josh had requested a meeting with him to get a head start on college applications. It was only the beginning of his junior year of high school, but he wanted to make sure he was set.

"Mr. Parker, I'm here to talk about college and my career," Josh said.

"Well, as a high school junior, you have a lot of important choices to make." He shuffled some papers around and hit the power button on the computer, then continued, "Such as choosing the right college for you. First thing's first, though, you need to decide what you want to do."

"I already know what I want to do," interrupted Josh. "I want to be a doctor. I want to help people."

"That's great!" Mr. Parker said as he glanced at his computer. Josh wasn't sure how much enthusiasm Mr. Parker genuinely had, or whether that was a statement he made to a lot of students. He glanced at Josh's file on his desk while he waited for his computer to boot up. "Well, your grades are terrific, you have plenty of after-school activities, and your attitude in class is pretty good. I think, with a lot of hard work, you should be able to achieve your goal."

"Good." Josh was relieved. "Now I need to know what colleges I can apply to." He added as an afterthought, "…and how much each would cost." He smiled as he began to formulate different plans for his future in his mind.

"Well, it depends on where you want to go to college. There are some great pre-med schools down south, but you have a few options—"

"I want to stay local, close to home." Josh was adamant about staying within driving distance of home. He didn't want Kathy and Chris left alone without his help in case there were any demonic attacks.

"Honestly, you're the only student I have ever met with who seems so certain about what he wants to do." Mr. Parker smiled and continued, "You look like you're on top of things, so I'm going to give you this website I found that'll help you find colleges." He pulled a piece of paper out of his printer and handed it to Josh. "Come and see me again when you've narrowed your search down to your top five college choices. If you need any help, feel free to stop by."

Josh left Mr. Parker's office and went straight to the library to look up the website.

* * *

As Josh and Chris walked home from school, they noticed a slick, black BMW parked in front of their house. With a fresh coat of wax and not a scratch on it, they knew exactly to whom it belonged: Will Brown, Kathy's husband.

In the year since Samantha had died, Kathy had voluntarily given up her powers, which relinquished the love spell Will had placed on her. All the events leading up to Samantha's death had come rushing back to Kathy, and she had demanded a divorce. Not that a legal termination of their marriage made much of a difference to a lovesick Dark Knight, but Kathy no longer wanted to be associated with him on any grounds.

Will had dark brown hair, so dark it was almost black. He always had a tan, and he had a noticeable scar on the right side of his neck. A result from a brawl he had in his early days of demonic activity.

Chris rolled his eyes at his brother as they walked up the driveway. "I wonder what he wants."

"Probably bugging Aunt Kathy again," Josh said as he stepped inside the door. "Let's hope he's not using his black magic."

"I don't think he is." They could hear them fighting from the kitchen. Kathy and Will were arguing once again. "That wouldn't help him if he's trying to prove he's good." They set their backpacks on the kitchen table and stepped into the living room where the yelling emanated from.

"I don't care if you still love me!" Kathy shouted at Will from across the vast, elegantly furnished room. "You lied to me, you tricked me, and you hexed me!" She counted off each one on her fingers.

"I swear to you, Kathryn, I haven't used my black magic in months! I don't know what I have to do to convince you!"

"See, that's just it." Kathy pointed at him. She kept her distance as he moved closer to her. "I shouldn't have to worry if my husband's ever going to go bad again and try to kill me in my sleep! Or my nephews!" She spotted the boys as they walked into the room.

"Great!" Will said, noticing Josh and Chris. "Just what I need, you two brats coming in here and screwing up my marriage."

"Your marriage was already screwed up." Josh was angry, but he kept his voice even and strong. "You know what you did."

"True," Will replied with an evil smirk. He leaned toward Josh. "It was your mother's fault. Her damn sister couldn't help but tell Kathy that she hated me."

"My sister hated you before she even met you! I ignored her and still kept seeing you, but only because you put a hex on me. I wish I had listened; I'd be a whole lot happier right now!"

"If I hadn't come along, you would still be a lonely woman living with her sister. You can thank me for the advancement of your powers too, before you pissed them all away!" Will spat. In a fit of rage, he picked up an antique end table and smashed it against a wall.

Kathy shrieked and then stared at him for a moment. "Get out of my house."

Will threw up his hands. "Fine. You think I'm so bad, then I'll be bad. I'm going to make your life a living hell, and you only have yourself to blame."

Will walked out the front door and down the front steps.

"Will," Kathy called after him, leaning against the front door. He turned to her.

"Go to hell." The front door slammed shut.

"Do you want me to blow him up for you?" Chris asked, breaking the small moment of silence after Will left.

"No, but I do want you boys to track him. I have his necklace to help you find him." She held up a chain with a gold wedding band hanging on it.

"Where'd you get that?" Chris asked.

"It was with some of his other stuff he left here. He came back today for it," Kathy said. She took a deep breath. "Do you think you can do that for me?"

Josh took the necklace and said, "Sure, but do you think it's a good idea? It's like we're looking for trouble. And we're never short on that."

"I know, but despite everything, I know Will won't hurt me," Kathy confessed. She closed her eyes and remembered the good times she and Will had. Despite the reason she fell in love with him, she did love him. It didn't change anything, though. He betrayed her and her family. This was the right choice.

"Do you want us to go after him if we find him?" asked Chris.

"All I want is for you to just watch him and make sure he's not doing anything evil or harmful to other people. I don't know how serious he is about returning to evil," Kathy said. She remembered the plans he had when they were first married and shuddered. "Will you guys do that for me?"

Josh nodded and walked upstairs to their magic room, which was Chris's old room. Now he shared a room with Josh so that all their magical items could be kept together in one room.

Sitting at a table, Josh pulled out the items he needed for the ritual. He handed Chris a heavy golden goblet and asked, "Can you fill this up for me?"

When Chris returned, Josh had the candles lit and aligned around the circle. He took the ring in his hand and muttered the incantation. He had used this spell several times. It was one of the few that his mother had had a chance to teach him, so he knew he would never forget it.

"Do you see him yet?" Chris asked, watching his brother focus.

"Not yet," Josh replied, "but while I'm looking, do me a favor and look up the things Aunt Kathy wrote in the magic book about Will."

"Why?" Chris asked.

Josh shrugged, turning his attention to Chris. "Maybe there's something we're overlooking? Or maybe there's something we don't know? She's been updating it like crazy lately. Every detail she can think of she adds, just in case."

Chris flipped through the pages of the battered old book. He stopped at Will's page and let out a howl of laughter.

"What's so funny?" Josh asked.

"I found him. She put him under 'family,' as in *Uncle* Will."

"Oh, yeah. That page was started before they were married," Josh said. "I found him. He's at work." Not only was he Will Brown the ruthless Dark Knight, and Kathy Walker's husband, but he was also a lawyer with a small practice.

Josh hovered over the book with his brother. "What'd you find? Anything new?"

The page was filled with little bullets of information about Will, with a giant picture of him in the center. The bullets at the top of the page listed all the good things Will had accomplished when Kathy was in love with him, but the second half of the profile listed all the evil things he'd done, past and present.

"Aunt Kathy is on a rampage with this. A lot of this stuff I didn't even know happened."

"'Extreme temper,'" Chris read out loud. "You think? He just smashed a table downstairs!"

"That's nothing. Remember when we found out he strangled that poor woman at that restaurant because she accidentally brought the wrong food to the table? Or how he punched out that guy at the gas station because he wanted to clean the windshield? Not to mention the fact that he's smart, so if he's not throwing a temper tantrum, he's planning something big."

"Damn. It's hard to believe that he could keep up the good-guy charade for so long."

"Well, the good thing is she's against him now," Josh replied. "And we have been able to find spells and potions to counteract his powers. We should be able to take him out with our powers, I think."

The Blood Moon

"You think so? This is going to be tough. Not only is he powerful, but he had some pull with Aunt Kathy before."

"I don't think we have to worry about that anymore. But we do have to tread carefully with this," Josh warned. "We need to keep our heads level and make smart choices. This isn't any ordinary enemy. This is personal."

* * *

Chris cruised into the house after school. His aunt was working and Josh was setting up for the homecoming dance, so he had the house to himself. He cranked up the stereo in the living room and ran upstairs to grab his laptop.

Passing the magic room, Chris decided it was probably a good idea to at least do a quick searching ritual to see if anything new had shown up. It had been a couple of days and Will was nowhere to be found. Chris could tell his aunt was getting worried, but it was out of their hands.

After he had lit the candles and filled a goblet, he held Will's ring in his hand and recited the spell:

I call on the strength of my power,
show Will's face in the water.

He chanted two more times before he opened his eyes and glanced at the goblet. Finally, Will had surfaced.

Chris patted down his pockets, searching for his phone.

Then he remembered he'd left it in his backpack. Jumping down the last few steps into the living room, Chris tore into his backpack. Hitting the power button on the stereo, he called Kathy.

"What's up?" Kathy's voice trilled on the other end.

"I think I found Will."

"All right." She paused, contemplating her schedule. "Uh…I can be home in about an hour. Watch him to make sure he doesn't move."

"Do we have a plan? Should I call Josh?" Chris asked.

"No." She hung up.

Chris returned to the circle and continued the ritual, making sure the connection wouldn't be lost. At least Will wasn't moving. He searched the location on his phone and saved it. It would only take ten minutes to get there.

Chris got a text from Kathy that told him to meet her outside. Within a few minutes, she pulled into the driveway and honked.

"So what's the plan?" Chris asked after he was in the car and had directed his aunt in the right direction.

"I don't know," Kathy said, biting her fingernail.

"What do you expect to happen when we get there?" Chris asked.

"I guess I just want to watch him. Make sure he's not up to anything."

"Uh-oh," Chris said, glancing out the window.

"What's wrong?" Kathy asked as they pulled up to a stoplight.

The Blood Moon

"I see Kaiser and the Queen. They're attacking someone!" Chris unbuckled his seatbelt and ran off into the street and between two buildings.

A dark bald man in a long black robe was standing next to a woman with long black hair who wore a shimmering red robe.

A woman with short blonde hair, and wearing a skirt, was laying on the ground, cowering with fear. Her purse had spilled out onto the ground, and her arm was bleeding. She had bruises on her arms and a black eye.

"Hey! Knock it off!" Chris shouted as he sprinted to the beaten victim.

"What are you going to do? *Witch*!" The pale woman in the red robe hissed. Her eyes flared red momentarily as she glared at him.

"I'm going to do my job," Chris said. He looked down at the woman on the ground behind him and said to the attackers, "Leave her alone."

"No," the man responded. "She's going to die, even if we need to kill you to get to her!"

"Kaiser, you and I both know that you can't kill me. You've tried many times, but you can't kill me or my brother. We're too powerful for you."

The Queen and Kaiser had been the Harper brothers' biggest threat, each side unable to beat the other. It was almost an unspoken agreement that they would stop trying to kill one another. But Chris was not about to turn his cheek to an unfair fight.

Kaiser raised both his open hands and shot a dark beam that

Chris easily dodged, even as he pulled the woman out of the way. He had increased his agility over the years with all the attacks.

"That doesn't mean we won't try," Kaiser said with a devious smile.

Kathy ran in from the other side of the alley. "Chris! Need a hand?"

"Take her to the hospital! I'll be right behind you."

The Queen waved her hand toward Chris, and he flew back past Kathy. He landed in a pile of garbage cans.

Just before Kathy could reach Chris, Kaiser shot an energy beam at her, and she jumped to the side as the beam shattered an old window. Kathy stumbled over to the woman and helped her off the ground.

Chris waved his hands in the direction of Kaiser and the Queen, trying to get them to sit still long enough for him to use his power and blow them up. Instead, he missed and the end of the fire escape that hung over their heads screeched and crumbled to the ground.

Chris glanced down to the street. They were starting to gain attention. "Aunt Kathy, we need to clear out!"

Kathy nodded and helped the woman out of the alley as fast as they could. Luckily, the nearest hospital was only two blocks away.

After Chris was sure the two women were safely away, he turned toward the villains. "Nice try, Queen," Chris said as he stood up and walked back toward her, "but the only reason you're so powerful is because you're feared. But honestly, your powers are even weaker than Kaiser's." Chris knew he needed to tread carefully. The Queen was a banshee, and her scream could be heard for miles.

"Are you willing to test that theory?" she asked. "I've been told I have a beautiful singing voice. I have a habit of knocking them dead."

Chris ignored her pun. He made a quick hand gesture and attempted to blow her up, but the energy fell short, and she just fell back onto the ground. He tried again, but Kaiser shot one of his black beams, and Chris was forced to jump out of the way. When he looked up, the Queen and Kaiser were gone.

* * *

Chris eventually caught up with Kathy in front of the hospital. She stood outside with her arms folded. Relief came over her face when she saw him.

"How'd it go?" she asked, pulling him into a hug. Even though her nephews were pretty experienced with their magic, she still worried. They were her responsibility now.

Chris looked uneasy as a group of people walked out of the building. He nodded across the street, and they took cover in an alley. They needed to talk in private.

"What the hell happened to you?" Kathy asked.

"What do you mean? After the Queen and Kaiser escaped, I came right here."

"No, I mean your arm!" Kathy shouted as she cradled his left arm to examine it. There was a gouge under the rip in his sweatshirt. Blood was running down, soiling his sleeve.

"Oh, I guess Kaiser did get me with his energy beam," Chris said as he looked at his wound. "Huh, what do you know! And I'm actually starting to feel the pain now." He started to weave back and forth. Kathy put her free hand on his shoulder to steady him.

As she held her nephew, she explained, "That's because he stole that power from a witch, and the pain doesn't come until later."

"Well, I should probably get this cleaned up, then we can go after Will," replied Chris.

"No. We shouldn't have gone after him in the first place." Kathy hated herself for being reckless. Chris was hurt, and it was all because she was impulsive. "You were right. I had no plan."

"What if he does something?" Chris started to protest, but Kathy cut him off.

"—I said no, Chris!"

He finally saw why she was so worried. He took a breath and said, "Did you erase that woman's memory?"

"Yeah." Kathy sighed. "It took me a while to remember the spell though. It sucks not having powers." She remembered the days when her sister would be able to do it without having to use a spell.

"It's what you had to do," Chris said. "At least you can still say spells."

"Yeah, I've already listed the pros and the cons about this

situation, but that doesn't make me feel any better." She gripped his good arm. "We need to get you home and get your arm taken care of before you do any worse damage to it. You could lose the use of your arm. We don't know if there's poison in his energy beams."

"Oh, that ship has sailed," Chris said calmly. "I haven't been able to use my arm since I started to feel the pain."

"Great!" she said sarcastically. She stared at his unfocused eyes as she thought of a plan. She had parked her car too far in the other direction. There was no way Chris was going to be able to walk that far.

"Call Josh," Chris said, breaking her train of thought.

"Good idea." She pulled out her cell phone and hit the number three speed dial to call her other nephew.

Chris sat down against the wall, his arm resting limply at his side.

When Kathy hung up she said, "Josh'll be here in about ten minutes. You think you're going to be okay until then?"

"I'm fine." Chris rested his head against the wall with his eyes closed.

"Are you sure? Because the hospital is right across the street."

"Yeah." Chris chuckled weakly. "How would we explain my arm? 'Oh, can you help me? I apparently didn't move fast enough when a demon tried to attack me.' It wouldn't go so smoothly."

"I was just asking," Kathy said. "I'll try to remember the healing spell, but if you don't think you can wait for Josh, we'll go to the hospital." She was almost positive at this point that the attack had poisoned him somehow. She wondered if a spell would be enough to get rid of the poison. They may need to make a potion or cream or something that would draw it out before they healed him.

"Aunt Kathy," Chris said, now opening his eyes to look at her, "I'll be fine. Stop worrying."

"Well, I promised your mother I would take care of you boys." Samantha had always been the calm one with stuff like this. She had always known exactly what to do.

"I think you should stop comparing yourself to her. You're two totally different people. You'll never be as good as her at some things, and there are things that she would've never been able to do that you do so easily."

"Yeah, I guess you're right," Kathy said with a smile.

"Can you believe that she's been gone a year next week?" Chris asked. "In some ways, it seems like it was just last week, and other times it feels like it's been forever."

"Wow. I never expected that this past year would go by so fast," Kathy said. "Even though you two have improved your magic a lot. You've mastered your powers, and I lost mine."

"It wasn't your fault, though. It was Will's. He's the one who manipulated you and—" Chris's voice faded. He knew the subject of Kathy losing her powers was a sore one, and he didn't want to overstep his boundaries.

"Yeah, and I have no idea when it'll be safe to call them back." She had voluntarily given up her powers. Will had placed a lust spell on her that made her overlook their very dark marriage. Ridding herself of her powers removed the spell. Now it was only Josh and Chris who had active powers. They weren't ready to handle that immense responsibility like that, but she didn't want to push them to use their magic, either. She wanted them to stay kids for a little bit longer.

Josh's car pulled over in front of them. He got out and walked around the car to open the door, but then he stopped and looked down the alley behind them and said, "Someone's here."

"What do you mean?" Chris asked as he got up with help from Kathy.

"I don't know. I just feel it," Josh said. He had his eyes peeled, scoping out the area.

"Any idea who?" Chris asked.

"It's Will," Kathy said. "I can feel the pull. He's close."

"C'mon." Josh helped his aunt lift his brother and shuffled over to the car. "I brought the magic book in case we needed it," he said.

Chris slumped down in the front seat.

"I think there might be more to his injury than what's on the surface," Kathy warned. She stood side by side with Josh and looked at the book. "Is this spell going to heal any infections or poisons?"

"It should," Josh confirmed, "if I'm reading this right." Some of the pages in the magic book were so old that they were written in Latin. Josh and Chris had gotten pretty proficient in the dead language, but they weren't exactly fluent. "Worth a shot, right?" He looked up at his aunt. She nodded her approval.

Josh stood in front of Chris and recited:

Curatio!

Chris's wound started to glow white. Seconds later it disappeared, and Chris opened his eyes, gasping for air.

He sat wide-eyed for a moment. Then he ran a hand through his red hair and sat up.

"How do you feel?" Kathy asked.

"Great."

"Your arm is fine?" she prodded.

He lifted his arm, made a fist, and spread his fingers out a couple of times.

"Good," she said. She turned and asked Josh if he still sensed Will. He was staring down the alley again.

"I feel him, but I can't pinpoint where he is," he responded, frustrated.

"I feel his pull, too," she said, walking down the alley. She turned a corner, and Josh and Chris followed close behind, ready for just about anything. Everything seemed too quiet. Not a rat or bird scuttled around. The only noise they heard was from the traffic on the street.

A man in a black cape came riding from deep in the alleyway on a black horse. He stopped right in front of the trio, the horse lurching, causing the witches to jump back.

"What are you doing, Will?" Kathy asked after she regained her composure.

"Just signed a deal with the devil," he replied. He held up a tattered piece of paper. "You thought I was kidding, didn't you?"

"Will, this is stupid," she exclaimed. "Can't you just move on?"

"I don't want to move on!" he shouted. "You were supposed to be my queen! Sitting beside me while I took the world by storm!"

Kathy took a step back, holding her arms out in front of her nephews like a mama bear protecting her cubs.

Chris stepped around Kathy's outstretched arms and said, "To get to her, you need to get through us first."

Will dismounted his horse and pulled back the hood on his cloak.

"That shouldn't be too hard," he scoffed.

"Arrogant!" Chris shouted as he tried to blow Will up. He was almost certain of the outcome, but he was so consumed with anger that it didn't matter.

Will's body expanded a little but soon went back to its normal size.

"You thought it would be that easy?" Will waved his hand, and Josh and Chris flew across the alleyway and into the wall. "See boys? It wasn't that hard to get past you."

Kathy backed up as Will approached her. She put out her hand. "If you hurt them, I swear, Will…"

"What?" Will smiled. Kathy wanted to slap the grin right off his face. "You're going to hurt me with your nonexistent powers?" He had cornered Kathy between two Dumpsters and a wall. "You don't have any powers." He put his arm against the wall, pinning her where she was.

"What do you want from me?" she asked, looking into his eyes.

"The offer still stands," he said, kissing her neck. "I want you back."

"Get away from me!" She pushed at his chest, but it was no use. "I'll never take you back!"

"Why? Because I'm evil?" Will asked.

"You lied to me," Kathy said, sliding under his arm away from his trap. "I never should've listened to you."

Will fell toward Kathy, who caught him in spite of herself. He was unconscious. Kathy looked behind Will and saw that Chris had tried to use his power on Will again but only managed to knock him out.

"Aunt Kathy, push him off you so I can really blow him up!"

"No." She let Will slip out of her grasp, propping him against the wall of the alley. "Let's go."

"But we have the upper hand here," Chris protested.

"We're going," Kathy said.

"But—" Josh began to question her too, but he saw the look on her face and decided not to.

"I don't understand," Chris continued.

"I need to think," she said, walking off.

Josh and Chris looked at each other and followed reluctantly.

CHAPTER FOUR

The next morning Kathy had left for work before Josh and Chris even got up. They came downstairs to find a note from her.

Went to work early.

"I'm worried about Aunt Kathy." Chris broke the long silence after they read the note.

"She'll be okay," Josh said, not exactly sure himself.

"But aren't you worried that she won't be able to let us get rid of him now? She wouldn't let me do it last night."

"Yeah, but last night was different. She actually saw him being attacked. Maybe she doesn't want to watch?"

"Aunt Kathy's not like that," Chris explained. "She would

want to come with us because he's so strong, and she wants to make sure we don't get hurt."

"That's true," Josh said. "I just hope she's dealing with it better today."

"I just hope she doesn't do anything drastic, like go looking for him."

"I have an idea," Josh said, walking out of the room.

Chris followed him to the magic book.

"We'll cast a protection spell on her. Just to be safe." Josh flipped through the book's pages.

"Hey, Josh," Chris started softly.

"Yeah?"

"Do you think…do you think she's still in love with him?"

Josh stopped and looked at his brother. "What makes you think that?"

Chris shrugged. "I know she gave up her powers in order to lift that spell, but what if she still loves him in spite of everything? Maybe she knows that the right thing to do is to cut him out of her life, but maybe it's not that easy?"

"Look," Josh said, wiping his face with his hand. "They were married. She really fell for him then. So much that it blinded her from everything else. I'm sure she still cares for him, but she won't let that stop her or us from doing what's right. This isn't easy for her. She's just got to process it for a while. She'll come around."

Chris sighed and nodded. "I hope you're right. Last time we almost lost her for good."

The Blood Moon

* * *

The boys had been right. Kathy left work early to find Will. She hoped there was still good somewhere inside of him. She just wanted to bring it out of him before he killed her, or someone else.

She drove to the alley where they had left Will the night before. She walked carefully along the building and kept her eyes open for anything that might jump out at her, whether it be Will or some street thug. She had a dozen spells on the tip of her tongue.

She found the spot where they had left Will and knelt down on the ground, hoping that he would come back to her there.

"Will," she said weakly, "if you can hear me, I need you to come out. I need to talk to you." She sat down against the wall and waited. "I need you."

She waited for twenty minutes and nothing happened. When she got to her car, her cell phone rang. It was her boss.

"Hello, Amy," Kathy answered.

"Kathy Brown! If you don't get your butt back over here, then I'll have to fire you!" Amy shouted through the phone.

Frustrated that Will wouldn't answer her call, and about the fact that she had so many unwanted ties to him that she'd created herself, Kathy groaned and interrupted her boss, "Actually, I took back my maiden name, Walker. And you told me you could handle everything without me."

"Excuse me, *Ms. Walker*, but was I finished speaking? If you don't get back over here now, you're fired! You've missed too many days already! I need someone reliable."

It was true. Kathy missed work a lot; not because she had a bad work ethic but because she needed to leave for various attacks and emergencies. It was yet another downside to her magical lifestyle.

"Well, I'm sorry, Amy, but I can't come back in right now," Kathy said.

"Then you're fired!" Amy shouted as she hung up the phone.

"Great." Kathy shook her head and put away her phone. She started the car and headed home.

As she approached the Bayfront Parkway entrance ramp, Will appeared in the passenger seat. She did a double take and swerved as she ascended the ramp.

"Will!" she shouted as she tried to pull over.

"Keep going," he said as he pointed to her foot, forcing it down on the gas pedal.

He grabbed the steering wheel and jerked it toward the edge of the bridge right next to the river.

"Will! Stop!" Kathy exclaimed.

She fought him, and the car swerved back into her lane, but Will did it again. This time the car flew off the bridge and plummeted toward the concrete earth.

Kathy screamed. In the midst of her screaming, she felt a hand on her neck, and suddenly her screams were echoing back to her.

She opened her eyes and saw parked cars surrounded by

concrete. She was in a parking building. Will stood next to her, his hand still on her neck.

"What? Where are we?" Kathy asked, brushing Will's hand off her.

"You were looking for me, right?" he asked, flashing his signature seductive smile that drove Kathy nuts. She used to find it charming, but now she found it revolting.

She groaned. "You know, you ruined my car and scared me half to death just because you can't answer my call?" She glared up at him and took a step back. "Shouldn't be surprised. You've never failed to let me down."

"Aw, stop. Is that really the memory you have of us? What about the love? What about the passion?"

"Uh, the only passion you had was destroying my family and manipulating me to be your dark queen," Kathy spat, recalling a few spells just in case.

"Sweetheart, I believe you had a helping hand in ruining that wonderful family of yours." Will smirked.

Kathy was disgusted. She stood back and looked him right in the eyes. "Screw you."

She turned and walked away from him. She wasn't sure where she was going, but it didn't matter as long as it was away from Will.

"We have an appointment with our lawyer," Will called out to her. "I wouldn't want you to be late for it."

Kathy scowled. "Well, then let's go," she called over her shoulder.

Inside, Kathy raced to the elevator, hoping to have a minute to herself. However, before the doors shut, Will was able to sneak in. As the elevator doors shut, he grabbed Kathy and put a knife to her neck, pinning her against the back wall of the elevator.

"Now, baby, you're going to give me a spell to get your nephews' powers," Will ordered. "I need them out of the way so I can get you back."

"I told you before, don't call me 'baby'!" She elbowed Will in the stomach and kicked the knife out of his hand. She didn't have enough time or room in the small elevator to pin Will against the wall. He probably would've overpowered her anyway, but she was able to grab the knife. With a firm grip, she pointed it at her ex.

"I swear, if you hurt my nephews, I'll make you wish you were dead," Kathy promised.

"You already do," Will said. "Just knowing I'm going to be without you makes me want to fight even harder to get you back." He held out one of his free hands and conjured a sword. "Let me go, or you leave me no choice."

"Never," Kathy said, her eyes fixated on his.

"Then I apologize for what I'm about to do." Will swung the sword sideways, cutting her stomach open.

Dropping the knife, she fell to the ground, her hands filling with blood. Suddenly her stomach started to heal. Will stared at her with his mouth wide open.

"What?" he gasped, astonished. "What spell did you cast?"

"Obviously, a pretty powerful one." Kathy smiled as she

jumped to her feet. "I won't hurt you if you get out of my life and never try to hurt me or my family again. Leave town and everything will be fine."

"I'm not leaving without you," Will said.

"Then I hope you enjoy the time you have left here on Earth, because as soon as I can, I'm sending you to hell!"

"Let's just make it through this meeting," Will said, "and I'll leave you alone...for a while."

As the elevator opened, Kathy said, "I'm not kidding, Will."

Will patted her cheek. "I know, sweetheart."

As Will left the elevator, Kathy reached down and grabbed the knife, sliding it in her back pocket.

* * *

When Kathy got home, Josh was in the kitchen, doing homework at the table.

"Where's Chris?" Kathy asked as she put her things down on the table across from Josh.

"Upstairs, on the computer."

"Chris," she yelled up the stairs, "come down here! I need to talk to you and your brother together!"

She returned to the kitchen, and Josh asked, "Can it wait? I really need to study."

"But we're going to need your powers," Kathy explained. She kissed the top of his head. "Sorry, babes."

"Oh good, you're home," Chris said as he walked into the

kitchen. He grabbed an apple from the bowl on the counter, shined it on his shirt, and took a bite. "What's up?" he asked with his mouth full.

"I'm trying to get some work done, and another magical problem pops up," Josh replied, annoyed.

"Not another," Kathy explained, "the same one as last night."

"Will," Chris noted, devouring another bite of his apple.

"Yeah, I went back to the alley looking for him today, but he wasn't there," Kathy explained.

"What!" Josh shouted.

"Yeah, but I also got fired and lost my car." She sighed. "It's been a long day."

"What!" Josh asked. "You got fired?"

"You lost your car?" Chris asked.

"I'm fine. Will actually drove it off the parkway, but he took us to our meeting for the divorce before it crashed."

"Is that what's all over TV?" Chris went to the living room and turned on the TV.

"What do you mean?" Kathy asked, following him.

"Your crash is all over the news! They're looking for you. They probably think you're dead," Chris explained.

She sighed, watching some of the coverage. "This is going to be a big mess to clean up. We're going to need a massive memory spell or something."

Chris shook his head. "Nah, the car burst into flames. Any identifying paperwork is long gone."

"What about the license plates?"

The Blood Moon

"Oh, right. Yeah, we'll want to summon those. Soon, too."

Kathy and Chris went back to Josh, who had attempted to continue his homework in their absence.

"So, anyway, Will attacked me in the elevator, and he said he'd leave me alone, but I don't believe him. That's why we're going to go to his apartment and attack him there. Actually, a weird thing happened in the elevator when he attacked me. He cut my stomach open, I felt the pain, then suddenly, I felt relief because it was healing by itself. I must've somehow cast a spell."

"Well, actually, we did," Chris admitted. "We cast a protection spell on you because we kinda thought you would go looking for him."

"Well, that was smart," Kathy said. "Thanks. But don't do it again. I can take care of myself."

"Obviously not," Josh said. "You would've died if we hadn't cast that spell. Going after him without telling us was really stupid."

"Well I didn't; so I'm safe." Kathy wrapped an arm around Chris's shoulders. "My specialty was time. I've altered it before, who cares if I do it again?"

"Hold on, Aunt Kathy, we need to find our heads here." Josh put up his hands as if to stop the conversation. "We're not thinking clearly at all. Yes, you used to be able to alter time, but you don't have your powers anymore. And even if you did, you still need to be safe, because you can't turn back time if you're dead! We need to stop being reckless. We were sloppy the day mom died, and look at the outcome."

Kathy looked up at the ceiling for a moment. When she focused back on Josh, she said, "You know, it's good to have a voice of reason in this family. You get that from your mother."

There was an awkward silence. Nobody knew what to add to the conversation or how to break the moment easily. So Chris just jumped right into it.

"I don't think it's such a good thing going after him tonight. I mean, obviously we're not at our strongest." He pointed to Josh, whose head was on the table inside his folded arms. "And if he really is going to leave us alone, we should take that as an advantage to go after the Queen."

"What!?" Josh screamed out as he jumped from the table. "Don't we ever get a break? I mean it's one after another. It seems that we keep knocking them down, but somehow more demons take their spots!"

"But if we don't do it, who else will?" Chris asked.

"We shouldn't have to be the only ones who do it!" Josh complained. "I mean isn't there anyone else to pick up the slack? Don't get me wrong, helping people is great, but when are we going to get a break?"

"Just use magic to help you," Chris said.

"I can't, then I won't learn the material," Josh said. "And our powers are meant to help others, not us."

"Who says? After all we do, why shouldn't we use magic to sweeten the pot? Make it worth our while," Chris said.

"Chris, that would get out of hand. Where would we draw the line?" Kathy asked.

"I'm not going to drag Josh through it all if he doesn't want to do this anymore," Chris said. "Something's got to give."

"Well, all I need right now to make it easier on me is sleep," Josh said. He began to pack up his books. "I was up all last night worrying about Aunt Kathy, and I can't think straight. I'm going to bed."

"Don't forget what I said!" Chris called up to Josh as he walked out of the kitchen.

"What are we going to do about Will?" Kathy asked.

"Well, the protection spell wears off after twenty-four hours, so you should be good for the rest of the night," Chris said. "We just need to hope that he doesn't come after you tomorrow."

"We need to make sure I'm well prepared for anything," Kathy said. "I'll be home alone all day, so I can rig the house with secret weapons and traps and hope he doesn't stumble across them."

"I think you should rig yourself with potions and spells that will only affect him."

Kathy nodded. "I shouldn't have gone after him today."

Chris pulled out the magic book and said, "You can't change what's done. We need protection. But first, the license plates!"

After summoning her plates, Kathy worked on potions as Chris flipped through pages in the dictionary to try and find rhyming words for different spells. They worked until midnight, when Kathy made Chris go to bed.

CHAPTER FIVE

Kathy was sound asleep with her head on the kitchen counter when the boys came downstairs the next morning.

Josh shook her until she woke up.

"Long night?" Chris asked.

Kathy stretched and looked around. "What time is it?"

"Seven o'clock," Josh said.

Kathy stretched and let out a roar of a yawn. "I finished the potion, now all I have to do is go after him."

"Well, you're not going after him by yourself," remarked Josh. He was fixing his aunt a cup of coffee. "In fact, you're not going after him at all. Wait until he comes after you again. You're—we're only asking for trouble by going after him."

"Well, I made enough potions to fill the house with them," replied Kathy. "And I have enough to carry three on me at all times."

THE BLOOD MOON

"Good, and we'll come home as soon as possible to make sure you're safe. Come on, Chris, let's get to school."

* * *

"Do you think Aunt Kathy will be safe today?" Chris asked.

Josh shrugged, glancing in his mirror and noting a car coming up fast behind them. "I think yesterday scared her enough to keep her distance."

"I guess you're—" Chris started, but Josh interrupted him.

"Oh shoot, it's Kaiser and the Queen!"

"Want me to blast them?" Chris asked as he spun around and tried to lean out the window.

Josh grabbed his shirt, pulling him back in. "No, that's too dangerous; let me try to lose them." Josh swerved the car all over the road to dodge the energy beams and look for an escape.

"Yeah, so much for safer, Josh," Chris remarked, white-knuckling the handle above the door.

Josh concentrated on the road as the Queen's car raced passed him and Chris and stopped right in front of them.

Slamming on the brakes, Josh held out his hand with his palm facing the Queen's car. Her car went flying back, and he stopped safely about ten feet away.

They got out of the car ready to fight. The Queen sauntered over, with her red cape flapping in the remaining breeze from Josh's magic. She stopped and met the boys' gaze. Kaiser appeared beside her in a puff of black smoke.

"Fancy meeting you here," she said. She turned to Kaiser and commanded, "Attack!"

Kaiser held out his arm and shot the green beam of energy at Josh. Josh put up his hand to create an air current to push it away, but instead, he erupted into a cyclone, drawing the beam in and shooting it out in random directions. Chris fell to the ground to duck for cover as the beam shot against a window in the Queen's car and another hit Kaiser in the leg. He fell to the ground, grabbing at his leg.

The cyclone ended and Josh returned to his regular form. His blond hair was windblown, and he was wide-eyed as he turned to Chris for an explanation. Chris shrugged.

The Queen glared at the boys and muttered a spell under her breath that sent her car soaring in the air before exploding. The boys ducked for cover as pieces of the car scattered around them. When they stood back up, the Queen and Kaiser were gone.

* * *

As the boys drove off to school, Chris complained about Josh's new ability. "A new power?"

Josh beamed with happiness. "It's not new! It's an extension of my wind specialty. Yours will grow, too." He rolled his eyes.

"Now I'm not the only one with cool powers!" Chris shouted as he threw his hands up in the air. "Thanks, Josh, you needed to go and spoil it for me."

"Chris, your power is still the strongest. And it doesn't really matter whose is better. I just don't know why the Queen decided to attack us today."

"We need to tell Aunt Kathy," Chris said.

"She'll probably hear about the car explosion on the news. We're making headlines all over the place," Josh said, worried.

"Do you think they're trying to expose us to get us off their trail?" Chris asked.

Josh shrugged. "I don't know. Maybe."

"We should go home and tell Aunt Kathy!" Chris said. "I mean, it sounds like something we need to address now!"

"No, we need to get to school. I have three tests today."

"Blow them off! You can make them up later! We have more important things to deal with."

"Go home then! I actually care about passing tests and being…being…normal!"

"We are definitely anything but normal," Chris stated with pride. "We've been witches our entire lives! Things aren't going to change. Deal with it."

The boys had been witches their whole lives. They were taught how to control and use their powers whenever it was appropriate. Fighting the bad guys was usually up to their mother and their aunt; that was until Samantha passed away.

"We haven't been dealing with these problems our entire lives. We just started fighting a year ago, when mom died. If we keep doing this, we're basically joining her, because we're doing exactly what she was doing when she died!"

"We're not joining her," Chris said sternly. "We're getting justice for her murder, and the murders of anyone else who died because of evil."

"Why should that be our responsibility? We're just kids! Just because we're equipped with powerful magic doesn't mean we're ready to fight such strong evils! Nobody would ever be ready for this!"

"I get it that you don't want to do this anymore, but look at all the good we've done, just in the past year," pleaded Chris. "And if you want to go to school now, then fine. But I'm going home, and I know you'll make the right choice."

"How do expect to get home?" Josh asked.

"Magic."

"Fine. Do what you gotta do to get home," Josh said as Chris started to mumble a spell to himself, "but if you get stuck somewhere in Timbuktu, don't expect me to come and save you!" He looked over and saw that Chris was gone.

* * *

"Aunt Kathy!" Chris called after materializing in the kitchen. He walked into the living room and jumped. The Queen and Kaiser were there along with another man wearing a suit. Chris stared at the new foe as the man grinned and rubbed his stubbly beard. Chris was momentarily blinded. When he refocused the man was gone.

That's when he saw her.

Kathy lay on the floor unconscious. He made to move toward her, but the Queen spoke up.

"What are you doing back here, *witch*?"

Chris scowled at her. "What did you do to her?" He pointed to his aunt's limp body on the floor.

The Queen threw her arm forward and sent Chris flying back toward the kitchen.

He scrambled to his feet and was about to attack, but the Queen and Kaiser were already gone.

"Aunt Kathy!" Chris screamed as he ran to her.

Through Chris's panic, he was able to realize what he needed to do.

He ran over to the phone in the living room and dialed the number for the school.

"I need to speak with my brother, Josh Harper!" Chris exclaimed. "Yes, it's an emergency! Better yet, just tell him to come home right now!"

Chris tried to check for a pulse, but his hands were shaking. He saw that she was breathing. He jumped when the phone rang.

"Hey, what's up? I'm on my way home," Josh said.

"Something's wrong with Aunt Kathy!" Chris shouted. "They did something to her! She's not moving!"

"Okay, Chris listen to me, call 9-1-1 and tell them that she fell down the stairs or something and that she's not moving," Josh explained.

"Okay, hurry home," Chris said. He hung up the phone.

* * *

"Where is she?" Josh asked as he burst through the door.

"They just left with her. She's on the way to the hospital," Chris said. "Where were you?" He was walking out the door, trying to hurry to get to his aunt.

"I got a speeding ticket," Josh explained. "Why are you here and not with Aunt Kathy?"

"I told them I'd wait for you. I didn't think you'd take so long getting here." Chris was climbing into the passenger seat of his brother's car.

"You should have gone with her, just in case she's possessed or something is supernaturally wrong with her." Josh ran to the driver's side and started his car.

"It doesn't matter. Let's go!"

Josh put the car in gear and flew out of the driveway, racing to the hospital, risking another speeding ticket.

* * *

When they got to the hospital, they needed to wait before they could go in to see their aunt.

When they finally got to see her, Kathy was sitting up and talking with the doctor, who was scribbling notes on her chart.

"Aunt Kathy, you're okay!" Chris walked into the room and reached down to give her a hug.

"Be careful," Dr. Salmon said. "Your aunt has a severe concussion. She's going to want to take it easy for the next week or so." She hung the chart at the end of Kathy's bed.

"Does that mean she can go home?" Chris asked.

"I don't think she can take it easy at home," Josh said, "and besides she's going to be home alone all day. If anything happens to her, it could be too late by the time we get there."

Dr. Salmon nodded in agreement. "That's a good point. But I actually want you to stay here so I can run a few more tests."

"Why?" Kathy asked.

"I don't want to worry you, but you didn't show any brain activity whatsoever. Usually, when people are unconscious or unresponsive, most people still have some level of cognitive activity. The results of your tests show you didn't. It's a miracle you were even still breathing." She smiled at Kathy and rubbed her arm. "I want to see what caused that, and until I do, you can't go home," she explained. She looked genuinely concerned, and Kathy was tempted to agree to stay, but she didn't think it would be wise to leave the boys home alone. She needed to be there, just in case.

"But I have to get home," Kathy argued. "My nephews need me, and I—I have responsibilities I can't do sitting here!"

"I apologize for the inconvenience. Your nephews will be fine, I'm sure." Dr. Salmon made it sound as if the decision was final.

"Yeah, I can drive us to school," Josh said.

"And I'll make us dinner," Chris said. "We won't have a problem without you."

"You know what I mean," Kathy said, glaring at Chris.

Chris shrugged. "At least you'll be safe here."

"Your nephews are always welcome to visit," the doctor reassured her. "It's just for a little while."

"Fine, I'll stay," Kathy agreed, throwing her hands in the air as a form of surrender. Even though she hated to sit around and leave her nephews alone, she knew that at the hospital she'd be safer with so many people coming and going.

Chapter Six

"How are you feeling today?" Josh asked as he and his brother entered their aunt's hospital room the next day after school.

"I feel fine, except for this little headache." Kathy sat up in the bed and smiled.

"Well, we survived without you." Chris took a seat next to her.

"That's good to hear. I've made up a few defensive spells that might help you if anything happens." She reached over and grabbed a spiral notebook and pen from the nightstand. She flipped a couple pages in and said, "Here's one that will make the victim's eyes itch; here's one to make his memory go blank for a few minutes; this one causes the victim's hands to swell, oh, and this one—"

Josh put his hand on the notebook to stop her from reading.

"Aunt Kathy, we get the point." He took the notebook from her and saw that she had pages and pages of spells.

"You must've had a lot of time on your hands," Chris said, reading over his brother's shoulder.

When Josh got to about the fifteenth page of spells, he saw that the next page was a long story. "What's this?" he asked.

"It's nothing!" Kathy grabbed the notebook away from him, and in the process whipped her head back. She yelped in pain and clutched the back of her neck.

Josh and Chris jumped up.

"Are you okay?" asked Chris.

"Yeah, I think I'm fine," she said, rubbing her neck as she leaned back against her mound of pillows.

Josh darted out of the room, calling over his shoulder, "I'm going to get help!"

"No, Josh, don't!" Kathy protested, but it was too late.

Chris stood back as the nurse ran in to check on her. Josh trailed behind.

"What's the matter? What happened?" the nurse said in a rushed tone.

"I kinda snapped my head back." Kathy had her eyes closed, and she held the back of her neck with her right hand.

The nurse let out a grumbling breath as she monitored Kathy's charts. When she was satisfied with her readings, she put a hand on Kathy's shoulder and helped her lean back against the bed. "Stay here, just like this. Don't move, I'll be right back. Boys, watch her." The nurse then rushed out of the room.

THE BLOOD MOON

A few seconds later, she reemerged holding a neck brace. Two other people followed her in.

"Boys, I'm going to need you to step back." The nurse waved her hand against the wall on the opposite side of the room, and the boys did as she asked.

A couple of nurses helped put the neck brace on Kathy, and once it was on, they questioned her on what hurt and what didn't. Eventually, all but one of the nurses left the room.

"Are you sure you're feeling better, Miss Walker?" the nurse asked.

Kathy tried to nod, but the neck brace made it difficult. "Yes," she finally answered. "Do I have to sleep in this?"

"You could've done some serious damage with your neck. We're going to check with the doctor, but she's likely going to want to run another test to see if you damaged it any further," the nurse explained. "Take it easy from now on."

Kathy smiled and thanked her. As the nurse exited the room, she motioned out the door to Josh and Chris. "Boys, a word?"

They followed her out into the hall.

"Your aunt is very lucky," the nurse started. "The way she came in here completely unresponsive, it's a miracle she's awake and moving around so well."

Josh and Chris glanced at each other, knowing full well that the Queen's magic was far from a miracle.

"If you two can't promise me that there will be no rough-housing when you come to visit, for your aunt's safety we're going to have to ask you not to visit anymore," the nurse said.

"No!" Chris blurted. He covered his mouth, and his face flared up when he saw a few people turn their heads toward him.

"We promise," Josh said. "It won't be a problem again."

Chris nodded in agreement.

The nurse smiled. "Good. I'm sure this won't be an issue any longer. However, the doctor will likely want to run some tests this evening, so I'm afraid you will no longer be able to visit with your aunt anymore today. You'll have a few minutes to say good-bye."

Josh nodded. "Of course." He led Chris back into Kathy's room where they said their good-byes and left for the night.

* * *

The next day Chris came to see Kathy alone. She was sitting up in bed, writing in her notebook.

"What are you writing?" He cocked his head to the side to try getting a glimpse, but she closed the notebook before he had the chance to catch anything.

"Nothing." She tucked the work under the covers opposite Chris. "Where's Josh?"

"A meeting or something. Student council, maybe? I don't know." Chris nodded at the neck brace she was wearing. "So what was the verdict once all the commotion settled down?"

"They put me in this stupid neck brace to make sure I keep still. Apparently I could've really done some damage when I whipped my head back like that." She spoke matter-of-factly, fidgeting with a stray thread on her blanket. "It's so uncomfortable, though."

"I bet." Chris was a little distracted by what was in the notebook, so he asked about it again.

Kathy sighed, contemplating whether she should tell him, then decided she might as well. "Seeing as though I don't own any real exciting books to read while I lie here in boredom, I decided that I might as well write my own." She reluctantly handed Chris the notebook and added, "It's not very good, just some scribbles, mostly."

Chris skimmed the pages as Kathy mumbled on about how it was a stupid idea.

He realized that she had been writing about him and Josh. Although she used different names, she used their same powers and personalities and situations.

Chris interrupted Kathy's rambling, "This is really good. You should do something with it."

"What? Really? You think it's good?" Kathy was surprised; she never really told anyone about her hobby, except Will, but she was almost positive he had forgotten about it.

"Seriously, you should try to turn this into a book, or short story to sell to a magazine, or something," Chris said. "I'd read it." That was saying something, because Chris wasn't an avid reader by any stretch of the imagination. But he'd make the exception if she was writing about them.

"Well, I have thought about it. It's a lot more fulfilling than working as a day-care teacher." Chris gave back the notebook and she continued, "I don't know. What if someone catches on that it's about you two? What if people ask questions?"

Chris rolled his eyes. "Yeah, cause this is so believable. Most people don't believe in magic. I'm sure no one will suspect these stories are true. You could be like that *Christmas Carol* guy and only submit little pieces like comics."

"Well, first I need to get out of here," said Kathy as the doctor walked in.

"How are you today, Miss Walker?"

"Incredibly bored." Kathy smiled. "But otherwise I'm feeling good."

Chris stood. "I should get home to do some homework. I'll be back tomorrow."

"Careful getting home. Tell Josh I missed him today," Kathy called as her nephew left.

* * *

Two days after Kathy was first admitted, the doctors ran their tests. All came back good, if not great. They were stumped as to why Kathy had more or less died and come back without any repercussions. Kathy and the boys knew that magic had come into play, so they weren't concerned at all. Their biggest problem was getting her back to full strength. Luckily, Kathy had persuaded the doctors to let her go home.

So the boys showed up bright and early Saturday morning to pick her up. As they stepped off the elevators on their aunt's floor, they noticed a pair of police officers talking to Kathy's doctor and nurse.

Josh could tell by the way Dr. Salmon looked at them that something was wrong. She had a green headband in her short dark hair. Her hands were deep in the pockets of her white lab coat.

"What's going on?" Josh asked, afraid of what the answer would be. Surely, if Kathy had taken a turn for the worse, they would've called them, right?

Tears welled up in the nurse's green eyes, and she raised a fist to her lips, clutching another patient's chart to her chest. She excused herself and disappeared into a bathroom down the hall.

"What is it? What's wrong?" Chris asked, growing more and more anxious the longer they waited in suspense.

"I'll let officers Roland and Peterson explain. I'm sorry, boys, but I need to check on my other patients." The doctor gave a sad smile and walked past them. Her lab coat blew in the breeze as she moved swiftly.

Josh was tired of the looks of sympathy. "Is somebody going to tell us what's going on?"

"We should go somewhere private," one of the cops suggested. He looked about midthirties, but he still had bright blond hair.

"No, just tell us what the hell's going on!" Josh demanded.

The other officer—a black man with a goatee and short-cropped hair—put up his hands to settle Josh down. "Okay..." He paused only for a second to think up how to start. "Your aunt is missing."

"What do you mean? This place has people coming and going all over the place!" Chris said, although at the moment this wing of the hospital was pretty quiet.

"Apparently the nurse went in this morning to give your aunt her breakfast, and she was gone," the blond cop, Officer Peterson, explained. "She was here for the morning rounds, so we know she disappeared sometime between seven and eight this morning."

Josh looked at his phone. Just after ten. "She's only been missing for a short time, then?"

Officer Roland nodded. "It's not a missing person's case yet, but definitely something we're going to check into."

The officers took the boys into a waiting room and questioned them about Kathy: Did she have any reason to run away? Was there anywhere she would go? Had anyone ever made any threats on her life?

After the questioning, the boys went home. Their heads were spinning with possibilities.

"What are you doing?" Chris asked for what seemed like the millionth time since he and Josh had left the hospital. They were in the magic room now, and Josh was flipping through the pages of the magic book.

"Someone said that it was as if someone popped in, grabbed Aunt Kathy, and then popped out again without being seen," Josh finally explained.

"So? Lots of people know how to do that. Well, lots of people we know."

"But none of those people want her." Josh continued his search in the giant tome.

"You think it's Will?" Chris walked over next to Josh to look at the book. Josh had stopped at the profile Kathy had written for him.

"Well, who else could it be?" Josh asked. "Nobody else is obsessed with her like he is. Maybe once he learned she was in the hospital, he figured it was the perfect time to strike? Get her while she's down."

"Aunt Kathy said he told her he was going to leave her alone. We should consider our other options. What about the Queen and Kaiser? What about that other guy who was here when she was attacked?" Chris asked. "Maybe they are the ones who took her. They were the ones who put her in the hospital to begin with."

"I was thinking about that, but it doesn't make sense," Josh explained. "I mean, why wouldn't they have taken her when they originally attacked her? Wouldn't they just attack again?"

"Maybe the new guy wanted her, and when he saw me, he disappeared before he could grab her. Maybe he came back to the hospital where she was vulnerable to finish the job?"

"It's been a couple days, though," Josh stated.

"But a hospital is not the most barren place," Chris prodded. "Maybe he didn't have a chance to take her until now?"

"I don't know. Either way, we're going to find Will and see what he knows," Josh said.

"Don't you think that's reckless? We're down a witch," Chris said.

"Then what do you expect us to do!" Josh snapped. "We owe it to her to try everything we can to get her back. I'm not losing her again."

Chris let out a deep breath. "Fine. I'll start tracking him. You look in the book for a spell that could take him out if need be."

Chris began the searching ritual. He went into Kathy's room, hoping that her energy would help channel the ritual's power and locate her sooner. He also wanted to get away from Josh. They didn't need to be bickering right now. They needed to find Kathy.

Josh flipped through the pages in the book, reading different spells and potions. He hoped to find just the right thing to bring his aunt home.

Their concentration was broken when the doorbell rang, making both boys jump.

Chris looked across the hall into the magic room and called, "Who is that?"

Josh stood. "Stay here and keep searching. I'll go check it out."

When Josh opened the door, he saw a man wearing a suit. When the man saw Josh, he flashed his white teeth through his beard.

He introduced himself as Eric Coleman.

"What can I help you with?" Josh kept the door between him and the stranger.

"I understand you live with Kathy Walker in this house?" The man took half a step forward, but Josh held his ground.

"Yeah, me and my brother. She's our aunt," Josh answered. "Why do you ask?"

"I also understand that your aunt was hospitalized a couple days ago, and that this morning she went missing," the man continued, ignoring Josh's question.

"Why don't you tell me why you're here?" Josh asked firmly, still leaning on the open door.

"I am wondering if you know where her husband is. He seems to have gone missing, too." Coleman turned toward Josh in time to see his mouth fall open.

Before he could speak, Chris yelled from upstairs, "Josh, I can't find him anywhere!" He bounded down the stairs and entered the living room.

"Witches, I assume?" Coleman asked. He pushed his way into the house.

Josh slammed the front door shut and waved his hand. A gust of wind came and pushed Coleman through the air into the next room.

"That was the guy who was here when Aunt Kathy was attacked!" Chris pointed at Coleman.

"Who the hell are you?" Josh asked.

"I already told you that," the lawyer answered with a smile, standing now.

"Tell us how you are involved with magic," Chris demanded. "Trust me, dude, I can do a lot worse than throw you across the room, so you better have a good answer."

"Well then, I should tell you that I am a witch as well," he replied.

"Right," Josh said, skeptical.

"I'm only half witch. My father was a mortal," he explained. "You cannot sense any danger from a mortal can you?"

Josh tilted his head. "No."

"What do you want with us?" Chris asked as he put up his hands, ready to defend himself and his brother.

"I need your help," Coleman confessed.

"Is Will really missing?" Josh asked.

"Yes, but that's not why I'm here."

"Then why are you here?" Josh asked.

"Just hear me out. I am working with the Queen and Kaiser, but I don't really like some of the things they make me do to people, nor do I like what they do to people with their magic."

"So you're bad and want to be good?" Josh asked.

"You're full of crap! You can't just flip sides like that!" Chris shouted.

"Being good or evil isn't genetic. Most people don't change, because it's how they were raised, and it's rooted in their way of life. It's not common, but sometimes it does happen," Coleman explained.

"Just shut up! No more excuses!" Chris yelled as he moved to strike.

Josh held out his arm in front of him.

"Your aunt has knowledge that isn't in your magic book, experiences that aren't recorded. She has gone through more magical problems than most," Coleman explained. "I think that's why she's missing."

"So they want her only so she can't help us?" Chris asked.

"Probably," Coleman admitted. "The Queen doesn't really tell me her whole plan because she thinks that half-breeds like me aren't as entitled to magic as pure witches."

"So we need to find the Queen and Kaiser, and that's how we'll find Aunt Kathy?" Josh asked.

Coleman nodded. "I think so."

"Do you have anything of hers we could use to find her?" Chris asked.

"I could show you where she is," Coleman admitted. "I live there, too."

"Then let's go," Chris said. "Is it close?" He reached over, grabbed his coat from the rack, and pulled out a few potions from a cabinet they had by the coat rack.

"Wait," Josh said. "How do we know this isn't a trap?"

"You'll just have to trust me," Coleman replied.

Josh scoffed.

Chris pulled Josh to the side. "What are you doing? He's going to take us to her."

"Doesn't it seem a little suspicious that he shows up right when she's missing and knows exactly where she is? We've never met him before, and maybe he was the one that put her in the hospital to begin with? You said yourself that you saw him here when it first happened."

"Yeah, but you said we need to try everything to get her back," Chris argued.

"Except this seems like a surefire way to get kidnapped ourselves. Maybe even killed," Josh said. "I want to find her too, but we can't be sloppy about it."

Chris sighed and nodded. His brother was right. He just hated to admit it. They finally had a lead on what happened to Kathy, but it was more than likely a trap.

Josh turned back to Coleman, who was pretending not to listen in on their conversation. "How can we be sure we can trust you?"

Coleman shook his head. "You can't. But what I will offer you is this." He produced a vial in the palm of his hand. "It's a potion powerful enough to kill me. It's yours. This way, you don't have to worry."

Josh was still skeptical and stared at Coleman right in the eyes.

"Look." Coleman uncorked the bottle and slowly tapped a drop on the back of his hand. As soon as the liquid made contact, smoke rose up and his skin burned. He shook the potion off his hand. Where the potion had hit was a deep shade of purple. He recorked the bottle and handed it to Josh. "There's your protection."

Josh grabbed the vial. It wasn't complete insurance, but it definitely helped. He only wished he had two of them so he and Chris could both have one.

"Okay, are we ready to go?" Chris asked.

"Wait." Coleman closed his eyes and said, "She's not there for some reason. Neither she nor Kaiser are there."

"Then where would she be?" Chris asked.

"Let me check." Coleman closed his eyes again and said, "They're at...they're at a run-down house...with some other guy."

"Is it close?" Josh asked.

"Yeah. A couple miles away." Coleman opened his eyes.

"Let's go get them!" Chris headed toward the door.

"Chris, wait," Josh said. "We have no way to defeat the Queen or Kaiser if they attack. Not to mention this other guy they're with."

"Then why don't we go check the book while Coleman tells one of us everything he knows about the Queen and Kaiser. Maybe we can come up with a spell or something."

Josh turned to Coleman. "If you help us, you will be stabbing the Queen in the back. That would mean that if our spell fails for some reason, you're probably going to be next to our names on her hit list."

Coleman took a deep breath. "It doesn't matter. I'm doing the right thing. We need to make sure that whatever spell you choose works. We won't have a second chance."

They went up to the magic room, and Chris looked through the book to find a match of Coleman's description of the man that was with the Queen and Kaiser. Josh tried to come up with a spell to take them out, but he always kept an eye on Coleman, holding the vial in his hand at all times. He didn't trust him. His transition to good seemed too easy.

* * *

The boys and Coleman rolled up to the old run-down house, which was just as Coleman had described. Josh cut the engine and stared out the window.

"I don't see anybody, but that doesn't mean that they're not in there somewhere," he said as he looked from inside his car. He was parked across the street from the old house. It was hard to see because the house was set far back from the road.

"Let's go," Chris said.

He got out of the car with Coleman and Josh following close behind. Josh caught up to his brother and grabbed his arm. He pulled him down by the side of an overgrown bush in the front yard.

"What if there's some magical barrier? We need to be careful," Josh warned.

"You tell me. Any danger?"

Josh looked around the neglected yard. There were a couple of rusty cars that had been abandoned, probably years ago. The rust and the overgrown foliage had nearly overtaken them. The grass was brown, and there were fallen leaves all over. But he still couldn't tell if there were any magical traps.

Finally, Coleman shook his head. "No. The only danger is what they're doing inside. They're trying to get into Kathy's head."

"Then we'll sneak up slowly," Chris suggested.

Coleman peeked his head over the top of the bush. "There's a dead tree up next to the house that we could hide behind if you sense anything, but other than that, there doesn't seem to be anything useful for us to use for protection. We'll need to be careful."

They left their hiding spot and ventured closer to the house. Coleman saw the broken windows, pointed to them, and then put his finger over his lips to tell the brothers to stay quiet.

The yard was covered with various objects that were now ruined after not being taken care of. There was a riding lawn mower stopped in the middle of the yard, a couple of bikes, plenty of branches that had fallen down, and an old shed at the end of the property that had seen better days.

The brothers and Coleman crept by the side of the house and came to the back door. Voices boomed from inside, and Chris ventured to the door and slowly tried to turn the knob. It wouldn't budge.

"Now what?" Coleman whispered. "Do we go to the front?"

"Nope!" Chris said as he held up his hands to blow the door up.

"Chris, wait!" Josh called.

Chris waved his hands and obliterated the door.

They charged into the house and stopped short in front of the stranger. They first noticed his deep crimson skin with tribal tattoos peeking out beneath a black robe. He was completely bald and wore a black goatee.

"Get out!" the man shouted in a garbled voice. He held out his hand and shot green acid at the boys and Coleman. They jumped out of the way, and the acid landed on what was left of the doorway. The part that was hit fizzed and melted.

"Holy crap!" Chris's eyes were wide, noting how close the acid had come to hitting him.

A giant energy beam shot from behind the red man and hit Coleman in the leg. He fell to the ground screaming, and Josh conjured a wind gust that sent their enemies flying back away from them. He saw at the last second that his power had pushed Kathy as well. Her limp body rolled and her brown hair flew into the air. He swore to himself, promising to be more careful next time he attacked.

"Eric Coleman?" A familiar voice asked from inside the house. "How dare you betray me!" The disembodied voice approached, and as it moved closer, the light revealed that it was the Queen.

"Run!" Chris yelled.

"Chris, get Coleman to the car. I'll keep these guys busy and meet up with you," Josh ordered.

"I have the stronger power, though!" Chris said as he blew up an energy beam and then closed his hand to make it reappear, bending it back to where it came from.

The red man stood up and shot acid at Chris. Josh used his new power to deflect it, and it flew out a broken window, melting the shards of glass that still remained in the window frame.

"Don't argue with me, Chris. Just do it!" Josh shouted once he had returned to his normal state.

Chris didn't say a word. He helped Coleman up, and they scrambled toward the car. Once Coleman was in the backseat, Chris hopped into the driver's seat.

THE BLOOD MOON

"Hang on!" He started the car, put it in gear, and raced down the overgrown lawn to the back of the house toward the fight.

Chris jerked the wheel to the left, and the car fishtailed in the yard. The passenger side was right outside the back door. He could see his brother inside. "Get in!"

Josh jumped into the passenger seat and started to deflect any attacks he could. Chris tried to speed away, but the tires dug into the ground, and the car refused to move. The Queen and Kaiser started to aim their attacks at parts of the house in hopes that it would collapse.

The new enemy stood up, grabbed Kaiser by the throat, and lifted him into the air.

"You are worthless," he screamed. "Although I do thank you for bringing that woman to me."

He threw Kaiser to the ground and held out his hand.

"Please, no!" Kaiser begged for mercy.

The red man was stern as he shot acid out of his hand, spraying Kaiser, leaving him screaming as his body was dismembered. The man motioned for Josh and Chris to come to him.

Chris walked out and Josh followed. "Chris, are you nuts?" Josh said in a loud whisper, grabbing his brother's arm.

Chris looked at his brother. "Aunt Kathy's still in there." He slipped his arm out of Josh's grasp and kept walking toward the strange and menacing demon.

The man faced the Queen, who lay across the threshold of the house. He put his arm around Chris and said, "Now, what are we going to do about this nuisance? She's been a problem for you two for a while now."

"We've…uh…actually come up with a way to defeat her," Chris stammered. He didn't like how close the man was to him.

"But I have a feeling you won't be prepared," he said. "See, I've been studying her just as long as I've been studying you two." He fished out a vial from inside his robe and handed it to Chris.

"What is that for?" Josh stepped next to his brother.

"We could do great things together, the three of us," he said, now putting his arms around both of them and drawing them in together. "We just need this bitch out of the way."

"Are you gonna get rid of her or should we?" Josh asked as he removed the red man's arm from his shoulder.

"I'll do it, just as soon as you take that potion," he insisted again.

"What is it?" Chris asked again.

"It will protect you," the red man said.

Hesitantly, Chris sipped it and handed the rest to Josh. It tasted horrible, and soon the brothers felt completely numb.

"I don't like this," Chris said, but he could only hear himself in his head. He wasn't even sure he spoke out loud.

The red man grabbed the Queen by her throat and lifted her up, just as he had done to Kaiser.

The Queen opened her mouth and let out a deadly screech. Josh and Chris could hear it despite the potion. Coleman screamed from inside the car as the windows shattered.

The red man screamed out in pain as he clenched her throat harder. He used his other hand to shoot acid into her stomach. The screech echoed, then died as the Queen was decimated.

THE BLOOD MOON

The numbness soon wore off for the brothers. They walked over to the red man, who leaned on his knees, gasping for breath.

Josh looked down at the stranger. "You helped us. Thank you."

"Don't...get used...to it," the red man choked between coughs.

"Josh, come here a second." Chris turned his back toward the red man and began to lead Josh away.

"What?"

"We can get rid of him now," Chris proposed. "We can make sure he won't bother us later. I think he's weak from her screaming, so I can just blow him up real quick."

Josh shook his head. "But he helped us. He possibly saved many people's lives, maybe even ours." He thought of all the potential harm the Queen could've done if she had lived.

"But how do you know that he won't try to kill us later?"

"We don't, but we'll make him a deal. We take Aunt Kathy and promise we'll leave him alone—for now—if he leaves us alone. If either of us breaks it, then we both can go after each other."

Chris shook his head, not liking the idea, but he knew they had no other viable option. They turned around and walked past the red man into the house.

Kathy lay on the dusty old wooden floor. Josh and Chris picked her up gently and carried her to the car.

Josh sighed when he saw the windows. "So much for my new car; I wonder how I should send this in for my insurance."

Chris chuckled; sometimes he could only laugh at how strange their lives would seem to the rest of the world.

"Where the hell…do you think…you're going…with her?" the red man asked weakly. "She's mine." He moved and reached for them but winced in pain.

"No, she's not. We're taking her back where she belongs," Josh replied after Kathy was safely in the car.

"We'll make you a deal," Chris continued. He folded his arms and leaned against the acid-burned doorway. "We get her without a problem, then we don't go after you, and you don't come after us. I mean it's obvious you're weak now. If we wanted to, we could kill you right now."

"So, is it a deal?" Josh asked as he held out his hand.

The stranger glared at him. After a long moment, he took Josh's hand and grumbled, "Deal."

* * *

As they drove away, Chris turned to Coleman and asked, "Are you all right?"

No answer.

"Coleman?" Chris asked again.

Silence.

Chris reached back to shake him, but as soon as he put a hand on Coleman, he felt warm liquid on his hand. It was covered in blood. Blood trickled from Coleman's ears and nose, and he wasn't breathing.

The Blood Moon

"Coleman's dead!"

"I didn't expect him to live," Josh said solemnly. He kept his eyes on the road. "He wasn't protected during the screech, so I figured since he wasn't nearly as strong as that red guy, so he wouldn't make it."

"That's too bad," Chris said, turning back around and wiping the blood on his jeans. "Now we've lost one of the only chances we've had for some help. If that made sense."

"I got it," Josh said as he drove.

"It sucks that we finally get someone else to help us out and…you know…" Chris put his feet up on the dashboard and lowered his seat to block most of the wind from hitting his face. "Usually, it's me and you against all things evil, but it was a nice change to have someone else on our side."

Chapter Seven

It was the beginning of November. Two weeks had passed since their encounter with the mysterious red-skinned man. Josh and Chris had returned their aunt to the hospital, unsure of what exactly had happened to her. It wasn't good news. Dr. Salmon told the boys she was in another coma, and they weren't sure why. She was going to be kept for further testing. Her mysterious disappearance had sparked an investigation. Luckily, the doctors at the hospital and some of the boys' neighbors provided an alibi for them, so the police didn't consider them suspects. After some routine questioning, influenced a little by some charms, the boys were off the hook with their aunt's kidnapping.

The brothers made sure that Eric Coleman received a proper burial after reporting to authorities that they found him dead in an alley. They were thankful that the investigation was quick and the death ruled a suicide. It appeared as if Coleman had jumped from the adjacent building.

After the two investigations, Josh and Chris had missed the opportunity to track the red man, and now they were at a loss of where their enemies were and what they were up to. The boys were no longer at full strength now that the police were involved. Neighbors continued to knock on the door and ask to help out, whether it be with a meal, a ride to school, or a place to stay. Josh appreciated it but didn't think it was wise to bring someone else into their magical lives. He didn't want to risk getting them in trouble or killed simply by association.

In order to ensure their protection, they put up a magical barrier around the house. They were trying to keep themselves protected from anything. They were not in a position to be attacked right now. And they had no idea who might be attacking. So many of their enemies had died, but new enemies had already come in to take their place.

Josh and Chris let down the barrier when they got home from school two weeks after they returned Kathy to the hospital. They jumped as a girl appeared in a swirl of white sparks. The girl had long straight brown hair that reached halfway down her back. She was dressed in jeans and a green V-neck T-shirt. Her expression was soft, yet serious.

"Who the hell are you?" Chris asked, putting up his hands, ready to defend. The anxiety of being attacked at any time had built up over the past two weeks.

"Don't worry. I'm a good guy," she said, folding her arms

across her chest. "Are you guys witches?"

"I…uh…what are you talking about?" Chris stuttered. Clearly, she was magical somehow, but it was best to play dumb until he could be sure. Of course, he was no actor.

"I'm a witch, too," she said, assuming Chris's comment was a confirmation.

"What do you want?" Josh asked. He didn't trust her.

"Why are you so rude?" she countered.

"Well, let's see; you barge in here using magic we don't recognize, then you ask us questions about being witches. We don't even know your name, and I'm sure you don't know ours!" He raised his hands, like his brother, ready to use his power.

"Relax. I'm not after you," she said with a smirk. "I understand your concern, but if you listen for just a second, we could talk and actually get to the point of why I'm here."

"All right. Talk." Chris's eyes were focused on hers, noting how intensely emerald they were.

She took a seat in one of the oversized chairs in the living room. The boys continued standing.

"So, where should we start?" the girl asked.

"Your name would be nice," Josh prompted. A little stunned by her casualness, he leaned against the arm of the chair on the opposite side of the room. His arms were sitting in his lap, ready to use his magic if need be.

Her expression changed as she thought about how to start her story. "Holly." She sighed, looking at the floor. "My name is Holly."

The Blood Moon

Chris waited, but when she didn't continue, he asked, "Do you have a last name?" He sat down on the couch and put his feet up on the coffee table. By the way she spoke, he no longer thought of her as a threat. Or at least he didn't want to. She was too beautiful.

"Bowen. Holly Bowen," she said nervously, still not making eye contact. They sat quietly. The boys weren't sure how else to continue. Finally, Holly looked at each of them and asked, "And yours?"

"I'm Chris Harper, and that's my brother Josh," Chris said pointing to Josh. "He gets a little cranky sometimes."

"Nice to meet you guys." Holly looked up at Chris and smiled.

Chris looked her in the eyes, and for a moment they were locked in each other's gaze. He could tell that Holly was not evil, but Josh was not as trusting.

"Let's get on with it," Josh barked. "Why are you here? How did you find us? Why did you find us?" He rattled off his questions so fast Holly couldn't answer. Finally, Josh gave her a chance to respond.

"Well, I came to Erie because my Dad told me it was too dangerous for me to stay in Salem," Holly explained.

"Like from the witch trials?" Chris asked.

"Nope, Salem, New York," Holly said.

"Why was it dangerous?" Josh asked.

"There is this evil witch that has been after my family since my great-grandmother attacked her," Holly explained. "Her name is Toxanna. She swore that she was going to kill every member of the Bowen family."

"So this witch has been attacking your family for…" Chris started to ask but got caught up with figuring out the math.

"Over eighty years," Holly finished with a nod. "Maybe longer."

"Has she succeeded so far?" Josh asked.

Holly dropped her eyes down to the floor remembering her late family. "The only people left are my uncle, my dad, and me." Her voice broke. "Really it's just me and my dad because my uncle got turned into a bird by Toxanna."

"A bird?" Chris asked.

"Yeah, when a witch comes close to death, and their magic is almost completely gone, they become a bird until their magic has fully healed. Almost like a rebirth, like a phoenix," Holly explained. "Anyway, she created this huge snowstorm, and I was kidnapped, and she nearly killed me. My father sent me to my mom's old mortal friend, Margaret. She knows about magic and stuff, but she doesn't talk about it. He says it would be safer, but I can't help thinking that I should've stayed and helped."

"So how did you find us?" Josh asked after a moment.

Holly explained, "I used a spell to find a powerful good witch in the area, and I found the two of you."

"Why were you looking for us?" Chris asked, leaning forward and resting his arms on his knees.

"I need your guys' help," she said. "My dad and my uncle could be in serious danger. They were training me so I could use the magic from my family line to take out Toxanna." Holly fought back tears while explaining. She wiped her eyes and then said, "And now I'm determined to help them. I will never be able to forgive myself if anything happens to them!"

Chris walked over to Holly and put his arm around her to comfort her. "We'll help," he said.

"Chris, can I talk to you?" Josh asked.

They walked out, leaving Holly alone in the living room.

"Are you seriously going to help her?" Josh asked, keeping his voice down.

"Well, yeah," Chris answered. "She needs the help, and so do we."

"How do you know she's not lying to us?" Josh asked. "I don't want to get killed just because you have a little crush!"

Chris glared at his brother. "I could tell by the way she was looking at me that she was telling the truth. And honestly I think we need her help more than she needs ours."

"No. We have each other." Josh took a step back to peek in the living room to see what Holly was doing. She was looking at the various family photos that hung on the wall.

"Exactly! Just imagine if I wasn't here to help you. Just imagine if you were here alone, and all you did all day long was think about what you're truly going through. We just lost Coleman, and he was only on our side for a short time. Think of how much we can benefit from this!"

Josh was still watching Holly gaze at the photos. "Fine. But if she gives off the hint of a threat, we're going to have to send her back to that snowstorm in Salem."

Chris nodded his head in agreement as the brothers rejoined Holly in the living room. She was looking at the last photo they had of Samantha, taken a year before she died. She had a genuine smile as she hugged Josh and Chris close to her. They were out in front of the Victorian house they lived in.

"Is this your mother?" Holly asked, pointing to the picture.

"Yeah, she's been gone about a year now," Josh said.

"I'm so sorry," she said. "My mother was killed before I was born."

"How could she die before you were born?" Chris asked. Then, sensing his carelessness, he added, "Are you adopted?"

"No, I'm not adopted." Holly smiled. "When my mother was pregnant with me, Toxanna kidnapped me from the womb," she explained. "So Toxanna gave birth to me and raised me until I was a year old. My dad got me back, but my mother never met me. Even as a baby."

"That's…interesting…" Josh mumbled.

"Our mother was killed by evil, too," Chris explained. "But we made sure we nabbed him before he could even brag about it."

Chris and Holly locked eyes until Josh slapped his brother's arm. "Follow me, maybe we can find a way to channel all your family's magic so we can finish off this witch quick to get her out of your hair." Josh headed upstairs to the magic room. Chris and Holly smiled at each other.

"We're going to help," Chris said. "Josh is just…cautious."

Holly smiled and mouthed, "Thank you."

When they got to the magic room, they looked through the magic book to see if they could find anything about Toxanna. They were startled when they saw that there was a mention of her in the magic book.

"That's weird," Josh commented.

"Why?" Holly asked. "Toxanna is a powerful witch."

"Yeah, but this was written by our ancestors. If Toxanna has a personal vendetta against your family, then how would she cross paths with anyone in our family?"

Holly shrugged. "Maybe she was a threat to more witches before she focused in on my family?"

Josh chewed on his lip. "Maybe."

The trio continued their research. What was provided in the book only supplied her specialty: water. There was no list of a spell or a potion or any ritual the witches could use to protect themselves from the evil witch. They were engrossed in their research when a man a little older than Josh appeared in a puff of white smoke. He wore a black leather jacket. His brown hair fell in his eyes, and he swept it up with his hand.

"Drew!" Holly exclaimed.

Before the brothers had a chance to react, five men appeared in a swirl of flames. They surrounded the room. They wore blue robes with single triangles on their chests.

"Told you she was trouble," Josh muttered to Chris. He put up his hands and created a windstorm that pushed two of the men into the hallway. The pages of the magic book flapped in the breeze.

Chris put up his hands and tried to blow up one of the men, but nothing happened.

"Your fire specialty won't work on us," one of the men explained.

Drew grabbed Holly's hand and disappeared in a puff of white smoke. The two remaining men turned on Josh and Chris.

"Duck!" Josh shouted to his brother.

Chris backed into a corner, which didn't sit well with him. It was such a small room, and there were so many enemies. The only exit was blocked by the two men Josh pushed into the hallway.

The pages of the magic book fluttered as Josh erupted into a small cyclone, knocking down the men as he moved throughout the tiny room. Shutters rattled and papers floated in the air like leaves. Suddenly Josh stopped and stumbled on his feet. He wasn't used to the new advancement of his power yet.

"You okay?" Chris asked, sizing up the doorway to see if they could make a break for it. He didn't think they could. He looked to the window. Too high to jump. And that would leave the men with the magic book.

Three of the men regained their bearings and turned on the brothers. One of them conjured a fireball and raised it to fire at them. Suddenly, he stopped and smoldered, emitting smoke to the ceiling that set off the fire alarms. Finally, in one last blast he exploded.

When the enemy was gone, Josh and Chris saw Drew and Holly standing in the doorway. The two men who were in the hallway were gone, and the two remaining men looked at each other and disappeared in a swirl of blue flame.

"What the hell was that?" Josh shouted at Drew and Holly. "You tell us that you're safe, and not even an hour later we're attacked?"

"It's my fault." Drew took a step closer to Josh, who put up his hand. He didn't say a word, but his eyes clearly said Don't.

"Who are you?" Chris asked. He kept his gaze on Drew; he didn't want to look at Holly. He felt betrayed.

"This is my trainer. He's a wizard," Holly said. "We should go downstairs and talk."

"You both need to leave," Josh said. His gaze was hard, and he raised his hands, ready to expel another wind gust.

"Woah, look, I have news about your aunt!" Drew threw up his hands in front of his face, hoping to stall Josh's attack.

Chris stepped forward. "What about her?"

"Is she married to a Dark Knight?"

"Sort of, yeah." Chris didn't add the divorce part.

"I was just at the hospital and saw him leave her room."

"You're lying," Josh said.

"She's in the ICU, right? Room 4?"

Josh raised an eyebrow. "Why were you there?"

Drew straightened up now that he had Josh's attention. He fixed his leather jacket. "I had a run in with the Fire Wizards—the men who were just here—and a civilian got hurt. None of my spells would heal the fire magic they used on her, so I took her to the ER. I was waiting to see if she was okay, and I sensed the knight there. That's when I noticed the woman in the next room was a witch."

"So how did you find us?" Chris asked.

"He was trying to find me," Holly explained. "That's how he ended up in Erie."

Josh lowered his hands. "So what's the deal with these…Fire Wizards?"

"Well, I was once one of them," Drew explained. "Before they were murderous, power-hungry *sorcerers*." He spit the last word like it left a bad taste in his mouth. "How much do you know about wizards? In general?"

"I know they can be just as powerful as witches, but they need wands and potions to channel the magical energy out," Chris stated. "They weren't using wands, though."

"Because they were bound together. The Fire Wizards are essentially a coven of wizards," Drew explained.

"I thought witches were the ones that belonged to covens?" Chris was more intrigued by Drew's story than he was threatened by him. Not like Josh, who was clenching his jaw.

"Mostly witches are the ones that belong in covens, but in this case they're wizards who came together to enhance their magical skill sets," Drew explained. "See, they each studied fire magic, so when they come together and use a binding spell, their power is enhanced. You get them each alone and they're not nearly as powerful."

"So fire magic is their specialty, like mine is, right?" Chris asked.

"Wizards don't work like that. Like you said, they use wands and spells to channel their magic. These guys have the fire spells mastered so that they don't even have to speak the charm before they shoot it out the end of their wands. And when they're together, they don't even need wands."

"So how come they followed you here? Or did you lead them here?" Josh asked.

"No, they followed me. They've been chasing me for some time now," Drew confessed. "I'm sorry that I brought them here. That was…irresponsible."

Something about Drew's story didn't add up. Josh pressed him further. "How about you tell us the whole story?"

Drew looked to the floor and smiled. His dark hair fell, and he pushed it back out of his face when he looked at the brothers again. "I was part of their coven, it's true. But they were different then. They used their power to fight evil. But something happened in the hierarchy of the Fire Wizards and they turned. Suddenly they were helping the bad guys. I didn't like it so I quit. They broke my wand, severed my connection from the group, and have been hunting me ever since."

"But we just killed one of them," Chris said.

"Those five were just a faction of the coven as a whole. I don't even know how large the whole coven is. Possibly hundreds of wizards. And you can't tell who belongs to it until it's too late," Drew explained. "So no, that one wizard I killed barely scratched the surface."

"This is your problem, not ours." Josh pointed to Holly. "We told her that we'd help her with Toxanna, but that's it. I'm not even sure we should've agreed to that, either."

"Josh…" Chris started to protest, but he stopped. His brother had a point. They had enough on their plate. It was best not to get any extra blood on their hands than they needed to. But he hated to send Drew and Holly to the dogs after they had helped them.

"The Fire Wizards are Drew's problem," Holly said, touching Drew's shoulder. "And I suppose Toxanna is my problem, but Drew has been helping me with Toxanna, and we still can't get rid of her. You guys could use our help, too. Why don't we agree to help each other?"

"No," Josh said. He busied himself by picking up the mess that he created from the attack. "You know your way out."

"Josh, we need to go check in on Will," Chris said. "Maybe Holly should come with us?"

"Yeah, I have a few things to take care of. I'll try to shake the Fire Wizards off my trail—off your trail. They won't be a problem for you," Drew said. He gave Holly a quick hug. "It's good to see you're okay. You know how to reach me." He pulled out a potion from his jacket pocket and drank it, disappearing in a puff of smoke.

"Who's Will?" Holly asked.

"A really bad guy," Josh said, setting the magic book back on the table.

Chris rolled his eyes at his brother. "He's our aunt's soon-to-be ex-husband. She hates him, but he still loves her. So now he's plotting ways to win her back using dark magic."

Josh rummaged through the scattered debris of the magic room and found a couple of bottles of potions that had labels on them. He read them and slipped them in his pocket. "All right, so we'll go to Will's. Scope things out to see if he's up to anything. If he went to see Aunt Kathy, he's got to be up to something."

* * *

"Why are all the windows smashed?" she asked as they got underway. Cold night wind swirled around inside the car.

"It's a long story," Josh said, gripping the wheel. He was still cooling down from the encounter with the Fire Wizards.

"Occupational hazard." Chris shrugged.

Holly rattled off a spell and waved her hand at the space where the windows had been. They reappeared, intact, as she said, "That's better," and moved her hair out of her face. "So what? You can't get your windows fixed?"

Chris was amazed at her casual use of power, and it took him a second to continue. "Basically, a bad guy killed our bad guys. She was a banshee and the windows shattered when she was killed."

Holly nodded, but didn't say anything. She was wondering if she had gotten in over her head with these boys.

Josh pulled into the apartment parking lot. "Let's go. Get ready for anything."

They got out and followed Josh to Will's apartment. He

fumbled with the lock, trying to pick it. Chris grumbled that he should just use his power, but with a click the door opened.

They entered the living room and turned on the lights. Will wasn't the cleanest person, but for a demonic warrior, his apartment looked pretty nice. Secondhand furniture filled the room. Blackout shades covered the windows, and there were at least a dozen pictures of Kathy throughout the small apartment. Other than the sound of traffic outside, the place was silent.

"He better not be at the hospital," Josh warned. "Chris, look in the bedroom, I got the closet and the bathroom. Holly, you watch the door."

She shut the door but decided against locking it. They might need to make a quick escape.

Chris came flying out of the bedroom, crashing into the opposite wall a few seconds later. He scrambled to his feet and ran to Holly.

"Why don't you witches leave me the hell alone!" Will growled as he emerged from the bedroom. He was dressed in gym shorts and a T-shirt, and he appeared to have been sleeping.

"He's the bad guy?" Holly was astonished. Chris didn't like the way Holly looked at Will. Jealously ripped through him as he discovered a new reason to hate Will.

"Who's the chick?" Will asked. "Replaced your aunt already?"

A force of wind shot through the apartment that sent Will crashing into a table, snapping it in half. Josh stepped out of the bathroom, hands extended, palms out.

Will stood. "Don't get too attached to her. She's next!" He conjured a sword and swung it in the air artfully.

He charged at Holly, and she held out her hands in panic. Will dropped the sword as if it were on fire. "How did you…?" He looked at Holly, stunned.

Josh used his power and knocked Will to the ground. He scooped up the sword and pointed it right at Will's neck. "Stay the hell away from Aunt Kathy. Next time, I won't hesitate."

* * *

"Did you see the look on Will's face? That was awesome," Chris raved as he plunked down on the couch and gnawed at his pizza later that night.

"Yeah, but do you think she knew she could do that?" Josh asked.

Chris shrugged. "Who cares?" A chunk of pizza was stuffed into the side of his cheek as he spoke. "She was protecting herself. Maybe she has a few spells and charms memorized herself?"

"But that was pretty powerful magic," Josh said as he put a slice of pizza on his plate.

"Good." Chris swallowed. "It's about time we start gaining allies. Powerful ones, too."

"Do we really trust her, though?"

Chris chewed another bite as he thought about it. He tried to maintain a level head, despite the way he felt. On one hand, she claimed to need their help with a demonic witch who had yet to show her face. On the other hand, she seemed to bring trouble almost immediately with Drew and the Fire Wizards. She and Drew even took off as soon as the wizards started attacking. Yet Drew was the one who'd killed one of them. Was that just a show? Chris couldn't tell. "I think we need more time to decide. We should definitely keep an eye on her. Drew too."

Josh nodded. "I don't trust him at all. I think he's trouble."

"I think you should stop worrying. He saved us today. Let's just count our blessings."

"I guess you're right," Josh agreed. "I just don't want us to be left vulnerable. Especially now. Mom's gone. Aunt Kathy's in a coma. Will is a freak and pretty much our only problem right now."

"Well, we have Toxanna to worry about," Chris reminded his brother.

"No, that's Holly's problem. We don't need to bring on a whole host of problems with more issues."

"Listen, she needs our help," Chris explained. "She has less family than we do. We have each other and Aunt Kathy. Granted Aunt Kathy's out of commission, but she's still here. All Holly has is her dad who, let's face it, is probably dead, and her uncle, the bird." Chris made a face. "What is he? A turkey? I mean, am I going to accidentally eat him in my sandwich next week?"

Josh smiled. He took a bite of his pizza, chewed a bit, then changed the subject. "Well, tomorrow we need to go to the hospital early and check up on Aunt Kathy."

"Hopefully, she'll be safe overnight," Chris added with a

mouthful. He swallowed and said, "Maybe tomorrow we should go and put a protection spell on her?"

Josh nodded. "We'd have to get the wording right to let the doctors do their work, but that's a good idea."

CHAPTER EIGHT

T he rain poured like someone was dumping a never-ending bucket of water all over the city. On their drive to the hospital, the boys heard flood warnings on the radio. They decided to park in the parking garage so they could stay dry. As they approached Kathy's room, they heard a familiar voice. Stopping short of the doorway, Josh said to Chris, "Is that Will?"

Chris's eyes bulged as he realized who it was. He nodded.

"Okay, just act natural. We can take care of this inside," Josh directed. The air had already started to stir as he grew even more agitated that Will was there.

They walked in and Chris shut the door behind them. Will stood over Kathy's unconscious body, holding her hand. Using a force of wind, Josh pushed Will away from her.

"Hello to you, too." Will smiled as he flattened his tie back down to his body. He had a black pinstriped shirt and a silver tie. "Your magic sure has intensified."

"Mine isn't the only magic that's grown," Josh replied.

Chris stood next to his brother and attempted to obliterate Will with his power, but Will's body simply expanded a little, as if he were a balloon being blown up, then quickly resumed its normal size.

Disappointed it didn't work, Chris glared at him. "What's your problem?"

"What problem?" Will asked. "You two are the ones who came in here and attacked me. I just wanted to visit my wife."

"Ex-wife," Chris corrected.

"You know what we mean, Will," Josh said. "Don't play dumb. You come in here every day, and you know she wants nothing to do with you."

Will stared at them for a second and then suddenly threw out his right hand and muttered a hex.

Black sparks came down from the ceiling and started to swirl around Josh and Chris. At first, the boys were startled by the sudden use of magic and began looking up at the ceiling where the sparks seemed to be coming from. Will's magic took hold, and both boys felt lightheaded. Chris collapsed on the floor, and Josh managed to get to a chair before he passed out.

* * *

Josh woke up to the sound of someone pounding on the door, desperate to get in. As he stirred, he noticed Chris on the floor and struggled to get to him. Groggy didn't even begin to explain the way he felt. Each limb felt like it weighed three hundred pounds.

Sliding to the floor, Josh crawled to his brother, ignoring the sounds of the fists on the door.

"You better answer that," Will said, towering over him. "Wouldn't want the doctors to prevent you from coming in here."

"Stay…away…" Josh mumbled.

Will put a hand to his ear. "I'm sorry, what was that? Didn't catch that." He smiled. "Have fun fixing this mess, boys." As he turned to leave, he was struck with the same hex that the boys were under and collapsed beside Chris.

Josh looked up and saw Drew. He was too weak to ask questions. He didn't have the energy to recoil when Drew placed his hand on Josh's forehead and muttered a charm under his breath. As Drew moved to Chris, Josh could feel relief flooding over him, helping him slowly regain his strength.

Josh sat back against the chair. The knocking at the door had stopped, and he wondered if the hospital staff had called the police.

As Chris came to, he fired off questions at Drew. "What's going on? Why are you here? What happened to Will? Why am I on the floor?"

"Easy," Drew said, kneeling beside him. "Give it a few minutes, you'll feel better."

"How did you know we were here?" Josh asked. He wasn't

quite ready to admit to himself or anyone else that Drew had saved them.

"Visiting the civilian from last night, sensed the knight again," Drew responded. "I heard the commotion outside, and I took care of it for you. Simple memory charm."

That explained the silence outside, but it didn't explain Will.

"How did you get in here with the door shut?" Josh asked. Chris was too tired to fire off any more questions, so his head bobbed back and forth between Josh and Drew.

Reaching into his leather jacket, Drew produced a small vial. "Teleportation potion. I have a ton of them made if you want to borrow one."

Josh put up his hand. "No thanks." He pointed to Will. "What did you do to him?"

Drew shrugged. "Same thing that happened to you."

"Why?"

"You know, I'm not a threat to you." Drew was getting angry.

Josh opened his mouth to protest, but he couldn't find a plausible argument. It was true that Drew brought the Fire Wizards to their house, but he had killed one of them. He'd also just saved them from Will.

"Do you know any truth spells?" Chris broke the silence.

Drew shrugged and nodded. "Yeah, a few. What do you have in mind?"

"An interrogation."

"In the hospital?" Josh asked.

"Why not? Drew fixed the situation outside, and it's not like it'd be any safer taking him home where we're more likely to be attacked. Let's stay in a crowded area while we can."

Josh threw up his hands in surrender. "Got any rope?"

"No need." Drew stood. "I can clear his head from the hex but leave his body cursed."

Josh didn't like that he threw around hex and curse like they were no big deal. Although, Chris did have a good idea, and this would be a good way to pump Will for answers.

Chris stood and staggered a little. Drew reached for him, but Chris put up his hand to stop him. "I got it. Just stood up too fast. C'mon, Josh, we need to get Will in the chair."

Josh stood and helped Chris lift Will into the chair. Drew stepped up to him and placed his hand on Will's forehead, just as he had Josh and Chris, and released magic into him.

Will came to with his full attitude. "You're a pretty smart wizard, aren't you? You certainly know your ancient spells. I must admit, I'm impressed."

"Why do you keep coming here?" Josh asked.

"I search her heart every time I come here," Will explained reluctantly. He seemed a little surprised at first. "A truth spell? How cute."

"Searching it for what?" Chris asked, ignoring Will's comment.

"I don't have to answer that. I don't have to say anything," Will said. He knew his way through the loopholes of spells like these.

Drew shrugged. "Sure. Of course, I also know a few wicked

curses myself." He leaned in close to Will's ear and lowered his voice so Josh and Chris wouldn't hear. "And I'm not that concerned with walking the line between good and evil." He stood up then. "So. It's up to you."

Josh and Chris exchanged worried glances.

"Love," Will answered. "Love for me. I want to know if she's really moved on."

"What did you find?" Josh asked. He was too curious to worry about more important questions.

"She still loves me," Will confessed, "but that might change when she finds out that I am the one who ordered the Queen to have Kathy put in a coma. Then she was kidnapped by Axon, and I went to get her back, but you two came and took her before I had the chance."

"Axon?" Chris asked. "Who's he?"

"He is the one who killed the Queen, Kaiser, and Eric Coleman. Eric would've been useful to me, but that's water under the bridge." Will tried to shrug, but the hex prevented him. "Anything else you boys wanna know about me? What's my real hair color? Exactly how much do I weigh? Oooh, I certainly kiss and tell after this little splurge of magic."

"Enough!" Josh didn't like how smug Will was. "We need to get rid of you so we can make sure Aunt Kathy's safe."

Will smiled. "Take your best shot, witch."

Josh whispered to Chris, "Do you know a spell?"

"I do." Drew opened his hand to the floor beneath Will's chair and spoke a charm. A hole appeared underneath Will, and he fell into it, disappearing into the blackness. The hole closed up behind him.

"Nice spell," Chris said. "How do you remember those crazy spells?"

"I have no other magic to rely on," Drew said.

Josh moved to his aunt's bedside. "Now that we got Will out of the way, we need to protect Aunt Kathy. We need to step up our protection on her so Will can't come near her. And if he does, at least cast a spell so he can't look in her heart. She's vulnerable now."

"What about the healing spell you cast on me before? Try it on her," Chris suggested.

Josh shook his head. "No, this is more serious than a simple spell."

Chris turned to Drew. "You have any ideas?"

He was leaning against the wall with his arms folded. "Didn't think they were welcome."

"They're not," Josh said.

"We'll take any help when it comes to Aunt Kathy." Chris shot his brother a look and turned back to Drew. "Please."

After some hesitation, Josh said, "Do you know a spell that is powerful enough to work?" He kept his eyes on Kathy.

"There's one that I'm thinking of, yeah. Should do the trick. Maybe not bring her out of the coma," Drew said. "I think that's the magic of drugs."

"Are there any side effects or anything?" Chris asked, knowing Josh didn't want to.

The Blood Moon

Drew stepped closer to them. "Maybe a little discomfort but nothing major. It's not that type of injury."

Finally, Josh looked at Drew. "Please help?"

He nodded and took Josh's place by Kathy's bedside. Laying a hand on her head, he muttered another charm. His hand started glowing white, and then Kathy's body started to glow white, too.

When the glow subsided, Drew stepped back. "Won't be long now. It just takes a few seconds to take effect. I'll leave you two alone." He pulled the teleportation vial out of his jacket and brought it to his lips.

"Hey," Josh said before he downed the potion, "thanks."

"Don't thank me yet," Drew said before he took the potion and disappeared in a puff of white smoke.

After Drew was gone, Kathy's monitors began shrieking with excitement. Chris opened the door and called into the hallway for help.

Kathy stirred and started pulling at the wires attached to her. Nurses flooded her bedside and pulled her breathing tube out and began to stabilize her.

* * *

"Glad to see you're awake," Chris said as he and Josh entered her room a couple of hours later.

"Me too," she replied, reaching for her throat. "My voice is a little raspy from the tube. I'm not supposed to talk, really. But how long was I out?"

"Two weeks." Josh took her hand.

"We have some things we want to tell you," Chris started.

"But that'll be saved until you get home from the hospital," Josh interrupted, shooting Chris a look. "We don't want to stress you out." He definitely didn't want her to know that they battled and interrogated Will right next to her unconscious body in a public place. She would not have approved of that.

"How did I end up in a coma?" Kathy asked. "The last thing I remember, I was going to an interview when I was attacked by that evil Queen." She stopped and looked down. When she looked back up at the two, she said, "But this…blond guy attacked me. He was the one who put me in the coma, wasn't he?" Then, before either of her nephews could answer, she said, "Yes, I know who it was. It was him. It was Eric Coleman, my lawyer. Is everyone in this world demonic!" She burst into a coughing fit that sent her monitors shrieking again. A nurse peeked her head in the room to make sure she was okay.

Josh squeezed her hand and shushed her softly. "Calm down. If you want to get out of here, you're going to need to stay calm."

Kathy took a deep breath and said, "Do you guys know what happened?"

"That's what we want to tell you," Chris started to say, but he was cut off by the entrance of Kathy's doctor.

"Glad to see you're awake, Miss Walker," the doctor said as she grabbed the chart off her bed and read it over.

"We're going to go," Josh announced. He stood and squeezed Kathy's hand. "C'mon, Chris."

CHAPTER NINE

So now you're on board with trusting Holly?" Chris asked. They were driving home, and Josh had just suggested that they ask Holly for help. The rain continued to pour down, and the thunder was beginning to roll in.

Josh shrugged. "Well, yeah. I mean, she helped us the last time we went to Will's place, and she hasn't given us any other reason not to trust her."

"But—like *you* said—she hasn't given us any reason to trust her, either."

Josh used his free hand to rub his face. "Look, Drew banished Will somewhere. We don't know how long he's going to be gone, so we need to act fast. We can't call Drew because we don't know if the Fire Wizards will follow him. Sure, Holly does have this demonic witch on her hands, but until now she hasn't made an attack."

"So basically Holly is the lesser of two evils," Chris said. Then, as an afterthought, added, "In a figurative sense."

As the rain slammed against the windshield and the wipers on Josh's car fluttered back and forth without making a difference, he gripped the wheel with both hands and kept his eyes on the road. He raised his voice over the sound of the rain. "Yeah. Do you have her number?"

"No. But we could just use a summoning spell or something. We'll find her one way or another," Chris said.

Josh pulled onto their street and into the driveway. They saw Holly huddled in the corner of the front patio under the small patch of roof that covered the cement steps, trying to avoid the rain.

By the time the brothers reached the door, they were already soaked.

"We were just going to call you," Chris said.

"What for?" she asked.

"We want to check out our uncle's house again," Chris explained. "We just ran into him again at the hospital."

Holly nodded. "Drew told me. Said you guys could probably use my help. I've been here a little while."

Josh pointed up. "The rain slowed us down getting home."

Holly looked out and watched the raindrops fall. "I know. She's coming, I know it."

"Who?" Chris asked.

"Toxanna. It always rains whenever she's nearby." Holly looked worried.

Josh nodded. "That's her specialty. And I'm assuming she's as powerful as you say she is by the size of the storm."

"You guys keep talking about specialties. What does that even mean?" Holly asked.

Josh and Chris exchanged looks before Chris asked, "You don't know what a specialty is?"

Holly shook her head no.

Josh scrunched his forehead. "So what have you and your family been doing with your magic, then?"

Holly shrugged. "Mostly potions and incantations. I guess back before Toxanna we used to be traveling psychics."

"Like the circus?" Josh blurted. Chris delivered a jab to the ribs. "Sorry."

Holly nodded. "More like carnivals, but yeah. Illusions, sleight of hand, that kind of stuff. Why, what about your family?"

"Our family has been battling people like Toxanna and Will for years. We were never part of any carnival," Josh started. "What we've learned over the years is that every witch has a specialty. Mine is wind, Chris's is fire, Aunt Kathy's is time, and Toxanna's is water. It starts off small, but with enough practice it can grow. Obviously Toxanna's specialty has grown quite a bit."

"Wait a minute." Holly raised her hand and then tucked some of her hair behind her ear. "So you're saying that I'm supposed to have a specialty? I don't have that kind of power! We've mostly relied on spells and potions. And I don't even know how I did that to Will the other day. It just sort of…happened."

"You haven't shown any other signs of focused magic?"

Chris asked. "It could be something like illusions, persuasion, anything like that. It doesn't have to be element based."

Holly shook her head. "No, not that I remember."

Josh shrugged. "Maybe you're telekinetic? Maybe that can grow into something else?"

"But I've never done that before! It didn't even feel like mine. It was…weird. I don't know," Holly stammered.

"Okay, let's just go inside, and we'll figure this out," Chris suggested.

Holly nodded.

Josh fumbled with his keys until Chris groaned. "What?"

He pointed to the street where a tiny old woman was making her way toward them with her bright yellow umbrella.

"Who's that?" Holly asked.

"Mrs. Kors. Our neighbor," Josh said. "Wait here."

Josh and Chris met her at the edge of the sidewalk.

"Here, stand under my umbrella," she offered, raising it a bit higher. Her gray curls were tucked underneath a pink floral scarf. The beige trench coat she wore nearly touched the ground, and the bottom was soaked with rainwater. She clutched it closed with her free hand.

The boys tried to duck under the umbrella, but it wasn't nearly big enough, and the rain still splattered them.

"What are you doing out?" Josh asked over the storm.

Mrs. Kors didn't hear them and shouted, a bit louder than necessary, "How are you boys doing? I heard from Marcy—you know Marcy. Short woman, volunteers over at the hospital?

Well, she heard that your aunt was admitted. What happened?"

Josh and Chris exchanged glances.

"Well, uh," Chris stammered.

She turned her ear and shouted, "What?"

Josh put a hand on her tiny shoulder and spoke up. "Everything's fine. Just a concussion. She was in a car accident. She should be home soon, hopefully."

"Oh, that's a shame! I had no idea. You boys could've stayed with me." She looked at them, waiting for them to accept the offer.

Again, the boys stammered and looked at one another for an escape. Finally, Holly appeared next to Chris. She had thrown on a jacket and pulled the hood over her head. "They've actually been staying with me for a few nights." She offered her hand. "I'm Holly. I live right over on Highview. I've been a friend of Josh and Chris's for a while now."

The old woman smiled. "Oh, well that's good. At least you boys aren't alone. You have a good friend here," she cooed. "Well, it was nice seeing you again, and nice meeting you, Holly. I need to get out of this rain before I get sick. You three should do the same! If you need anything, give me a call." She turned and shuffled back over to her house across the street.

After the three of them had dried off from the rain, they went in the magic room and huddled around the magic book. Josh flipped through the pages and stopped when he got to the profile on William Brown. He found what he wanted.

"Here it is," he said. "Here's all the information we have on him."

"Let's get busy on a spell," Chris said.

"What if that's not enough?" Holly asked. "What if there is no way to defeat him?"

"Then we'll combine a potion, a spell, and all three of our powers," Josh suggested. "There is a way to defeat everyone. It's just our job to find out what that is."

"I'll grab a dictionary and come up with a spell," Chris said as he crossed the hall to his and Josh's room.

"You and I are going to work on a potion," Holly told Josh as she grabbed the magic book and walked downstairs to the kitchen. Josh followed her.

* * *

In the kitchen Holly made a list of the ingredients she needed and handed it to Josh.

"You got any of these?" she asked.

"Snake venom? Dragon scales? Owl feathers?" He read off the list. "Who has this kind of stuff?"

"I do…or did," Holly replied. "My dad went a little overboard when my mom died. He made a potion for everything because he refused to use spells. That was my mom's thing. Needless to say, he has a well-supplied kitchen, but I'm guessing by the look on your face you don't, right?" Josh shook his head, and she continued, "I'm going to guess you have simple ingredients like garlic, vinegar, milk, and eggs? Stuff like that?"

"Yeah," Josh said as he hunted through the cupboards and

the fridge. He put all the ingredients she mentioned on the counter next to the stove.

Holly filled a pot up with water and set it on the stove to boil.

"Drew relies a lot on potions, too," Holly stated. She looked through the list. "I'm sure he'd have most of this stuff. Let me call him."

Josh wanted to protest, but he figured they needed to start trusting Drew—and Holly—until they gave them more reason not to.

She stepped into the next room as she spoke to him and returned. "He'll be over soon."

"Is he the one who taught you your magic?" Josh asked.

"Him and my dad, yeah." She nodded. "My dad owned his own restaurant, so it was hard for him to teach me after school. That's why he hired Drew."

"My mom was the expert on potions," Josh said. "She began teaching me a bit, but—"

In a puff of smoke, Drew appeared next to Holly with a cloth bag. He passed it off to her. "I don't have time to chat; I'm kind of in the middle of a chase." He drank a potion and was gone just as quick as he had appeared.

"Was that Drew?" Chris asked as he walked into the kitchen with a piece of folded-up paper in his hand.

"Just missed him." Holly added some milk and vinegar to the potion, then she cracked the eggs one-handed and dumped them in as well, shells and all. She wiped her hands and looked at the book for the next ingredient. "This might be a little more difficult."

"What?" Josh asked, stepping toward the book to try to catch a glimpse.

She pointed at the last line in the potion recipe. "In order to make this specific to Will, we need some of his DNA. A piece of hair, a fingernail, cheek swab, blood…"

"Toothbrush?" Chris asked.

Holly shrugged. "I don't see why not."

"I'll be right back." He took off upstairs and returned a moment later with a beat-up toothbrush. "He left a lot of stuff." He handed it to Holly. "We were going to use this to clean the toilet—"

"Gross!" She shouted and dropped it in the potion.

"We haven't yet!" Chris laughed.

Josh couldn't help but smile, too. Maybe getting outside help wasn't such a bad idea. Holly wasn't solely focused on killing Toxanna; she was willing to help him and Chris with their enemies, too. Maybe this partnership could work out after all.

Holly added a few more ingredients to the potion, which had become a thick brown paste.

"Looks different than what we're used to seeing," Josh commented.

"This is actually the best substance you can get. When it splatters, not only can you see it better than liquid, but it sits on their skin longer and speeds up the execution," Holly explained.

Josh peered in the pot and nodded. He turned to Chris. "Do you have a spell?"

Holly turned off the stove and added garlic powder to the stinking mix.

"Yeah, I'm not too sure how this is going to work, though," Chris said. "What if Aunt Kathy wants to do it?"

"Do you want to wait to find out? What if he hurts her?" Josh asked.

"No, but I do want to wait until she's home."

"I'll finish the potion; you guys go to the hospital and cast a protection spell on her," Holly suggested as she dropped three drops of snake venom into the pot.

"Good idea," replied Josh. "I'll go get the spell. Meet me out front, Chris."

* * *

After Josh and Chris left, Holly had finished brewing the potion and filled several vials. She was sitting in the living room reading a magazine when she noticed a puddle of water slowly inching its way across the hardwood floor. She put the magazine down, and sat up as the water began bubbling and a person started to form out of it headfirst. He had blue skin and was completely bald. He wore all black and had a small collection of markings on his forearms.

"Nice to see you again, Holly Bowen," he said.

"Zamball?" Holly shouted as she jumped up off the couch. "How the hell did you find me?" She was trying to slowly get to the kitchen to escape out the back door.

In an instant, he was by her side. He grabbed her arm and squeezed hard.

"I have very powerful magic, remember?" Zamball replied as he sneered at her.

"Let go of me," Holly warned as she whipped her arm around trying to break free.

"Sorry. I'm going to need you to come with me. Back home to our mother."

Together they materialized back into water and disappeared, leaving a puddle on the carpet.

* * *

When Josh and Chris returned, they called for Holly.

"That's weird. If she left, I'm sure she would've locked up," Chris said.

Josh was having his doubts again. He started panicking. Just when he thought they could trust her, she up and disappeared the moment she had the house to herself. She probably took the magic book. Maybe even the potion they had made together.

"Oh, this is bad," Chris said after he stepped on the puddle in the living room. "You look upstairs for her; I'll search down here."

Josh bolted upstairs, and Chris ran to the kitchen.

Nothing was touched in the kitchen. The back door was shut, and there didn't seem to be any other sign of a struggle. The puddle scared Chris. Holly had been nervous the continuous rain was a sign of Toxanna. She had probably been right.

Josh bounded down the stairs. "Damn, she's not up there.

But luckily the book and everything in the magic room is still in place."

"That's good." Chris sighed. "But we still have no idea where she is."

Drew appeared in a puff of smoke. "Finally lost them!" he cheered. When he saw the looks on the brothers' faces he asked, "What's wrong?"

They showed him the puddle in the living room and filled him in on what had happened in the hour since they had last seen him.

Drew chewed on the inside of his cheek, thinking. Finally, he said, "Okay, the water is probably not Toxanna's. There would be much more water damage if it was hers. Now her son, Zamball—"

"Zamball?" Chris blurted with a snort.

Drew wasn't laughing. "Yes." He turned to Josh and continued, "Zamball has the power to turn himself into water to get through tight places. I'm guessing it was him."

"Okay. So now what?" Josh asked.

"I heard some rumors today about the rain. Did Holly tell you about that?" Drew asked.

"Yeah, she said the rain is usually a sign that Toxanna is nearby," Chris responded. "It's been raining for a few days now and nothing's happened." He was kicking himself for not being more prepared for a potential attack. Everything with Will and Kathy was tying up their time.

"Right, but if what I heard is true, Toxanna has partnered

with some pretty powerful forces here in Erie," Drew explained. "That's why it's been a few days before she made an attack. She's usually not that patient."

"Who has she partnered with?" Josh asked.

Drew shook his head. "I don't know. But when the Fire Wizards were chasing me today, they made sure to stay clear of this area. I'm guessing Holly's close."

Josh and Chris looked at each other. They were both thinking the same thing.

Chris was the one who finally spoke up. "We know where she is."

CHAPTER TEN

Josh, Chris, and Drew pulled in the driveway of Axon's house. They were hidden behind a line of tall bushes along the drive-way blocking the view from the house.

"This is it," Chris said. He made a move to exit the car, but Josh grabbed the sleeve of his hoodie.

"Wait! We need a game plan first."

"Fine, I'll blast through the front door. You go through the back, and we attack them from both sides," Chris ordered. "Okay? Good. Let's go." He didn't wait for an answer. He got out of the car and ran to the front door.

Josh and Drew exchanged glances before chasing after him.

"Wait for me! Remember to wait!" Josh whispered loudly as he ran in a crouch past Chris to the back of the house.

When Josh was at the back door, he shouted, "Now!" and

Chris blasted the door, obliterating it to nothing. He leaped through the smoke and saw Josh on the other side of the giant room, inside the house. Drew appeared in the doorway behind Josh, a potion in each hand.

Holly was standing next to Zamball, and their hands were tied to one another with a thick black rope. There was a woman in a dark cloak in front of them. She was chanting from a hand-held book in her right hand, and her left hand was stretched out toward Holly.

Standing next to Axon was a woman with dark green hair. She wore black lipstick and a leather skirt that went down to her knees, as well as a strapless leather top.

The demonic pair started walking away from each other and toward the boys.

Axon focused on Chris until Josh cried out, "Hey! Axon, I thought you said you'd leave us alone? We haven't touched you!"

Axon turned toward Josh, charging at him. Josh focused his magic on an overturned chair and blew it at him.

The chair crashed against Axon's forearm and the demon continued in his pursuit.

The woman with green hair watched as the chair struck Axon, then turned to see Chris moving toward Holly. Quickly, the woman took a stance between Chris and Holly.

Once he saw the woman stand near Chris, Drew sprinted over to him and stood next to him.

Chris gave Drew a dirty look. What, did Drew think he couldn't handle this on his own?

"I just came here for my friend over there." Chris gestured to Holly and continued, "So if you don't mind, step aside." It was not a request, but the woman didn't budge.

"Chris…" Drew warned.

"You little witches think you're so tough don't you?" she asked. "I've had over eighty years to rid the world of Bowen witches. I can just as easily start with your line!" She raised her arms up and cackled. The intensity of the storm picked up outside, and the wind howled amid the thunder clacking. "Prepare to die!"

"Toxanna?" Chris mumbled.

"Yes," Drew said.

Chris's heart started racing. If Toxanna was here, it meant bad news for Holly's family.

Chris looked up and noted the dusty chandelier that was hanging by its last thread from the ceiling as Toxanna lifted her arms to summon magic. He looked over at Drew and nodded up. Without saying a word, they formulated the plan.

As Toxanna shot her burst of water in the direction of the boys, each of them fell to the floor and managed to dodge the attack.

Drew popped up to his feet and noted the chandelier. He motioned for Toxanna to come closer. "Come get me."

Toxanna stepped forward, directly under the chandelier. Chris lifted his hands and used his power to sever the chain holding the chandelier to the ceiling. It came crashing down on Toxanna, knocking her out. The clattering rain outside immediately stopped.

"Thanks," Chris muttered to Drew. He didn't want to admit it, but he would've been toast without him at that moment.

Turning to face Holly, Chris focused all his energy on the woman in the black cloak chanting in front of Zamball and his bound prisoner. Behind Chris, Drew chanted a strengthening spell toward him. With a tremendous effort, Chris was able to blow the priestess to pieces. Holly remained oblivious, staring into nothingness. Zamball, however, was well aware of his surroundings.

"Witch! What the hell did you do?" he shouted, dragging Holly along by their bound hands as he moved. "Oh, you're still alive," Zamball said to Drew. He pulled a long stick—his wand—out of his pocket and pointed it at Chris. A powerful stream of water shot out of the end of it. Chris put up his hands and used his energy to break up the water stream, sending mist all over the room. The sudden burst of rain blinded Zamball.

Drew extended his hand at the rope tying Holly to her captor and muttered a charm. The rope went limp and fell from their arms. Holly collapsed on the ground. Chris and Drew both moved to help her but stopped short.

"No!" Zamball screamed, balling his hands into fists by his sides. "You didn't let the Dark Priestess finish her ceremony!" Once again he pointed his wand at Chris and Drew.

Chris put up his hands just in case, but he was afraid to use his magic full blast with Holly so close. He shuffled his feet and saw a broken picture frame on the ground. "I'm just here for Holly, and once I get her away from you, all of us will be gone," he said.

THE BLOOD MOON

"You're not taking her anywhere!" Zamball shouted and sent another powerful stream of water at Chris. Drew pushed Chris out of the water and took the hit, crashing onto the floor soaking wet. He grabbed at his chest as he gasped for air.

Chris managed to land right next to the broken picture frame. As Zamball was admiring his successful attack on Drew, Chris hurled the frame at him which made perfect contact with Zamball's face.

Chris scrambled to Holly's side, taking hold of her arm and helping her up. She was coming out of whatever spell had entranced her, but she was still out of it. With one of his arms around Holly's waist, Chris stopped by Drew and asked, "You okay?"

Drew nodded, his hair sticking to his face. "Get her out."

Chris nodded and stumbled with Holly outside and into Josh's car. She was exhausted, muttering under her breath. Chris couldn't make it out.

When he had safely delivered Holly, Chris ran back inside to help his brother. He arrived just in time. Josh's face was covered in blood, and he was backed into a corner.

Drew was just starting to stand. He wobbled and held the wall for support. Chris told him to go protect Holly.

Axon lifted his hand to shoot acid at Josh, but Chris raised his hands and used the last of his magical energy to decimate Axon's hand. Writhing in pain, Axon fell to his knees.

"You stupid witch!" Axon hollered.

Chris didn't have a chance to offer his own retort. He was

interrupted by yet another enemy who leaped from the rafters in the ceiling and landed in front of Axon, spreading his thick, leathery wings out to protect Axon. The creature had sharp, pointed claws and big ears like an elf. He was bald except for a few wiry hairs around his ears.

"No more," the creature groaned. He conjured a fireball in his hand and attempted to throw it at Chris.

Chris put up his hands to blow it up, but he was too drained from the day's battle. Luckily, Josh was now by his side and was able to create a small windstorm within the house that put out the fireball. The room went dark as the fireball disappeared.

By now, Josh was able to throw the creature against the wall with his power.

As the brothers moved toward the door, Toxanna started to wake up. She waited until Josh and Chris were nearby, then she conjured a water ball filled with electric currents and fired it at Chris. Josh lifted his hand and used his power to create a wind force from his palm, preventing the enhanced water ball from going anywhere. Instead, it rained all over her, and she screamed as her skin sizzled. The brothers ran for the door and escaped to the car. They sped off with Holly and Drew passed out in the backseat.

* * *

When they got home, Chris wrapped his arm around Holly's waist and her arm over his shoulder and helped her into the house. He sat her down on the couch and got her a glass of water.

By now Drew was waking up too, and he was able to get inside with Josh's help before he collapsed on the couch, exhausted.

"What happened?" Chris was sitting on the coffee table.

Josh was busy looking in the mirror over the fireplace, nursing his wounds. It was only a minor cut across his forehead. Head wounds always looked worse because there was so much blood. Something he didn't need to go to any classes to learn.

"Well, I was here waiting for you two, and Zamball popped up," Holly explained, grasping her cup with both hands.

"How do you know him?" Josh asked. He was dabbing at the cut with a wet towel.

"He's Toxanna's son," Holly said. "He used to disguise himself as a student and come to my school to check up on me."

"Eventually, I found out and exposed him," Drew added.

"Which was the beginning of the end of my time in Salem," Holly finished.

"So what did he want from you?" Chris asked. He was leaning in closer and closer to Holly with each sentence.

"He wanted to marry me." Holly's voice broke. She sat for a moment and wiped at her eyes. "We reappeared—I guess at Axon's house—and this Dark Priestess showed up and I couldn't move. I could see and hear everything, I just couldn't move." Her hand shook.

Drew sat up. "That's some pretty powerful magic. Not the type of thing Toxanna dabbles in, either. She's gotta be getting some extra help. And not just from Axon."

"Of course," Josh grumbled, taking a seat on the edge of the chair.

"What happened after that?" Chris pressed.

Holly took a deep breath and continued, "Toxanna trapped me in an ice cube. Then when the priestess tied our hands together to start the ceremony, I was unfrozen, but I...I can't remember the rest. It's all a blur." She dropped her head and closed her eyes again, then when she looked up, she said, "The last thing I remember was you saving me and helping me to the car, Chris."

Chris couldn't contain the giant smile that burst across his face. He leaned back a bit hoping she wouldn't spot how red he was. "Well...you know, it was nothing—no problem."

Drew rolled his eyes.

"No, it was definitely something," Josh said. "You seemed pretty pissed. There was nothing left of the front door because you blew it to absolutely nothing. You've never done that before. Look at yourself. You're exhausted. We've never been that drained before."

Drew raised his hand in the air. "Actually...that power boost was my doing. I put a strength charm on you. The exhaustion is just sort of a side effect."

"What!" Josh stood and loomed over Drew. He was outraged. Who did this guy think he was to cast spells on them without warning them first?

"Relax! It saved the day!" Drew protested.

"Never do that again. Do you hear me?" Josh was in Drew's face. His heart was pounding, making the gash on his head start to bleed again.

"I'm sorry, but it was necessary at the time," Drew defended himself. "Chris's power is, well, powerful. He just needed an extra boost. I won't do it again. Next time you guys can die on your own accord."

"Get out," Josh demanded.

"Josh…" Chris sighed. He wasn't happy about Drew using his magic on them either, but it did help.

Josh continued to stare at Drew. Finally, Chris said, "Look, Drew. I don't like it that you did that, either. Just don't do it again. Okay?"

Drew put up his hands in surrender.

They sat in silence for a minute until Holly asked, "Have you talked to your aunt?"

"No, not yet," replied Josh. "I mean we did when we cast the spell on her, which, by the way, she wasn't happy about."

"Hypocrite," Drew muttered and Josh shot him a look.

"This is different. She's family."

"Doesn't seem that different to me," Drew countered, which resulted in the two of them yelling at each other.

"Enough!" Chris shouted. When the two of them finally stopped arguing, he continued, "Drew, I think you should go home."

With an exaggerated effort, Drew stood. "Fine. Holly, call me if you need anything." He drank a potion and disappeared.

CHAPTER ELEVEN

Chris was still in his tired morning haze as he hunched over his bowl of cereal and read the front page of the paper. That was usually all of the newspaper that he read. He didn't care for the rest of it. If he needed to know something, Josh or Kathy usually clued him in.

His morning peace crumbled when Holly walked in the back door and beckoned, "Aren't you ready yet?"

"Shh!" Chris warned. "I want Josh to sleep in a little. He's been so annoyingly cranky the past couple of days. He needs to relax today." He lifted the bowl to his mouth, drinking what was left of the sugary milk.

She scrunched up her forehead. "But he's probably going to spend the day studying." In the short time Holly had known Josh, she figured that he didn't spend a lot of time relaxing.

"Don't ask me." Chris shrugged as he got up and put his cereal bowl in the sink. "He finds a way to relax by studying. Anyway, I told Aunt Kathy I'd be there soon, so are you ready?"

Holly nodded.

"Remember to make us reappear across the street from the hospital, so we won't draw attention," Chris reminded her.

"I know! It's not my first time using magic!" She groaned as she dug a potion out of the bag that was slung over her shoulder and resting on her opposite hip.

She took Chris's hand—which Chris wasn't expecting, and which made it almost instantly grow clammy as he cursed himself for his sweating palms—and sipped half the potion. She handed it off for Chris to finish the other half. They both disappeared in a giant white flash.

* * *

They reappeared in the alley across from the hospital where Josh, Chris, and Kathy had last fought Will together.

"Let's go," Chris said. Still holding her hand, he led her all the way to his aunt's room. He was surprised that she didn't say anything about their handholding.

As they walked into Kathy's room, they stopped momentarily. The sheets were ruffled, but the bed was empty. Chris noticed the bathroom door was shut and breathed a sigh of relief. Will hadn't been back here. He wouldn't dare now that Kathy was conscious.

Behind them the door clicked shut. Chris and Holly turned and saw that Toxanna had followed them in. Her vibrant green hair was tucked under a surgical cap. She wore black scrubs and a stethoscope. She had been waiting for them.

"What are you doing here?" Holly demanded. She pulled her hand out of Chris's and put both of them in front of her, ready to deliver any attack she could think of.

Toxanna smirked at the two of them, inching her way closer. Chris and Holly continued to back away from the demonic witch. Neither of them were back to full strength since the attack the day before.

"Who are you and what are you doing here?" Kathy growled as she emerged from the bathroom fully dressed.

"My husband requests your presence," Toxanna explained.

"Your husband?" Holly scoffed. She couldn't imagine Toxanna having a husband. She tried to picture Toxanna as a 1950s housewife, but her usual tall leather boots crept into Holly's mind and ruined the image. Of course Holly knew that Toxanna had been married before, but that had been before Holly was even born.

"Who's your husband?" Kathy asked.

Chris didn't let Toxanna answer. "She's not going anywhere with you!" He stepped in front of his aunt.

"If she doesn't come with me now, his master will come after her himself," Toxanna warned. She held a fierce stare with Chris. "Trust me when I say that you don't want that."

"Master?" Chris asked.

"He's a bounty hunter," Toxanna explained, her mouth turning up to a smile, "and this time, he was sent after you."

"Then maybe your husband shouldn't be such a coward and come get me himself." Kathy locked eyes with the evil witch. "Instead he sends his wife to fight his battles."

Toxanna lunged at Kathy. Holding her glare on Toxanna, Kathy concentrated and, for the first time in a year, she accessed her power to stop time and froze her in midair.

"You have your powers back?" Chris looked at his aunt with concern. Had she brought them back too soon? What if the curse on her had returned? What if it returned again after a short period of time? How did she know it was safe to bring them back?

"Yeah. My nurse told me Will was here a few times while I was out, and I figured that if he needed to check up on me personally, then his spell was probably wiped clean from me," she explained.

"What if you're wrong?" Chris asked.

"How did you have the tools to do it?" Holly added.

Kathy smiled and put a hand on Chris's shoulder, looking into his eyes. "I'm not wrong." She turned to Holly. "Who's your friend?"

"Oh, this is Holly. She's a witch from New York. Actually, Toxanna is kind of her family foe."

Kathy pointed to the witch, who was still frozen midair. "Toxanna?"

Chris and Holly nodded.

Extending her hand to Holly, Kathy introduced herself. "Nice to meet you. You've been helping out my nephews, then?"

Holly nodded. "I'm trying. They've been helping me out as well. Seems like our enemies are sort of uniting."

Kathy smiled. "Of course. So, what are we going to do about…Toxanna?" She struggled with the name. Some of these names just got weirder. "My nurse will be here soon for the release paperwork."

"I have an idea," Holly said as she produced a small journal from her bag. She flipped through a few pages of handwritten notes until she found what she was looking for. Reaching her palm out toward Toxanna, she muttered a few words in Latin.

In a white flash Toxanna was gone. Holly snapped the journal closed. "Banishment spell. Should leave us enough time to get home."

"Nicely done," Kathy admired.

* * *

The group landed with a thud on the sidewalk in front of the house.

Kathy rubbed her neck. "Yeah, this is just what they meant by take it easy. I must be rusty." With her specialty, Kathy was able to move through time and space, including the present which came in handy as a teleportation power.

Storm clouds thundered above them, and puddles formed in the street as the rain poured.

THE BLOOD MOON

Their attention turned toward Josh, who sat on the front steps with his head resting on one of his hands. After being out in the rain for some time, he had decided that it was better not to fight it. He was already soaked. No reason to hide from the rain. "It's about time!" He threw up his hands in exasperation.

"We were only gone, like, forty-five minutes!" Chris defended himself, but then he noticed his brother's expression. He became concerned. "What happened? Why are we outside?"

"Will," Josh spat. "I'd just sat down to study when he picked me up and threw me outside. I didn't have time to even use my powers against him!"

"So why don't you go back inside and kick his butt?" Holly asked.

"Because the door is sealed," Josh explained. He was annoyed by the whole situation. Couldn't he just have one day off? From magic, at least. He was going to spend the day studying. Not exactly kicking back. No wonder people thought he was stressed.

"Well, if Will is here, then it's the perfect time to search his apartment for anything he might be cooking up for us," Kathy said. She slung her hair over her shoulder and curled it with her hands to get it out of her face, wringing out some of the rainwater. "Time for me to rejoin the races. Josh, you come with me. Chris and Holly will stay—"

"We should check out Axon's house, too," Chris cut in. He turned to Josh. "Toxanna was at the hospital. Apparently she's a newlywed, and she's after Aunt Kathy. Since we last saw Toxanna at Axon's house, maybe they're working together and we'll find her there."

"Be careful," Josh warned. "We don't know what to expect there. That guy creeps me out."

"How are you going to get there?" Holly asked Josh.

"My specialty is time. It's grown from simply stopping time to transporting myself to another spot in the present," Kathy explained. She shrugged. "Basically, I can teleport."

Holly smiled. "That's so cool!"

"What's your specialty?" Kathy asked. Josh and Chris exchanged glances. Kathy noticed. "What?"

Holly shrugged. "I don't know what it is. I didn't even know witches had specialties until I met these two." She waved her hand at the brothers.

"Oh…" Kathy was surprised. She had never heard of such an inexperienced witch. She obviously knew enough about the supernatural that she wasn't a total novice. But specialties were something that every witch knew about. She wasn't sure how much she could trust Holly, but then again she was just a teenager. How malicious could she be?

"Well we're going to have to figure that out so we can help you practice it," Kathy finally said. "But right now we have other things to handle." She reached for Josh's hand and said, "You two be careful." In a flash of red light she and Josh were gone.

"Why is it such a big deal that I know my specialty? I don't even think I have one," Holly asked Chris.

"Every witch has one. And if you've been practicing magic,

it's not just going to disappear," Chris explained. "The sooner we figure out what it is the sooner we can help you expand it." He shrugged. "Maybe it just hasn't developed yet? I just got mine last year." He stared at the ground, remembering the horrible attack that had resulted in his mother's death.

"Maybe…I guess I could ask Drew. He might know," Holly added.

"Drew, right," he mumbled.

* * *

Holly and Chris reappeared at the front of Axon's run-down house. The rain wasn't as heavy here. They walked through the front door that Chris had blown off earlier. Nobody was inside, which raised Chris's suspicions. If Toxanna had come for Kathy, wouldn't the rest of her crew be waiting for her? Or was the attempt to marry Holly and Zamball off a one-time deal? What if Axon had killed off another one of their enemies? In the demonic hierarchy, it was hard to keep track of who despised whom more.

"Keep your eyes open and your voice down," Chris whispered. "Stay close to me so that neither one of us gets jumped." The only sound was the rain splattering the roof and the water dripping from their clothes.

Holly nodded and followed, resting a hand on Chris's shoulder as he crept farther into the house.

The gargoyle flew down from the rafters and landed in front of Chris. Holly let out a quick shriek and reached for Chris's arm when he jumped also.

"Why do you insist on coming back here?" the gargoyle demanded in a menacing groan. "Do you have a death wish?"

"Who are you?" Chris asked.

But before he could answer, Holly asked, "Devon, what are you doing here?"

"I follow my queen, Toxanna," the creature answered. He held up his hand, conjured a fireball, and threw it at Holly.

Chris stopped it before it hit her. He closed his hands and reconjured the fireball toward Devon.

The fireball hit Devon in the shoulder, and he fell to the ground.

"Stay away from me, witch!" Devon yelled.

Holly and Chris stood on either side of the fallen creature and looked down at him. "Where are Toxanna and Axon?" Chris demanded.

"You, of all people, should know," Devon answered.

"Hmm…nope! That answer's not good enough!" Chris said as he blew up Devon's hand. Devon shouted out in pain and Chris said, "Now, I could keep going all the way up your arm until you're gone. Really, I don't care if you die. Make it easy for yourself and tell us."

"She's…she's with Victoria," Devon answered between haggard breaths. He cradled his bleeding limb.

"Victoria?" Holly asked.

"Do you know a Victoria?" Chris asked Holly.

"No, I don't think I do," she answered.

Chris turned his attention back to Devon. "I warned you," Chris tried to blow up more of Devon's arm, but Holly pushed his hand out of the way and Chris blew up part of the wall. The explosion shook the rest of the walls of the house and the two witches looked around, wondering if the ceiling was going to cave in on them. "What are you doing?" Chris barked.

"Maybe he's speaking in code," Holly suggested.

"What does it mean?" Chris asked Devon.

"I told you all I know," Devon replied.

"I don't think you did," Holly said. She looked Devon in the eyes for a moment, then turned to Chris. "Okay, we need to think because he's not going to tell us any more."

"I don't know a Victoria, though," Chris argued.

Holly chewed her bottom lip, thinking. She was interrupted when Drew appeared in a puff of white smoke. "You guys have a problem." He was talking to Chris.

Chris couldn't help but resent him. Sure he was a major help, but he and Holly had history. No matter how superficial it felt, he wasn't sure he'd ever be happy to see Drew pop up.

"What?" Chris asked coldly.

"There is a whole lot of evil emanating from your house," Drew said. "My guess from the rain is that it's Toxanna, but not just her." He looked around. "Maybe Axon, too? Either way, not good."

Chris groaned. "And we know Will's in there. Josh saw him." So now their three biggest enemies were joined together. Was Axon Toxanna's new husband? Chris couldn't even imagine how that pairing would work.

"We need to find a way back inside the house," Holly said. "What's in there that they would want?"

Chris shrugged. "Maybe the magic book? But that's white magic. Will would stay away from that stuff."

Holly looked at Drew. "Do you know any spells to remove a house-sealing spell?"

Drew ran his hand through his brown hair. It was matted to his head from the rain. "I could probably whip one up," he responded. "I'd have to take a look at the spell on the house first, though."

"We have to go. Josh and Aunt Kathy are probably on their way back," Chris said.

"Not if I get there first!" Devon shouted as he jumped to his feet and tried to fly out of the house before Holly and Chris could disappear.

Chris blew up part of Devon's right wing, and the creature fell to the ground.

"Chances are we'll get there before you," Chris said.

"Can you give us a lift back to Chris's?" Holly asked Drew.

"Uh…sure." Drew hesitated. Holly held out her hand but Drew ignored it, opting to put his hand on each of their shoulders instead. In a puff of white smoke, they were gone.

* * *

THE BLOOD MOON

When they reappeared, Josh was standing next to Kathy in front of the house in the pouring rain. Their faces were stricken with fear.

"Toxanna and Axon are the ones inside with Will!" Chris shouted to his brother over the roar of the storm.

"We figured," Josh said, his arms folded, staring at the front door.

"Who is this?" Kathy asked, pointing to Drew. She had been gone for a couple weeks and her nephews had already found two new friends. It sounded too good to be true, and she was not about to trust them easily. Luckily, it didn't seem like the boys trusted Drew that much, either.

"A friend of mine from back home," Holly answered. "He's a wizard. He thinks he can come up with a spell to let us in the house."

"Really?" Josh asked. "Every spell I've tried doesn't work. And it's not like we can light candles and do a ritual out here."

Drew nodded. "One of them is probably feeding the spell from inside. As long as they're in there, the spell will stick. But"—he produced a small pouch from his jacket pocket—"we can create a doorway inside." He walked to the front door and sprinkled a brown powder in front of the doorway, muttering to himself as he did so.

"What is that?" Chris asked.

When Drew was finished spreading the powder, he said, "Sage. It's used for healing and protection. It's best when it's burned as incense, but in this case I think the powder will work just as well." He mumbled more foreign words and extended his hands to the door. Slowly, he reached for the doorknob.

"I think it worked," Holly cheered once Drew had his hand on the knob.

"Quiet!" Kathy whispered as they entered the house.

"Where is everyone?" Holly asked. She looked around nervously. There was nothing but silence.

"They're still here, I can sense it," Drew warned.

"Josh and Chris, you check down here. Holly and I will go upstairs and check by the magic book," Kathy ordered. "Hopefully, that's not what they're after."

"What do I do?" Drew asked.

Kathy studied him for a moment. "Stick with the boys."

They split up. Josh, Chris, and Drew crept into the kitchen and spotted Zamball. He was mixing a potion at the stove.

"Hey!" Josh shouted as he threw his hand up and created a wind gust, blowing Zamball and everything on the kitchen counter across the room. "I believe that's ours."

Zamball sprang to his feet and scrambled up the stairs.

"Aunt Kathy, watch out!" Chris shouted up the stairs.

"I got him," Drew said, chasing after the wizard.

"Quiet!" Josh said to Chris as he slowly stepped toward the living room. He cringed every time their sneakers squeaked on the tiled floor.

"Where are they?" Chris asked. Between the five of them, they had almost the whole house covered, and no sighting yet. It was not a good sign.

"Not upstairs," Holly announced as she, Kathy, and Drew

came down the stairs into the kitchen.

"Where's Zamball?" Josh asked.

Drew shook his head, raking his wet hair out of his eyes with his fingers. "Lost him. He must've turned into a puddle of something."

"What do they want from us?" Chris asked.

"I'm not sure. Maybe the house? Or maybe the book." Josh considered.

"Nope, the book's fine," Kathy said. She had the large tome in her hands, propped against her stomach.

"Maybe our magic?" Chris suggested. It was a thought that had occurred to him before. Will was known for collecting powers. Usually from other demonic beings, but who was to say that he wouldn't take theirs? If Will couldn't convince them to join him, why not just take their powers and be done with the hassle?

"Or the house's magic," Josh added.

"What do you mean?" Holly asked.

"Well, the house has been in our family for generations, and our family have always been witches, so if you take a century and a half of spells being cast and magic happening, the house must've picked up a lot of the magic like a sponge," Josh explained. "The house itself is powerful. Especially to people who need power."

"Is there a basement?" Drew asked.

Kathy's eyes widened. They never used the basement, so it wasn't on her mind. "Yeah."

They followed her to the basement. Devon, Zamball, Will,

Toxanna, and Axon were all in a circle, heads down, eyes closed, chanting. They were so entranced that none of them looked up when the five of them came down the stairs.

"Hey!" Josh shouted, and he sent Devon flying across the basement with his power.

"I heard there's a party here, and we weren't invited," Chris said as he tried to blow up Toxanna. Axon grabbed her arm and turned transparent with her. The attack missed them and dissolved against the wall, the house obviously absorbing the magic.

Chris stood stupefied for a moment. He had never noticed the house absorbing the magic before.

"You see, you stupid witches, you're powerless against me," Axon said. "And I'd appreciate it if you don't try to kill my bride."

Holly groaned at the bride comment. "Are you kidding me?"

"I think it's about time you shut up, witch!" Toxanna screamed as she pointed at the five of them. A dark green beam shot out of her finger, wrapped around each of the witches, and transformed into a chain that bound them together. A power she'd acquired from another witch. Holly wondered if it was one of her ancestors.

When she was sure her enemies were contained, Toxanna turned around and started chanting again.

"Can you move your hands?" Josh whispered to Chris.

"No, I can't even move my fingers," Chris replied. "I think we're paralyzed." Panic set in as Chris tried to squirm.

"I can't move, either," Holly cried. "She must have us under some spell."

"Does anyone know a spell?" Kathy asked.

"I might," Drew said, closing his eyes and leaning his head back. "Might take a second, though."

Their enemies stopped chanting and turned around with their hands open, ready to do battle.

White sparks floated out of Josh, Chris, Holly, and Kathy and over to Will, Toxanna, Axon, and Zamball. Drew began to mutter to himself in Latin, hoping that his ability to do spells wasn't gone. He had no active powers since the Fire Wizards disowned him, so without spells, he was sunk.

Toxanna threw her head back and cackled. "I finally have your powers!"

"Hey, where are my powers?" Devon complained.

"You're just a minion, so you don't deserve any. And besides, you weren't chanting with us," Will said. "Thanks for your powers, babe." He smirked at his ex-wife and walked over to her.

Drew had finally finished chanting, and the chains fell limp at their feet. The five of them stood back and tried to eye their escape.

Will tried to grab Kathy's hand, but she reached back and sucker punched him right in the nose. Blood poured down his face as he cradled his throbbing face. "Don't touch me!" she warned as the other four headed up the stairs.

On Kathy's way up, Will grabbed her ankle. She frantically kicked at him until finally making contact with his hand, and he set her free. Will reached with his other hand and grabbed her kicking leg. He didn't leg go this time and dragged her down the wooden stairs. He wrapped his arms around her tightly, preventing her from punching him again. It didn't stop Kathy from trying, and it certainly didn't stop her from calling Will a few choice words.

"This is not fair!" Toxanna whined. "They're supposed to be dropping like flies!"

"Enjoy the hunt, sweetheart," Axon cooed. "The chase makes it sport." He flashed her an evil smile.

"We don't even know who got what power," Toxanna said.

"Just try and use them," Axon suggested. He put up his hands and tried to blow up Kathy, but she froze in her frenzy.

"You got her powers?" Will asked, stepping away from Kathy. "Then what did I get?"

The air began to stir in the dank basement.

"This is unacceptable!" Toxanna shouted. The wind grew stronger as she grew angrier. "I thought I'd have the Bowen witch's power!"

"You must have the oldest boy's," Axon declared.

Will put up his hands and blew up the wooden two-by-four that served as the handrail for the stairs. "And I have the strongest power." He smiled. "Good. This could work out just fine after all."

"What about the fourth witch?" Axon asked.

Will, Toxanna, and Axon turned and looked at Zamball. "You must have them," Toxanna said. "Son, you know what to do."

Zamball nodded at his mother and ran up the stairs after the rest of the witches.

THE BLOOD MOON

Will grabbed Kathy, pulling her out of the influence of Axon's borrowed magic. With his arms wrapped around her waist, and Kathy thrashing, Will carried her up the stairs.

As Will set Kathy on her feet at the top of the stairs, he reached for her to restrain her again. Kathy whipped her legs behind her, tripping Will and bringing him on top of her on the floor.

Kathy scrambled from under Will and sprang to her feet. All the anger that she had built up against Will was finally seeing an outlet.

"I don't want to hurt you!" Will shouted.

"Leave me alone!" She ran from the room, throwing the kitchen barstool to the floor as an obstacle.

Josh, Chris, Holly, and Drew were all waiting for Kathy in the magic room. She shut the door and leaned against it, gasping for breath.

"Where's Zamball?" Kathy asked.

"We haven't seen him," Chris said.

"I'll go look for him," Drew volunteered.

"No," Kathy gasped. "We might need you."

"Aunt Kathy, are you okay?" Chris asked, seeing blood stuck to the side of Kathy's face. She must've hit her head on the stairs in the scuffle with Will.

"Yeah," she gasped. "Now we have to get our powers back."

"I have an idea. Where's the book?" Chris asked.

"We…uh…left it downstairs," Holly remembered.

"Could we call it up here?" Josh asked. "We need a spell."

"There's no time!" Kathy shouted. "We've locked ourselves in a corner, and they're on their way up!"

"Do you have any more teleportation potions?" Holly asked Drew.

"Plenty," Drew nodded.

"No, we're not going to run away from this," Kathy stated.

"Drew, teleport down and grab the book and bring it back here for us," Holly instructed.

"Hurry!" Kathy warned. "They're really pissed. The spell didn't work the way they wanted." She regretted sending him down to potential danger, but she knew she was the only other option and Will had his sight set on her.

Drew nodded and drank one of his potions, disappearing in a puff of white smoke.

Axon started banging on the door. "Let me in, witch!"

"We have to barricade the door!" Josh said. Chris helped him push furniture in front of the door.

The witches could hear explosions coming from the hall. Since Will had just received Chris's powers, he was not able to control them yet.

Drew reappeared in a puff of white smoke and handed the magic book off to Chris. He frantically flipped through the pages as the crashes from outside the door grew more intense.

The door to the room shattered, and Will stood in the doorway. "Hi, honey, I'm home." He flashed his perfect smile.

Kathy stood in front of her nephews, Holly, and Drew and tried not to think about their slim chances of escaping. Especially with Toxanna, Axon, and Zamball likely right behind Will.

"You have our powers, just leave us alone," Kathy said.

THE BLOOD MOON

"See, I know you witches," Will said as he sauntered into the room, easily pushing the furniture that blocked the doorway out of his way. "I know you wouldn't leave it alone. Certainly the boys wouldn't. Just look what they did to our marriage."

"Our marriage was an evil union right from the start, and you know it." Kathy spoke sternly, locking eyes on Will.

As Kathy and Will bantered back and forth, Chris measured how dangerous it would be to go out the window.

"I think I recall you telling me that you loved being my queen, isn't that right?" Will's eyes shifted up to Chris. "Don't think about going out the window, or you'll feel the strength of your own power."

Chris gulped. His hands were shaking. He wondered if Drew had any potions up his sleeve, but he looked just as nervous as the rest of them.

"Now, if the five of you could join me downstairs, we could finish what we started," Will said, knowing full well that they wouldn't go without a fight.

Drew handed Holly a potion without Will noticing. "Drink," Drew mouthed.

Behind her back, Holly fumbled with the cork for a minute before drinking the potion. It tasted horrible, and she wasn't sure what it did, but she trusted Drew. She looked down at her hands and saw that she was turning transparent, just as Axon had previously.

"Hey! Where did she go?" Will demanded.

Once Holly realized what the potion was doing to her, she

reached over and grabbed Drew's hand, who turned transparent himself. She took Chris's hand as well and allowed him to become transparent.

"Where did they go?" Will's temper was rising. "How are you witches doing this? I have your powers!"

Kathy couldn't see Holly, Drew, and Chris disappearing behind her. When she turned to look, Will backhanded her, throwing her to the floor.

"Hey!" Josh shouted, running at Will. He was able to throw a successful punch to Will's gut before Will hurled him across the room. Josh crashed into a lamp in the corner and lay limp.

"Josh!" Chris shouted. Will heard it but couldn't see where it was coming from.

"C'mon," Holly urged, squeezing Chris's hand. Together, the three of them moved over to the magic book.

Will was now towering over Josh, squishing his face in his hand, muttering threats to him as he lifted him slightly off the floor.

Chris dropped Holly's hand and kicked Will in the back. Josh crumpled on the floor, and Chris helped him stand. Kathy joined Holly and searched through the book.

Chris helped his brother to a chair and turned just in time to duck away from Will's oncoming fist. Standing at the bookshelf, Chris pulled off the thick volumes and launched them at Will.

Will stumbled back into the hallway as Toxanna and the rest of the crew emerged in the doorway.

"Found it!" Kathy shouted and lowered the book to Josh so

he could read. Chris and Holly gathered around them.

Together, they recited:

> *I call forth from space and time,*
> *the powers that are rightfully mine.*
> *Bring them now to me here.*
> *Return what is mine, and what I hold dear.*

White sparks came from Will and the other enemies in the hallway and returned to Josh, Chris, Kathy, and Holly in a rush of warmth that spread throughout their bodies.

"Showtime," Chris said as Axon walked through the door. He tried to blow up Axon but was only able to inflict a small cut on the evil man's arm.

"Don't go so big," Drew suggested. "Try something small. Blow up his arm first, and then his other one until he's in so much pain that he can't take it and you can blow him up completely."

"That's torture!" Josh said. That was not the way they practiced magic, and it was not something they were about to start.

"Do you have a better way?" Chris asked. He wasn't about to wait for an answer. Josh was in bad shape, and Chris was going to make Will and the rest of them pay for it.

"Yeah, a spell."

Toxanna was conjuring a ball of water between her hands.

"Fine, give me the spell to defeat him."

"I don't have one," Josh admitted.

"Look out!" Holly shouted as Toxanna threw the giant ball of water at them.

Josh extended his hand toward the attack and used his power to break up the water, sending mist throughout the room.

"Boys, you get Axon, and we'll get the others," Kathy shouted. "We'll take the book. There may be a spell to kill one of them in here."

They split up, Josh, Chris, and Drew went downstairs with Axon chasing them, and Kathy and Holly led Toxanna and Zamball upstairs to the attic.

* * *

Downstairs, Josh, Chris, and Drew were busy trying to fight off both Devon and Axon. When Devon threw a fireball, Josh used his power to throw it back at Axon. They weren't making any headway with their attack because Devon was able to cure Axon after every hit.

"Josh, we need to take out Devon before we start on Axon!" Chris called over to his brother.

"Don't worry. I'll handle it," Josh responded. He didn't have a chance to move because Axon extended his arm toward Josh and pinned him against the wall.

"Hey!" Chris shouted, moving toward Axon, but Devon fired attacks at Chris, which prevented him from defending his brother.

Drew pulled a vial out of his pocket and hurled it at Axon. The blast sent everyone flying, hitting the walls.

Axon stood and gripped his left shoulder, which was now

bleeding down his muscled arm. Chris crawled over to Josh, but Axon waved his hand and Chris crashed into a lamp in the corner. Shards of glass pierced into his arm and he slowly reached down and plucked them out.

Looking over at Drew, Axon smiled. He hadn't killed him, but the wizard was unconscious. Either way, not something he needed to worry about. He raised his hand at Josh and dragged him up against the wall again, pinning him in place with his magic. He walked over to Josh and held his throat, choking him.

"Hey!" Chris cried out, throwing an explosive attack Axon's way. Chris's magic clearly hurt Axon, as he let go of Josh and staggered back.

Josh collapsed on the floor, gasping for breath.

"What happened to our deal?" Chris said. "You leave us alone, we leave you alone." Devon flew feet-first into Chris, knocking him to the ground.

Still kneeling on the floor, Josh used both hands to produce a gust to send Devon flying across the living room. His magic pushed Devon right out the front window.

"Damn," Josh said as he ran over to his brother. "Chris, are you okay?" He rolled Chris over onto his back and saw blood oozing from a gash on Chris's face. Josh cursed out Devon as he turned his attention to Axon.

"Would you like to finish the job?" Axon asked, smirking. He inched his way closer to Josh, tossing broken pieces of furniture out of his way.

"You won't touch him." Josh stood and met Axon's stare.

"Oh no, of course not," Axon said, throwing up his hands in a shrug. "He's out of my way. You, on the other hand…"

Josh threw Axon across the room. "Stay away from us!"

Axon stood. "Impressive," he said, crossing the room faster now. "Enjoy your powers while you still have them."

"Hey!" Drew shouted from Josh's right.

When Axon turned, Chris used his magic to annihilate Axon's leg. Their enemy crumbled to the floor, writhing in pain.

Josh helped his brother off the ground. "You okay?"

"For now," Chris answered. "Let's nail this bastard."

"Remember what I said, go after smaller things like his arms and legs," Drew advised. He was clutching his ankle.

Chris nodded and then blew up Axon's other leg. The force knocked him off balance, but Josh caught him and put his arm around his brother to steady him. He grabbed Chris's left arm and wrapped it around his neck and held it to keep him up.

"Okay, you only need a few more hits," Josh said trying to keep his brother standing.

"Okay…I got this," Chris said as he picked his head up and blew up Axon's right arm.

Axon shouted out in pain and spit acid toward Josh and Chris. Drew shouted out a charm, and the acid took a sharp left turn and shot out the broken window that Devon had flown through.

"You think just by killing me that this will all be over!" Axon shouted. "You have no idea how many people are involved!"

"Come on, Chris, you can do this," Josh encouraged. Inside

he was panicking. Hoping Devon didn't wake up before Chris was able to finish Axon off. If Devon attacked, they'd be done for. Chris was in no position to fight.

Chris blew up Axon's other arm. His eyes were unfocused. Josh continued to encourage him, but Chris's eyes rolled backward and he slumped down, passed out.

"Chris, wake up!" Josh shouted. He sat his brother down on the torn-up couch and shook him a little to try and get him to wake up. Nothing.

Axon was still lying on the floor, cursing at Josh.

Fear gripped Josh. Chris had the power to defeat Axon but wasn't up to strength. He looked over at Drew in panic.

"I'm no healer!" Drew said. He pulled out a few potions from his pocket and tossed them one by one to Josh. "Here, try these on Axon!"

Josh hesitated. He didn't want to get any closer to Axon than he had to. He uncorked the potion and splattered it at Axon. The demon's skin bubbled, and he continued to scream.

Josh looked up at the ceiling and shouted to Kathy, hoping she would hear him, but he doubted she could.

Devon jumped up on the windowsill and showed his yellow, razor-sharp teeth.

Josh fumbled with the cork from one of the potions Drew gave him, but before he had a chance to do anything, Devon was on top of him, dripping saliva into Josh's face as he hissed at him.

Josh frantically tried to fight Devon off, but the gargoyle had him pinned. Josh swung his leg out and kicked at anything that might possibly fall on top of Devon and weaken his hold over him. Nothing worked until Devon screeched in Josh's face, dripping more saliva onto him. In one swift move, Josh pushed Devon off him and Devon fell on the floor, flat on his back.

Standing now, Josh saw that Drew had thrown a potion from where he was sitting. Josh nodded at him, a silent thank you.

Devon was now on his feet again, but Josh was able to use his power to push him out of the window again. This time, he ran to the window1 and created a powerful gust of wind that broke off a tree branch and pinned Devon to the ground.

Satisfied that Devon was taken care of for the moment, Josh turned his attention back inside.

Axon was still screaming and cursing, and Chris was still out cold.

With his heart racing, Josh ran upstairs in search of his aunt.

"Hey, where are you going!" Drew called to him as he left the room.

Chapter Twelve

Upstairs in the attic, Kathy froze each of Toxanna and Zamball's attacks, while Holly flipped through the magic book looking for a spell. She was tucked behind a stack of boxes, trying to hide from their enemies.

"Aunt Kathy!" Josh shouted as he sent Zamball flying across the room. He ran to his aunt, who reached up to attend Josh's wounds on his face. "Chris passed out, and I need to heal him so he can finish Axon. Where's the book?"

Toxanna fired a powerful burst of water at Josh and Kathy, pushing them hard against the wall and drenching them. Zamball stepped in front of his mother, who tried to make a run for the door, but Josh was able to throw both of them back in a sudden burst of his own magic.

"We've got to get down to Chris." Kathy jumped to her feet.

She swept her wet hair out of her face and ran to the door. Josh and Holly followed, but Toxanna grabbed Holly's ankle as she exited. Holly fell on the stairs, the magic book rolling to the bottom.

"Holly!" Josh called, but Drew was at the bottom of the stairs, limping on his ankle.

"I've got her! You go help your aunt!" Josh hesitated and Drew shouted, "Go!"

Toxanna dragged Holly into the attic and slammed the door shut. Drew propped the book under his arm and waved his hand in front of the doorknob, speaking a charm that swung the door open immediately. He entered and was immediately attacked by Zamball.

The two wizards wrestled on the floor, until finally Drew was on top of Zamball and brought the thick magic down hard on top of his face. The dark wizard's eyes closed, and his head rolled back, his body going limp.

When Drew stood he saw Toxanna had her hand over Holly's mouth, drowning her from the inside. He grabbed his final potion from his pocket and hurled it at Toxanna's back. The evil witch let go of Holly and reached for her back in pain. Drew slid over to Holly, who was coughing up water.

"You okay?" Drew asked, wrapping an arm around her. Toxanna was still clutching at the burning potion on her back, so they had a little time.

Holly nodded and coughed some more water.

"We need to find a spell," Drew said. He was on his knees

with the Harpers' magic book on his lap. He flipped through the pages, looking for just the right spell.

"How do you…" She broke into a coughing fit again. "How do you…know it's…in there?"

He shrugged. "That's what your father said." Holly looked at him curiously. How would her father know there would be a spell in the Harpers' magic book? He didn't even know them! Josh and Chris had certainly never heard of Toxanna, and all the times she had looked through their book, she'd never seen any mention of a spell that could kill her archenemy.

She broke into another coughing fit as Toxanna began to advance on them once again.

"Just try to relax." Drew tried to soothe Holly. If she couldn't speak, she couldn't perform the spell. Plus, he needed to find a black candle.

Drew finally found the spell and set the book down behind a box. He put a small box on top of it to hold the page in case any further scuffle lost it.

Drew looked up and saw Toxanna fire an attack at them, but Holly muttered one of the spells she'd learned from Drew, and there was a protective dome around them. The water splashed over the dome, but Holly and Drew remained untouched.

Digging through the box to his right, Drew finally found a black candle. He knew the Harpers must have a stockpile of them somewhere. He spoke a quick charm and lit the candle. He placed it in front of Holly and then passed her the book.

"Read," he ordered.

Family united. We speak as one.
This evil here, we must shun.
The war has been too long a fight.
Get this evil out of our sight.

Toxanna was thrown back so hard that she broke through the wall and fell to the ground next to the unconscious Devon outside.

"Is she dead?" Holly asked.

"I'm not sure," Drew admitted. "I doubt it." He looked at the spell again. "I thought it was supposed to summon your family to kill her?"

"Chris!" Holly remembered and ran downstairs to find him, the protective bubble breaking as she exited it.

When Drew finally hobbled down the two flights of stairs to join her, he discovered that Chris was bleeding heavily. His sweatshirt was now soaked with blood, and he was getting more and more pale as time passed.

"Where's the book?" Drew asked.

"How will that help?" Holly asked.

"I might be able to whip up a potion that would stop the bleeding, but we need to act fast," Drew said. "Go! My ankle's too messed up to go myself." Holly raced upstairs.

"You think you can save him?" Kathy asked. She was kneeling next to Chris, cradling his head in her lap.

"Hopefully, but we have to hurry," Drew said. "Josh, get a pot of water boiling."

"What about Axon?" Josh asked, moving to the kitchen.

Obviously, Chris came first, but how were they supposed to work with a demon lying in the living room?

Kathy looked up and said, "He should stay frozen. If not, I'll be here to do it again."

Josh nodded and went to the kitchen to start the potion. Drew turned to follow but stopped and asked Kathy, "Did you see where Will went?"

Kathy suddenly realized that they had lost track of him in the chaos. "No. Last time I saw him is when we called our powers back. Maybe he took off once he realized his plan failed?"

Drew ran his hand through his brown hair. It was matted to his face; he wasn't sure if it was from Toxanna's water attacks or blood. "Okay, one thing at a time now." He limped off to the kitchen.

Ten minutes later Drew, Josh, and Holly returned to the living room.

"Hurry!" Kathy urged. Tears were building up in the corners of her eyes. She couldn't let Chris die. She had made a promise to her sister.

Holly knelt next to Kathy and Chris. Propping his mouth open, Holly tried to get most of the potion in it. Her hand was shaking so much that some of the purple potion rolled down the sides of Chris's face.

The four of them stared at Chris, waiting for something to happen.

"It's not working!" Holly panicked.

"Give it some more time," Drew urged, but he wasn't sure if

it would work. This potion was the extent of his healing abilities.

Finally, after what seemed like an eternity, the gashes on Chris's neck and arms sealed up, and the color returned to his face. The only evidence of the injury were the slashes in his shirt.

"He's okay. Go ahead and wake him," Drew said. "His body thinks he still needs to be unconscious from the wounds, but he doesn't have to be anymore."

Kathy gently shook her nephew's body that was laying across her lap. Chris woke up with a jerk. He sat bolt upright and gave a vacant stare before dropping his head and rubbing his eyes. He shook his head as if to clear his thoughts. "What happened?"

Relieved to see he was awake, Kathy started crying and wrapped her arms around him, squeezing tight.

"What's going on?" Chris mumbled in Kathy's arm.

"You passed out after being attacked by Devon," Josh explained. He felt ten times better now that Chris was up and talking again.

"Drew saved you," Holly added.

"Oh," Chris said, searching the room for Drew. "Thanks." He sat up on the couch, holding his hand to his forehead. Kathy sat next to him, one hand still on his shoulder.

"Of course," Drew said.

The room was silent as they watched Chris get his bearings. Finally Holly spoke up, "You need to finish off Axon."

"I don't know if Chris is up for that," Josh interjected.

"Well, we can't just leave him here!" Holly argued.

"No, I can do it," Chris said. He attempted to stand, but as his knees buckled. Josh and Kathy each grabbed an arm to support him.

Chris focused his attack on Axon. After a moment he said, "I can't."

"Why?" Josh asked. "It's so easy. He's not that strong. He just knows how to keep secrets. That's why he's been a problem. We could've taken him out before, but we decided to leave him and look what happened." He regretted his words almost immediately. He didn't want to push Chris too hard, but they had Axon in the palm of their hands again. He didn't want to let this opportunity slip.

"Yeah, it kept Toxanna busy so we could get Aunt Kathy out of the hospital and get her home safely," Chris reminded his brother.

Kathy chewed on her bottom lip and shifted her eyes from Chris to the ground—he was right.

"But keeping a…a…malevolent force here is dangerous," Josh argued, "especially since he's injured."

"But it doesn't seem right," Chris said. "Before I was attacking in self-defense, and now I'm attacking because I have the power to."

"But he's evil," Kathy said sympathetically.

"Just because he's evil, doesn't mean he has done anything absolutely horrible to us," Chris said. "It's just natural for him to do something like that."

"Chris, he almost killed you," Kathy urged.

He stared at the floor, not saying a word. He couldn't bring himself to do it. Sure, it would be simple, but was that the reason they should execute him?

"You're right," Josh said, "but we can't just try to kill him halfway and then stop. That's torture."

"But what about—" Chris protested but was interrupted.

Devon came flying back through the window and tried to attack Chris, but Josh sent him flying back out the broken window.

Kathy's power wore off, and Axon began to scream, "You witches put me here, and when I am healed I will make sure you suffer just like me!" He started spitting acid out and melting the ceiling above him.

"Chris, blow him up!" Josh demanded. "Before he hurts anyone!"

Chris sighed and, with a quick flick of his hand, blew him up. The yelling and acid stopped.

"Thank you," Josh said.

Chris still looked uncertain.

"Hey, you did the right thing." Holly rested a reassuring hand on his shoulder.

* * *

As Toxanna and Devon lay unconscious on the ground outside, the witches and Drew hovered over them, unsure of what to do. Asking Chris to use his power was out of the question. They were all drained from the day's battle—especially Chris. He wouldn't have done it under these circumstances even if he was up to full power.

"What are you going to do about the house?" Drew asked.

"The house usually fixes itself," Josh explained. "That's why Will was here to begin with. The house has collected the residual energy from all the years of magic, and it's almost magical itself."

Kathy nodded. "Comes in handy."

Chris was fidgeting with his fingers and had a blank expression on his face.

"Chris, what's wrong? You've been quiet," observed Kathy. She slung her arm around him and squeezed.

"Huh?" Kathy scared him. "Oh, I'm, uh, just starting to grasp the idea of how dangerous this is for all of us."

"Well, yeah, people barge into our house all the time to take over or try to kill us and stuff," Josh said.

"Not just that," Chris said. He was playing with his fingers again. "My hands are lethal weapons. If I make a wrong move, I could severely hurt someone. And because of that, I almost died today." He shrugged. "I don't know. It's been a long day. I'm going to bed."

"What about these guys?" Josh asked, nodding at Toxanna and Devon.

"Too bad we don't have a spell to kill them," Holly said. She wished that she could end her family's long struggle with the evil witch right now, but she didn't know how. It made her feel powerless.

"I got it," Drew said. He spoke a banishment charm. A giant

hole appeared underneath Toxanna and Devon, and they fell into it. Afterward, the hole disappeared.

After Chris went upstairs, Josh said, "I've never seen him like this."

"I think he just needs a good night's sleep," Holly said. "And so do I. I'll be back tomorrow."

Chapter Thirteen

Chris had been quiet, which was completely out of character. When he came home from school the next day, he plopped on the couch and stared at the ceiling.

The house had rebuilt itself. They'd awoken that morning, and all of the windows were intact and any holes in the walls had been filled. The furniture was still a mess when Chris left for school, but he realized he was lying on a new couch.

"You're home!"

Chris jumped at the sudden exclamation. In his surprise he shattered one of the newly replaced windows with his power. He ran a hand through his red hair.

"Sorry." Holly giggled. "Good thing about the house, though. Everything looks great. Well, I helped your aunt fix the furniture."

"What are you doing here?" Chris asked. It came out harsher than he intended. He could tell by the hurt look on Holly's face. "Sorry, that's not what I meant."

She came around the side of the couch and made to sit down. Chris sat up to give Holly some room. "Are you okay?" she asked.

"I'm fine," Chris answered. They both knew he was lying.

"No, you're not. Something's up. Spill." She kept her green eyes on him.

Chris sighed and then said, "It's stupid. I'll be fine." He tried to stand up, but Holly pushed him back down on the couch, pressing on his chest and sitting on his stomach so he wouldn't move.

"You don't think I'm going to let you get out of this that easily, do you?"

Chris's face flared as she stared down at him. She smiled and asked, "Is this about what happened yesterday?"

He didn't answer, which was answer enough for Holly.

"Okay, so things got scary for a second, but everything worked out. Whatever Drew whipped up worked, right? No lasting side effects?"

"I'm fine. But what if I had died? What would you guys do? What would Aunt Kathy have to tell people? Then Will would win and—"

Holly put a finger to his lips and shushed him. "The fact is you didn't die. Drew was able to help. This is why we need to help each other. Toxanna probably would've killed me—or married me off to Zamball—if it wasn't for you and Josh." She cradled his face in her hands. "You were saved, and you need to continue to fight."

"But I don't know if it's worth the risk." He reached up and held her hands by his face.

"If that's not, then what is?" Holly asked. "Think about it. You of all people love magic. Forget about me and Drew. You're telling me that your family is not something you'd risk your life for?" She smiled at him and squeezed his hands. "Think about it. If you give up on magic, then your mother's death will mean nothing, and you will leave your brother and your aunt alone. They need you. We all do."

* * *

Too old. Too pricey. Too ugly. Was finding a rental car that difficult? The problem was that Kathy had her hospital bill coming and hadn't yet found a new job. Even though she was a witch, she still couldn't make money appear out of nowhere. That wouldn't be right, and she didn't want to be personally responsible for economic inflation.

At least she didn't have to pay for the repairs to the house. That would've cost a pretty penny that she didn't have. The furniture was the result of a little white magic between her and Holly. The young witch was proving to be a powerful asset to their fighting force. Kathy still wasn't too sure about Holly's wizard friend, Drew. He had helped save the day a couple of times, but she hadn't spent enough time with him to get too good a feel for him.

Kathy was grateful for Holly. Or at least she assumed it was Holly. Chris was finally starting to act like himself again, and she had a feeling that Holly was the reason. Just another reason why she liked that girl.

Finally, she gave up on the car search, opened a new tab on her browser, and started researching potential jobs. She wasn't qualified in anything. At least, not anything that would produce a steady paycheck. She was certainly skilled in the creation of potions and spells, but she couldn't put that on a résumé.

Her curiosity got the better of her and her search shifted to links for freelance writers. She discovered a literary magazine that was looking for a serial writer. She filled out the preliminary application online but was interrupted when Holly walked in.

"Hey," Kathy greeted. She was a little startled to see her since it was one in the afternoon. "Don't you go to school?"

"Not really. Didn't exactly have a chance to have my transcript sent down here when I was fleeing," Holly responded. "And besides, I was trying not to leave a paper trail."

"Doesn't your friend—" Kathy started.

"Margaret?"

"Yeah, doesn't she think it's odd that you don't go to school?"

Holly shrugged. "I find things to do. But"—she held up her hands as if to stop from being interrupted—"that's what I'm here to talk to you about. Margaret's missing."

"You don't sound that upset," Kathy commented. She closed her laptop and walked to the sink to rinse out her teacup.

"There's a slight possibility that she's just running late from work," Holly said with a cringe. She didn't want to come off as a worrier. "It's just that if she's going to be late, she usually calls."

"Well, how late is she?" Kathy asked, leaning against the sink.

"She usually opens the store, so she'd be home by now." Holly glanced at the clock on the wall. "Mmm, maybe two hours?" Kathy dropped her head low and gave Holly a look. "You don't understand, she's usually very punctual!"

Kathy held up her hands. "Okay. Let's cover our bases before we assume it was some malicious scheme. Let's do the tracking ritual. If nothing comes up, then we consider our other options, okay?"

Holly nodded. "Thanks. I know something is off."

* * *

"Dude, you're seriously in way too many clubs," Chris whined as he entered the house. They had gotten home late because Josh had to help the art club set up for their upcoming art show. Chris had sat around for two hours waiting.

"You could've taken the bus," Josh countered. He had heard Chris's griping the whole way home.

Chris paid him no mind. "Why are you even in the art club? It's not even like you're featured in the show tomorrow."

"I told you, it's for a well-rounded college application," Josh said.

They walked into the kitchen and stopped dead.

"I expected to see you cooking dinner," Chris said. He lit up when he saw Holly and flashed her a giant smile.

Kathy was stirring something on the stove. A big poof of black smoke came up, and she backed up and swatted it away. They had taken out the fire alarm in their house after setting it off too many times with potions. The house fixed itself if there was any fire damage, so they didn't have to worry about it.

"No time for dinner," Kathy said. "Make a sandwich if you're hungry. We have work to do tonight. I'll make dinner tomorrow."

"Why does it seem that we're always in here making potions?" Chris asked. He grabbed a loaf of bread from the counter and began preparing a PB&J.

"Because we are." Kathy dropped three more ingredients into the pot that was bubbling on the stove.

"So what's up?" Josh asked from the kitchen table. He was emptying his backpack.

"Margaret, the friend I'm living with, has been kidnapped," answered Holly.

"We're hoping by Will," Kathy added.

"Hoping? Are you crazy?" Josh couldn't believe what he'd heard.

"Will didn't do it," Chris said. "He's smarter than that. If he is really trying to lie low, then he wouldn't dare do anything at all. Even something as stupid as this. It's probably Toxanna. She's not as smart." He looked at Holly real quick and added, "Not saying you're family is dumb for not being able to kill her all these years...but, you were just...uh, under unfortunate circumstances—"

"Yeah, I get it, Chris." Holly rolled her eyes and continued, "We already canceled Toxanna out, though, because she's weak," she explained. Then her eyes got really big as realization hit her. "I have an idea." She dashed upstairs.

While she was gone, Chris asked Kathy, "So what's the potion for?"

"We're going to use it to look for Margaret. If it works, we should be able to pour it on something she owned and use that to locate her," Kathy explained.

Holly came back down a few minutes later with the book opened and said, "I can use this spell to defeat Toxanna for good."

"But earlier this week, you couldn't defeat her," Chris reminded her. "Is this a different spell?"

"No. But I'm going to summon my family first to have them say it with me," Holly explained. "Last time it was only me, but if my whole family says it with me, it would be more powerful. It's my family that has the connection to her, so that would be strongest. I think if you guys said the spell with me, it might actually weaken it."

"You could tweak that spell and have them automatically summoned when you say it," Kathy suggested as she turned off the stove. "Potion's done."

"Great idea!" Holly was getting excited. After her family had been persecuted for all these years, she was finally going to bring an end to it. "Kathy and Josh, stay here and work on the spell. Chris and I will get her keys or something." She grabbed Chris's hand and raced out the door.

* * *

"I still don't understand why we didn't use magic to come here," Chris whined as they walked up the sidewalk to Margaret's house, although he certainly wasn't objecting to the hand-in-hand walk.

"I'm running out of potions!" Holly said. She needed to brew some more, but she barely had any time to catch her breath lately, so mixing up extra potions was out of the question.

Her eyes flashed to the window as they neared the door. Voices. Two men. She pushed Chris down behind the bushes lining the walk, putting a finger to her lips to silence him. She leaned down and whispered softly, "We'll sneak in the back. Follow me."

They circled around the quaint little house with brown siding and green trim. Margaret prided herself on her real-life gingerbread house. The flowers were perfectly aligned along the walk to the front door and around the sides of the house. Whenever she had a free moment, Margaret would be outside working on her garden. Even though Holly didn't know her as well as her father did, she couldn't help but feel a sense of pride in Margaret's work.

They made sure to stay close to the house and out of sight of any windows. At the back door, Holly reached for the right key gingerly, making sure to not let them jingle.

Slowly and silently she unlocked the door and opened it enough to allow them to enter. Chris went in first and stood by the door until Holly was by his side.

The voices were coming from the living room at the end of the hall. Holly pointed to the coat closet, and the two of them squeezed in. There was just enough room for them amid the fluffy winter coats. Sitting silently, keeping the sound of their breathing low to help them hear, they listened.

"I don't see the point of planting this here," one of them grumbled. He sounded like he needed to clear his throat, but Holly imagined that clearing his throat wouldn't fix the rasp.

"By planting this here, it will lead the witches straight to the woman and that dumb broad," the other explained. His voice was smoother, softer, but direct. He didn't sound like the type of person to be questioned. "They won't miss the opportunity to kill her, and she'll be out of his way."

Chris and Holly could see a fiery light through the outline of the door for only a brief second. A familiar voice asked, "What did I tell you about staying at one place too long? Those damn witches are everywhere, and especially here, and especially now. You should go," the new arrival ordered.

"Yes, my lord," came the response in unison from the other two.

The fiery light flashed again and then disappeared. Chris looked down at Holly, who was only inches away. "You think it's safe?"

Holly nodded, not sure herself. She opened the door anyway and felt a rush of fresh, cool air. Slowly, they proceeded to the kitchen and picked up a set of car keys.

"Do you think this is what they planted?" Chris asked.

"I don't know"—Holly shrugged—"but I don't care."

"Why?" Chris asked. "It sounds like a trap."

"But the trap is not for us," she said. "It sounds like it's for Toxanna. Whoever was here wants her gone, and if they're going to lead us to her, then we shouldn't miss this opportunity."

"But after Toxanna's out of the way, they'll be after us," Chris argued.

"By then we'll know who they are," Holly said.

"He sounded familiar. Did you recognize the voice?" Chris asked.

Holly shook her head no. Chris couldn't help but think that if Josh had been there, he would have been able to figure it out.

* * *

Back at Chris's house, Kathy and Josh had already revised the spell and were waiting in the kitchen. Thunder began rolling in. A storm was definitely coming, which made Holly more nervous for Margaret's safety.

"Good. You're home," Kathy greeted them. She had just pulled out four blue candles and was taking them to the living room, which Josh had cleared of furniture.

"What'd you bring?" Josh asked. He carried a small golden goblet filled with water to his aunt.

Holly handed Josh the car keys and said, "We found something else out, too."

192

The Blood Moon

"What's that?" Kathy was placing each of the candles specifically around her.

"Apparently, someone is trying to take over the evil kingdom, or whatever they have going on," Chris explained. "There's a new power that is planning on taking us out."

"Not surprising. Now that the Queen is dead, the bad guys are probably scrambling for a new leader," Kathy said. She lit each of the candles with a match. "Usually, it's the person who killed her, but that would be Axon, and Chris killed him."

"Who is it?" Josh asked. He passed off the goblet to his aunt just as another crack of thunder sounded.

"We don't know. We couldn't make out their voices," Holly explained. "They said that they planted something—probably those keys—to lead us to Toxanna so we could kill her and get her out of the way for us and them. By the sound of this storm, she's ready for a war."

"So it's a trap?" Josh asked.

"That's what I said!" Chris threw up his hands in exasperation.

"For Toxanna, not for us," Holly replied, shooting Chris a look. "By the time this new threat gets to power, we will already know about them. Maybe even know how to defeat them."

"But that's putting the spotlight on us," Kathy said. "And by the time they take power, their strength might have grown. We need to take care of this soon."

"You cannot honestly tell me you're going to make me give up an opportunity like this to get rid of Toxanna?" Holly demanded. She wasn't happy. The Harpers got their revenge for their mother's death, why weren't they letting her do the same for her entire family? "After all that my family has been through? This has been going on for over eighty years!" A clap of thunder erupted just as Holly slammed her hands down on the back of the couch. She felt strangely empowered by it, even though she knew she had nothing to do with it.

Holly had heard stories about how her family had faced severe threats from Toxanna for many years. Since Pamela Bowen had first attacked her, Toxanna focused on each member of her family, slowly working her way through Pamela's relatives until Toxanna finally got the better of the white witch. Killing Pamela didn't stop Toxanna from continuing her vengeance on the entire Bowen family, even as the family continued to grow. Up until Toxanna's husband was killed by Simon, Holly's father, Toxanna was on a roll, nearly wiping out the entire family. But now Holly had the upper hand, and she didn't want to lose it.

"I'm sorry, but it's not as black and white anymore," Kathy tried to explain, but Holly didn't want to hear it; she stood glaring at Kathy with her arms folded. "There's a third party involved now."

"Yeah, and we have the opportunity to eliminate one of them!" Holly argued.

Kathy kept her stance. She liked Holly, but at this moment she was being stubborn. The girl had tunnel vision when it came to killing Toxanna, and Kathy didn't want to slip up again. She saw firsthand with Samantha what happened when they were sloppy.

The Blood Moon

More thunder boomed overhead. The storm was going to start any minute.

"No, I'm not jumping into this until we have all of our bases covered," Kathy declared. "We figure out who is setting this trap and how to avoid it before we go in there guns-a-blazing."

"You guys do what you want," Holly said. She snatched up her bag from the floor. "I'll do this myself." She raced out the back door before they could stop her.

* * *

Kathy's heart raced as she pushed the pedal in Josh's car down farther. The downpour was brutal. The storm was in full force, and Kathy sped down the wet roads with the wipers on full blast. She was livid and worried at the same time. How could Holly be so stupid? She was just one witch, and she didn't even have the spell they reworked to take out Toxanna. And what if she needed backup? Drew was not going to be able to take on Toxanna and whoever was hunting her. What would happen if they did succeed in killing the water witch? What said the new threat wouldn't turn on Holly?

"Aunt Kathy, take it easy," Josh warned. She had insisted on driving and backed out of the driveway before he and Chris were even buckled. Chris was no help either. He had brewed up some of their strongest potions after Drew didn't respond to the summoning. He wasn't even sure if Holly had done her homework yet. Had she searched for Toxanna's location like they had?

Josh breathed a sigh of relief when they pulled up to the alley across from the hospital—the same one they frequented lately with all the attacks. The three witches passed around potions between them and then stepped out into the pouring rain.

"Stay close," Kathy warned. "Be careful."

As they walked deeper into the square behind the buildings, they noticed Devon perched above them on the corner of one. Zamball and Toxanna were still nowhere to be seen.

Chris pointed to Devon, who was looking out into the night sky. He wasn't sure if Devon didn't see them or was just ignoring them, waiting for some sort of plan to be set in motion.

Josh put up both hands and created a gust of wind that forced Devon to leap into the air. The wind whipped the rain against the witches' faces. Using his leathery wings, Devon soared down into the square.

"Where's Toxanna?" Kathy asked.

Before Devon could answer, Drew and Holly appeared in a puff of white smoke. Holly pulled out a piece of paper and read:

> *Somewhere hidden in these waters,*
> *therein lies an evil power.*
> *Return her to her human form*
> *to win this battle and end the war.*

A manhole cover shot into the sky as water erupted from the pipes beneath them, creating a geyser. Once the rush of water subsided, the puddles it created began to rise and take the shape of Toxanna and Zamball.

The Blood Moon

"Powerful spell," Toxanna admired. "Come here to kill me?" The rain didn't seem to stick to her. It was as if an invisible force field surrounded her and protected her from it.

"As a matter of fact we have," Josh confirmed.

Toxanna jumped when Josh spoke. She turned and faced the three witches.

"I know you three can't," Toxanna said. She opened her hand and shot a burst of water, soaking them more than they already were. Amid the attack, Zamball moved to grab Holly, but Drew fired a potion at him to stop him.

"Where is she?" Holly demanded when the attack had stopped. She locked eyes with Toxanna.

"Where is who?" Toxanna asked. She held her elbow with one arm and looked at her nails with the other. She looked bored.

"You know who I'm talking about," Holly said. Her knuckles were white from squeezing the potions in her hands.

"I really don't know what you're talking about," Toxanna said. "Now, if you're going to kill me…" She moved her fingers in way that said Come here.

Holly raised a fist, ready to throw the potion, but Josh stopped her. "This is too anticlimactic," he said.

"What are you saying?" Holly asked.

"It seems too easy," Josh explained. "After all the trouble she's put your family through, this is how it ends?"

"You were always too smart for your own good," Toxanna said. The witches were bewildered as Toxanna reached toward the sky, stretching.

"How are you…" Chris couldn't finish. Last time they'd seen her, she'd been nearly on her deathbed. Two minutes ago she seemed ready to die.

"I cast a strength spell. Granted it only lasts twenty-four hours, but it's remarkable. I am stronger than Superman!" Toxanna walked over and picked up the Dumpster that was in the corner and threw it at the five of them.

The witches scattered as the Dumpster smashed into Josh's car, sending shards of glass everywhere.

"Damn it," Josh muttered, looking up at Toxanna. He summoned his strength and created a small cyclone and sent it in her direction. Again, the wind caused the rain to stab into them like needles. She jumped into the air and turned into water vapor. She reappeared normally after the cyclone dissipated.

"Where's your son?" Kathy asked.

Toxanna smiled and didn't respond.

Holly looked to Chris. He knew exactly what she meant without any words being spoken. Chris tried to blow up Toxanna, but she burst into water before reassembling.

"Nice try," she said. Water erupted from the palm of her hand and froze as she conjured an ice sword. She swung at Holly, but Holly reached for a metal pole that lay on the cement next to her and quickly held it up to block Toxanna's attack.

"Chris!" she shrieked, looking for help.

Nervously, Chris chanted a spell:

The Blood Moon

A white glow came over Holly and evaporated.

"That'll take care of her," Chris said. "Now we need to find Zamball and figure out a way to take out Devon." He ran a hand through his wet hair. His sweatshirt was heavy on him in the rain and the chill sent a shiver up his spine.

"I'll see if I can find Zamball," Kathy said as she ran past Holly and Toxanna down the alley.

"So we need to get rid of Devon," Josh said. "That'll be simple." He shivered. The cold rain gave him goose bumps.

"Might be harder than you think," Drew said, joining Josh and Chris.

The puddles around their feet rose and formed six men in the same way Toxanna and Zamball had appeared minutes before. They didn't have any defining features other than the shape of men. Obviously the product of Toxanna's magic.

"So are you guys Toxanna's college friends?" Chris asked sarcastically.

"We each take two?" Josh proposed. He took a step back, quickly scanning them all and picking out the toughest ones to take on himself. Chris, on the other hand, had his hands up, ready for a fight.

"Sure, I'll come help you when I'm done," Chris joked. He noticed that Devon took off over the buildings. "Devon's leaving," he added, but the other two were too preoccupied with their newfound water enemies to notice.

Drew shot potions at the water men, but nothing seemed to be damaging them enough. Josh tried to blow them away, but they changed into water vapor and reappeared once the attack passed. Chris wasn't having much luck, either. Every time he blasted one of them up, they reemerged from the puddle the explosion created. Whatever attacks were hurled at them didn't seem to be making a difference.

"Okay, blowing them up doesn't work," Chris said as the three of them were cornered back-to-back. Their water-puddle enemies circled around them.

"Nothing is working," Josh added. Water ran down the bridge of his nose and dripped like a leaky faucet.

"We need to think about another way to get rid of them. Holly needs help!" Drew said.

"What about a sponge?" Chris asked. "To absorb the water, I mean."

"Good thinking," Josh said, "but we're going to need a giant one." He created a wind force that broke up a stream of water into mist.

"I'm thinking. Sponge…lunge…I got it!" Chris shouted. Then he recited:

We want a giant sponge,
to clean up this life-size grunge.

In a swirl of white sparks, a giant yellow sponge appeared in front of them.

"Corny spell," Josh said. "I can't believe it worked."

"Yeah, well it did, now it's your turn," Chris ordered. "I'll blast the water attacks, and you guys get them with the sponge."

Drew and Josh each took hold of a side of the sponge and collected the water remains of the enemies after Chris blew them up. After a few minutes of wrangling, all six of the attackers were trapped in the sponge.

"Now what?" Chris asked.

"Obliterate it," Josh suggested. He held his arms, shivering. They needed to get someplace warm and dry soon.

"Or we could leave it here and have the sun evaporate them," Drew suggested.

Kathy appeared in a red flash next to Josh. "I couldn't find Zamball," she said. "Maybe he jumped off their bandwagon?"

"Would he ditch his mother like that?" Josh asked but never got an answer.

Holly screamed and fell to the ground. Toxanna was holding the ice sword at her throat. Holly's pole was just out of her reach.

Chris blew up the end of Toxanna's sword, and when Toxanna looked up at Chris, Holly took the opportunity to grab her sword and slice off Toxanna's arm.

Toxanna fell and a black cloud seeped out of the end of her arm as the strength spell left her. "No, come back!" she cried out. "I promise I'll do better the second time around!" In an instant, the rain stopped and the witches stood in a circle around Toxanna, wet and cold.

"The second time?" Holly asked. "Lady, there isn't going to be a second time for you. Kathy!"

Kathy tried to freeze Toxanna, but the evil witch was too strong to bring to a complete stop.

Kathy slipped out the piece of paper with the reworked spell and handed it to Holly. The ink had faded and the water made the page soggy, but it was all they had. They were not going to let Toxanna get away. "Here, this should work."

Holly recited:

> *Bowen witches; spiritual beings.*
> *I call you down with this greeting.*
> *We unite, and speak as one.*
> *Toxanna here is well done.*
> *Family spirits with all your might,*
> *I call you now to finish the fight.*

The moonlight shone through the night sky, and blue streams of light came down and surrounded Holly, then pierced into Toxanna. Screaming, Toxanna's body burst into a million pieces that hit nearby walls and shattered like ice.

After Toxanna was gone, the spirits briefly surrounded Holly before flying back into the night sky.

The witches were silent. Holly stood with her shoulders slumped, staring at the space where Toxanna had stood moments ago.

"Are you okay?" Drew asked, touching her shoulder. He

hesitated when she didn't turn to him like she always had.

"They were here," Holly said. "My entire family was here. For the first time in my life, I felt safe." Chris walked over and grabbed her hand. She put her arm around his waist and squeezed tight. She closed her eyes and thought of the family she missed so much. She stopped the killings. Her family wouldn't suffer any longer. She leaned her head into Chris's chest and sobbed silently.

Chapter Fourteen

It was the end of November, and the weather was certainly showing it. The streets were lined by soft snow that brought peace to the entire city of Erie. Now that Toxanna and the supernatural thunderstorms were gone, the witches embraced the snow.

"Gotcha!" Holly shrieked in laughter as her snowball hit Chris square in the back. He had his arm up to swing in the opposite direction. He hadn't seen her sneak around behind him.

"Hey!" Chris shouted, chasing after her. Since Toxanna was gone, they had a lot more free time to relax and catch their breath. Chris and Holly were spending a lot more time together because of it. He didn't want to think about the possibility that she might go back to Salem soon.

They ran to the playground and climbed on top of the caged

castle. Before Chris could get up the ladder, Holly had shot another snowball at him, hitting him right in the face. Chris wiped off the wetness and said, "Are you using magic? No fair!"

Holly smiled and ducked inside the kiddie fortress. Chris was in such a hurry to chase after her that he forgot that he wasn't toddler-sized anymore and smacked his head against the low-hanging roof. The slippery plastic of the playground set sent his feet out from under him, and he landed flat on his back. He put up his hands. "Okay, okay! I'm out! You win!"

"I'm not falling for that!" Holly said from below. Chris couldn't quite make out where she was.

"No, seriously, Holly, come help me up!"

"Okay, fine." She climbed up the ladder and burst into laughter. "Wait until I tell Josh about this. He is not going to let you live this down!"

"Just shut up and help." Chris smiled. He reached up a gloved hand and Holly took it, pulling until she collapsed on the ground next to him.

"You did that on purpose," she said.

"C'mon, you know me better than to fall for the ol' 'come help me up' trick."

Holly smiled and their eyes locked.

"Will you go out with me?" He blurted it out faster than he expected, and he hoped that she wouldn't make him ask again.

Of course, she did. "What?" She heard him just fine the first time. But she wanted to buy some more time to come up with her answer. She liked him, but were they just kidding themselves by getting involved any further? If her father was alive, she couldn't leave him alone in Salem. Especially since the threat to their family was gone. He had lost too much already. But then there was Chris…

"I said…asked…if you might want to, maybe, go out with me sometime?" This time, it was definitely much slower. Suddenly, Chris felt hot lying on the snow. He could feel his face get red.

Holly flashed him another smile and grabbed his hand. She wished they both weren't wearing gloves. "Of course. Just as long as you walk me home. It's getting dark, and your aunt will probably be wondering where we are."

Kathy had taken Holly under her wing in more ways than just the supernatural now that Margaret was gone. The poor woman's body had been found a few days after Toxanna had died. The police were investigating the murder. Luckily, after the first round of routine questions, Holly was ruled out as a suspect.

Now Holly had moved in with Drew in a small apartment in the city but was over at the Harpers' most of the time. Chris wasn't too happy about Holly and Drew living together, but there wasn't anything he could do. They just didn't have the room at his house. Plus, Drew was Holly's only good connection from back home. Someone she knew and trusted. More so than she had with Margaret. It also helped that Drew was rarely home because he was dodging the Fire Wizards still. Every once in a while he would pop in with enough time to get a good night's sleep before taking off somewhere in the morning.

Chris and Holly wandered back to his house on the outskirts of town. Arm in arm the whole way, keeping each other warm.

THE BLOOD MOON

* * *

Kathy pulled up to the theater in her brand-new compact car. Thanks to Samantha's smart investing, Kathy had enough money to finally buy herself a new one. Now that Josh's car had been smashed too, they were desperate for a set of wheels.

Chris and Holly hopped out of the car. Kathy rolled down the window and shouted across the passenger seat, "Have fun! Call me if you change your mind about the bus!" She added as an afterthought, "Or anything else!"

She was nervous about this date. Maybe even more nervous than Chris and Holly were. For one, this parenting thing was still something Kathy was adjusting to. Samantha had been the responsible one. Kathy was always the one who was just looking to have fun. That's why it was so hard for Kathy to see Sammy's little boy off on his first date. Something Samantha would have loved to see for herself—should have seen herself.

Beyond her sister, Kathy worried how Chris and Holly's relationship would pan out. She didn't want either of them to get hurt, and she didn't know how their alliance as witches would work if Chris and Holly were no longer on good terms. They couldn't afford to lose another ally, no matter how selfish it sounded.

Despite all this, Kathy rolled up the window, took a deep breath, and drove off. She waved as she pulled away.

Chris waved back and muttered, "She's being so weird."

Holly shrugged. "It shows she cares. C'mon, what do you want to see?"

Chris insisted on paying, but Holly wasn't having that.

"Fine, you buy the tickets and the snacks for the movie, and I buy dinner," she suggested. "I've seen your piggy bank; you're as broke as I am." She laughed and reached for his arm.

After the movie, they decided to walk down to the restaurant rather than take a bus. The whole way they were hand-in-hand.

The restaurant was nothing fancy. Just a chain restaurant that Kathy had a gift card for. She insisted that they use it since Chris refused any money.

"You know what I find odd?" Chris asked after they ordered their food.

"What's that?" Holly asked.

"In a somewhat nice restaurant like this, you order your food and eat it, and then pay, but at a gross fast-food place you pay and then you get your food." He was nervous, he didn't quite know what to talk about. "It's easier for the nice places to dine and ditch than it is for the gross places."

"Is that all you want to talk about?"

"No, but I don't know what to talk about. I've never really been on a date before." Chris could feel his face burning with his confession.

"Neither have I," Holly admitted.

Chris smiled and reached for her hand on the table.

They gazed at one another until Holly spoke up. "So you pretty much know about my whole family because of the whole Toxanna thing, but I don't really know about yours. What were your parents like? I want to know more about your life before me."

The Blood Moon

Chris was shocked that she was asking about his family. Nobody ever asked. They all knew that it was somewhat of a sore subject with him. With the exception of Josh and Kathy, he didn't have much of a family.

Noticing Chris's hesitation, she added, "Unless of course you're not comfortable with that."

Chris smiled. "No, it's okay. Well, my mom is dead, as you know. We live with my aunt and fend off attacks from her psycho ex-husband." He forced a smile to lighten up the evening.

"No! I know that part already. I've known you for a couple months now! What about your dad?" She was wary about this; she wasn't sure how he'd react. Nobody mentioned his dad either. Somehow everyone knew not to.

Chris took a deep breath. He didn't like talking about his dad. But Holly had laid her cards on the table from day one. It was time for him to do the same. "My dad…I wish he and I had the same relationship as you and your dad. But to be honest, I'm not his biggest fan."

"Oh." Holly had no idea, but in a way that explained why she never heard him say anything about his dad. Nor were there any pictures of him at their house.

"It's not that bad really. He was just never around. He left my mom a few years ago. Right about the time Josh started showing signs of magic." Chris paused because their waitress brought over their food. After she was out of earshot, he continued, "He left my mom for many reasons. He didn't like that she wouldn't let him sell the house. He didn't like it that Aunt Kathy lived with us. He didn't like it that she was a witch, either. Although Aunt Kathy told us that he somewhat accepted the fact that Mom was a witch, but he couldn't handle having sons as witches."

"Chris, I'm sorry." She covered their entwined hands with her free one.

"Can we change the subject? I don't want you to feel bad for me. I'm over it. I've accepted the fact that my father is not in my life anymore." As he spoke, Holly's hold on his hand tightened.

"Sure," Holly said. She gave his hand one last squeeze before letting go and looking at the plate in front of her. "Looks good, doesn't it?"

"Mmm," Chris mumbled, his first forkful already in his mouth. "So, I told you something I'm not used to sharing, how about you do the same?"

"Um…sure, I suppose that's fair." Her head was spinning with what she had left out. Finally, it clicked before Chris could even articulate the question.

"What's the deal with you and Drew? You guys obviously have more of a history than teacher-student." He reached for his water, hoping that he hadn't just upset her.

"Well…" Holly started before slipping another bite in her mouth, buying time to think of the best way to approach the subject. She didn't think talking about her previous relationship was something she should be doing on a date. "Drew came into my life when I first learned I was a witch. My dad thought keeping my powers from me would prevent me from being Toxanna's target."

"Obviously that didn't work," Chris commented. He wished he could take back his question, but he was too curious to know the answer.

"No," Holly said. "Once I knew I was a witch, my dad thought it would be better for me to know how to use my powers in case—when Toxanna attacked. At the time, Drew was still on good terms with the Fire Wizards, before they were corrupted. So he became my teacher. My dad had his own restaurant, so we were alone a lot and…yeah…" She really wanted to stop talking about Drew, but Chris was leaning closer and closer, waiting for her to say the words she didn't want to.

"Yeah…what?"

"We dated for a short while, if you could call it that." Holly shrugged. "He showed me some pretty neat tricks with magic—not that that stuff was useful against Toxanna. We never formally dated like this. It just sort of happened because he was there." She shrugged again, trying to play it off. "Once the Fire Wizards had turned and Drew was exiled, we broke it off. He thought I'd be a target. I only looked him up again when I moved in with Margaret and was desperate for help."

"Oh." Chris didn't know how to respond. He still wanted to know more but didn't push it. This was definitely not how he wanted things to go tonight.

She reached for his hand again. "But look, Chris. I never liked Drew half as much as I like you. I'm not just saying that. I'm living with him and here I am with you."

"Right." He nodded and drove his fork into his chicken.

"You're right. Can't blame me for asking, right?"

They moved on and continued the rest of the date laughing and telling funny stories about their childhoods.

"I'm serious!" Holly laughed. "The first thing I did with my magic was turn Zamball's girlfriend into a dog!"

Chris asked between snorts of his own laughter, "How did you manage that one? And a better question is how could Zamball get a girlfriend?"

Holly's laugh subsided so she could explain. "Well, he disguised himself as this really cute guy named Elliott. Everyone wanted to date him, but this popular girl was dating him. I called her a bitch and ended up turning her into a dog!" She started laughing hysterically again. The story wasn't even that funny, but they were having a lot of fun together, which made everything ten times funnier.

Their laughter ended once the manager came to their table and told them it was closing time. They looked around and saw that they were the only ones left in the restaurant. They hadn't even noticed anyone else had left.

They walked to a nearby bus stop and sat on the cold metal bench to wait. Holly leaned in to Chris, partially to stay warm, but mostly just to be near him.

"Tonight was a lot of fun," she said, resting her head on his shoulder. Her hands were buried in her pockets.

"Aren't you glad you finally decided to go out with me?" Chris joked.

"We should do this again sometime soon. It's good to have a

nice night away from all the magic mayhem." She shivered in the cold, and Chris wrapped his arms around her.

"The next time we both are free, we'll go," Chris promised.

They sat in silence enjoying the peaceful night with each other until the bus came.

Once they were seated, Chris looked Holly in the eyes and said, "Tonight was a lot of fun."

Holly laughed. "I already said that."

"Well, I mean it. Every time I'm with you, I'm so much happier," Chris confessed.

Holly leaned in and kissed him. "You're sweet, but if you keep saying how much I make you happy, I'm going to start to wonder if you're the girl in this relationship." She laughed. "I even bought you dinner."

Chris smiled.

"So how was your date?" Holly asked.

"It was…okay," Chris said.

They were the last people off the bus.

When they got to the front door, Holly said, "You know you didn't need to walk me to the door."

"Well, since I live here, I thought it'd be a nice gesture."

Holly kissed him again.

When they got inside, Kathy yelled at them for being out so late.

"I tried calling Holly's cell phone, but that didn't get me far because you never turned it on!" Kathy waved her phone in the air. She was relieved they were all right but angry they never returned her calls.

Josh was lying on the couch enjoying his brother's punishment all too much.

Holly pulled her cell phone out of her pocket and said, "Oh, I guess I forgot to turn it on." When she turned it on, she saw that she had twenty-three missed calls and fifteen messages.

"Sorry, Aunt Kathy. But look, we're safe," Chris said, holding up his arms and turning around to show off that he wasn't hurt at all.

"Are we in trouble?" Holly asked.

"No, but next time I'm driving you," she said. She changed her tone and asked, "Did you have fun?"

Chris looked at Holly and then back to Kathy and said, "It was okay."

Chapter Fifteen

"Where's Aunt Kathy?" Chris asked when he and Josh came home from school the following week.

"She's at her inter—" Josh stopped dead when his foot hit a puddle in the living room. "Let's not overreact, it could've been Aunt Kathy. She might've dropped something and didn't get a chance to clean it up yet." He didn't even believe the possible explanation, but he didn't want to panic.

"Do you think it was Zamball?" Chris asked.

Josh sighed. "Probably. What other person do you know that could do that?"

"Toxanna," Holly answered. She had emerged from the kitchen and startled the boys. "Sorry, let myself in. I was bored at Drew's."

"Oh." Josh had almost forgotten about Toxanna's specialty. It had been almost three weeks since Holly had defeated her family nemesis. "It can't be her. That'd be impossible, right?" He wasn't quite sure himself.

No one answered him. They all just stared at the puddle, realizing that their small moment of peace was now over.

"So our main suspect is Zamball," Chris said, breaking the silence. "Let's not blow this out of proportion. Josh, you continue to work on your homework or whatever you do. Holly, you don't need to deal with this, either. We still don't know for sure if this is Zamball."

"I think I should help," Holly said. "I'll look in all the diaries and all the notes my family took on Zamball, and you use the water to see if you can find him."

Chris nodded. They separated and went straight to work. He used an eyedropper to gather some of the water, and Holly left to gather her journals from Drew's apartment.

* * *

After spending some time searching, Chris came down to the kitchen and said, "It definitely was Zamball, but I can't find him."

"How do you know it was Zamball?" Josh asked. He was doing homework at the table.

"I did a small ritual to see if any demonic traces were in it," Chris explained.

They heard a crash from the living room. The brothers looked at each other with panic in their eyes.

"Where's Holly?" Josh asked.

They sprinted to the living room and found Devon, his hand gripped tightly around Holly's throat. His wings had grown back once again, and they were neatly tucked behind him.

Holly was frantically trying to rip his hand off her neck, but it was no use. Devon's hold was strong. She was getting blue in the face, and her efforts to free herself weren't helping.

Chris blew up Devon's arm, and Holly fell to the ground, unconscious. When Devon screamed out in pain, Josh sent him flying out the front door.

Chris knelt down next to Holly to check her pulse just as Kathy walked in the front door, wearing a black suit jacket and pants. Her purse was slung over her shoulder, and she had a smile on her face until she saw Holly. "What's wrong?"

Josh ignored his aunt and asked, "Is she okay?" He was looking over his brother's shoulder. The color was rushing back to Holly's face. A good sign.

"Yeah, she'll be fine," Chris confirmed.

Josh turned to his aunt. "Keep an eye on her. We need to borrow your car."

Kathy fumbled in her purse until she produced her keys. They still had the tag from the dealership. She handed them over to Josh. "Where are you going?"

Josh pulled on Chris's shoulder to break him away from Holly and ran out the front door. "We need to follow him!"

* * *

Devon tried flying high in the air so he could hide himself, but there weren't any clouds. No matter how high he flew, Josh and Chris were still able to spot him. They chased him down the street and back to the alley where Toxanna had met her demise.

Devon landed in the alley, and the boys got out of the car, ready to fight.

"Do you really think I'm that stupid?" Devon asked. His back was to the brothers, and he was nursing his damaged limb.

"I'll take that as a rhetorical question," Chris said sarcastically.

"Why'd you lead us here?" Josh asked.

"I wanted to take you to the place where I was when my life changed," Devon explained. He turned his head over his shoulder but still didn't face them.

"He doesn't know anything," Chris said as he attempted to blow Devon up, but Josh pushed him, and Chris's attack blew up a streetlight instead.

"No, leave him," Josh said. He addressed Devon, "Who do you work for now?"

Devon finally turned and faced them. Josh didn't like the confidence he had. With his good hand, Devon conjured a fireball and threw it at Josh.

Josh sent it back at Devon's head. When the demon ducked, the boys tackled him. It took them a while to contain him. His thrashing and the power of his wings prevented them from holding him, but eventually they got him. They both lay on top of Devon and questioned him.

"Now, as I was saying," Josh said, "who do you work for?" He lay on Devon's back, holding his wings in place.

"I'm still not going to tell you, witch," the creature answered with a laugh.

"Maybe you should rethink that answer," Chris said.

"Or you'll do what?" Devon asked.

Chris grabbed one of Devon's legs and annihilated his foot. The demon screamed.

"So what'll it be?" Josh asked. "If you don't talk, we'll just keep blowing up each of your limbs until you tell us. We'll get it out of you eventually."

"When the sun is black and the moon is red, a man will emerge from the shadows to triumphantly spread the darkness."

"What is that?" Chris asked, annoyed. He was fighting to grab Devon's other leg to blow up his other foot. His hand was already covered in Devon's blood.

"Chris, relax. I'm thinking," Josh said, looking at his brother. "It sounds like a prophecy of some sort."

"Yes," Devon said. "Now let me go. I gave you what you wanted!"

"No, we're taking you home with us until we figure out what to do with you," Chris said.

A water puddle ran underneath Devon, and a hand appeared out of the water, pulling Devon inside. The boys slumped on the hard concrete once Devon had vanished.

"Zamball's at it again," Chris said. "Should we go after him?"

"No," Josh said. He sat on the ground and stared at the spot where Devon had disappeared. "He told us the prophecy; now it's our job to stop it."

Chapter Sixteen

The furniture was pushed aside in the living room, and Holly delivered a kick into Kathy's open hand.

"What's going on here?" Josh asked. He tossed his jacket over the back of the couch.

"I was mad Devon was able to come up from behind me and jump me so easily, so I asked Kathy to teach me self-defense," Holly explained. She had changed her clothes and was now wearing shorts and a tank top. She had pulled her hair out of her face and in a loose bun.

"Aren't you taking this a little too far?" Chris asked.

"No. I still don't know what my specialty is. I think this is a good skill to know," Holly explained. "But I actually used a spell for a quick lesson, so I pretty much know how to do everything. Kathy's helping me practice." She clapped her hands together and rubbed them. "Okay, let's try that flip. Which one of you two wants to help?"

Josh slipped into the kitchen and left Chris standing there.

"What! Me? No!" Chris protested. "What if I blow something up?"

"We'll deal with it later," Holly said as she grabbed his hand and pulled him into the center of the living room.

Chris took a deep breath and asked, "What do I do?"

"Just run at her," Kathy instructed.

Chris warily ran toward Holly. The next thing he knew, he was on the floor looking up at them.

"Cool," Holly cheered. She clapped her hands together as if to brush off the dust. "I did it! Now go take a break. I'm going to need some more help in a couple of minutes."

Chris stayed on the floor for a minute or two regaining his bearings. When he finally found the strength to get up, he walked into the kitchen and saw Josh writing down the prophecy they'd just heard.

"Okay, well this is simple," Josh said. "'When the sun is black...' That's got to be an eclipse."

Chris plopped into the chair next to Josh and opened his brother's laptop. He typed into the Internet browser search bar and said, "Does this have anything to do with the blood moons we've been having?"

"'...and the moon is red...'" Josh recited. "It's got to be the blood moon. When is that?" He leaned over to look at the computer screen. "That's not until April."

Chris grabbed the piece of paper that Josh had written the prophecy on. "'...a man will emerge from the shadows to triumphantly spread the darkness.' That's pretty simple. Do you think Devon was paraphrasing?"

Josh leaned back in his chair. "Either way, we got the gist of it. Isn't there usually a location with prophecies?"

Chris shook his head. "Not always. And like I said, he was probably paraphrasing." He stood and grabbed a water bottle out of the fridge. "Okay, I gotta go be the punching bag."

"Have fun," Josh called over his shoulder. He reached for the magic book on the counter and flipped through it to look for more information about prophecies. There wasn't much in the book that could help him.

His concentration was broken by Drew's voice. He hadn't heard him come in. He jumped. "Whoa! Way to sneak up on me like that!"

"Sorry. Where's Holly?" Drew ran a hand through his unkempt hair. He looked sick, like he had been on the run for too long.

"Are you okay?" Josh asked. "Why don't you sit down?"

"No! I'm here for Holly." Drew pounded his fist on the counter. "Sorry. I just really need to see her. Soon—I don't have a lot of time."

"Is it the Fire Wizards?" Josh asked. He didn't like that Drew was bringing them to the house, but he felt bad for the guy. Drew obviously couldn't handle a whole coven of wizards on his own.

"Holly!" Drew shouted. He wasn't getting anywhere with

Josh. He stalked into the living room.

"Drew! I haven't seen you in weeks! Where have you been?" Holly asked. She moved toward him, but he put up his hand.

"Holly, I—" Drew didn't have time to finish before five men wearing blue robes appeared in a swirl of flames.

"Not here!" Drew said.

"You know why we're here," one of them said.

"We're not picky, either," another one added, scanning the room.

Yet another one threw a fireball at Holly, but Chris stopped it with his power before it could hit her, blowing the fireball up.

"Get the hell out of my house!" Kathy shouted as she kicked one of them down.

Another one of the men tried to tackle Josh, but Holly kicked him in the stomach.

Josh used his power to send the other three flying across the room.

"There are five of us and five of them. If we each get one, they shouldn't be a problem," Chris said.

They split up and went into different rooms.

Holly muttered a short incantation and conjured a sword. One of the men in blue robes created a fire sword. They squared off and started fighting. As their swords clashed, embers filled the air. Whenever the enemy's blade came too close, Holly could feel the heat emanating from the magic sword.

In the kitchen, Chris used his power to blow up the fireballs that were coming at him, then reversed his magic and sent the fireballs back in the direction they'd come from. His attacker was good at dodging the fireballs that were sent back his way, causing the wall opposite Chris to erupt in flames.

Josh was fending off attacks by forming a small cyclone to collect the fireballs in. He was able to stop the attacks, but he had no way of attacking the man at all.

Using her newly restored powers, Kathy froze the attacker and his fireballs and then teleported behind them. Once she was out of the danger zone, she teleported her attacker to the spot she had been in when he first attacked, and then she unfroze them. The fireballs that were intended for her hit her enemy instead.

In the foyer, Drew was mumbling spells and charms under his breath to confuse his target. Instead of focusing on the incoming attacks, he instilled temporary paranoia in the man, which caused him to retreat.

Eventually, everyone convened back in the living room. One of the men in the blue robes looked at Holly before turning his attention to Drew. "This isn't over," he said just before he and the other four men disappeared in a swirl of blue flames.

"What the hell, Drew?" Chris demanded, trying to catch his breath. The adrenaline sped up his heart rate, and he needed a second to cool down. He leaned forward with his hands on his knees.

"Chris," Kathy parented.

"Still haven't shaken those Fire Wizards yet?" Josh asked.

"No. But that's not why I'm here. I'm sorry for troubling you with them. I've told you that already," Drew said. "I'm just here to bring Holly back."

"Back to Salem?" Holly asked.

"Yeah. Your father called on me. He wants to make sure you're safe."

"Even more reason for her to stay here," Chris said.

"Why?" Drew asked.

"Because if she's near you, she's in danger," Josh said. "Since you won't tell anyone about these Fire Wizards, she could walk into the middle of a crossfire and get hurt."

"Why do you think I've been staying away from the apartment? I don't want Holly getting hurt!" Drew countered.

"And yet you show up here, and not even five minutes later the Fire Wizards show up," Chris said. He had his arms folded and stared at Drew.

"Guys, my dad and my uncle are the only family I have left," Holly said, nearly whispering. She was actually surprised herself that they heard her with the tension in the room. "I can't just leave them." She was still processing the fact that her father was alive after all.

"She's right," agreed Kathy. She put her arm around Holly's shoulder.

"But what about us?" Chris asked. "You can't just leave me all alone. And how are we supposed to cope without you? Toxanna may be gone, but Zamball and Devon now have a grudge against us. Something you started, and now you're just going to leave us?"

Holly stared at the floor for a minute, taking everything in.

Then she spoke quietly. "I'm sorry, but I need to go back."

"How can you just ditch us like that?" Chris argued. He felt betrayed, backstabbed, like he had been a fool. Here he was flirting and hoping that what he and Holly had together would keep her in Erie, but in the end she was still going back to Salem. With Drew.

"We need your help!" Josh added.

"Guys, she's got to go back." Kathy was annoyed with her nephews for being so inconsiderate.

"You can't honestly say you're not going to feel guilty when you get back home," Chris said.

"Why would she?" Drew asked. "Toxanna's gone. What's keeping her here?"

"She's leaving her friends—who treated her as family—high and dry because her father misses her," Chris explained. He turned and addressed Holly. "I get that you want to be with your father. Really, I do. But wouldn't you feel guilty because you brought problems here, and then you left us after the problems got worse?"

"Why can't you guys just say good-bye?" Holly asked. "I'm going back, and…I just have to go back."

"Let's go." Drew tried to put his arm around her, but she moved away from him.

"No, we'll go tomorrow," Holly said. "I owe them that. Just take me back to the apartment so I can pack."

Chris stormed off to the kitchen.

"Great, so I'll be back early tomorrow," Drew said.

"What's wrong with you?" Josh asked. "How can you just tear her away from us like this? And you say you care about her?"

"I would die for that girl, so don't you dare tell me I don't care for her." Drew spoke in a stern, even tone. "And besides, her family deserves to see her. They've already lost enough." With that, he disappeared in a swirl of white smoke.

Josh and Kathy joined Chris in the kitchen.

Josh asked, "Are you okay?"

"Let's not make a big deal about this." Chris's voice broke. He turned his back on his brother and aunt and walked upstairs.

Josh turned to Kathy. "What are we going to do about him?"

"I don't know," Kathy admitted. "All I know is that this is going to hurt him for a while."

* * *

The next morning, Holly was packed and ready to go. Drew had returned and was ready to take them back. She stood in the Harpers' doorway. Kathy, Josh, and Chris were waiting to say their good-byes. Chris had his arms folded and wouldn't look Drew or Holly in the eyes.

She said her good-byes to Kathy and Josh. When it came time for Chris, he just waved and walked away.

"Chris, just say good-bye so this won't be any harder," Holly said, tears welling up in her eyes.

"I know a way to make it a lot easier," Chris said.

"I can't stay," Holly said. "You wouldn't know. You have family here. I don't!"

"We're your family," Chris pleaded.

"Chris, my family has been fighting Toxanna for eighty years," Holly reminded him. "We have been fighting for the right to a normal life, away from Toxanna and her army. Now we have that. I can't just leave my dad again. He's been through so much. We've finally earned our right to a normal life."

Chris sighed and then said, "I hate that you're leaving. I hate that you're dumping the rest of your problems on us. But I guess I can't stop you from going. As long as you promise to visit. I mean, you need to help us defeat Zamball and Devon sometime. We deserve a normal life too, don't we?"

"I promise," she said. She hugged him and then, on impulse, kissed him. "Bye." She took Drew's hand, and together they disappeared in a swirl of white smoke.

"Bye," Chris said after the smoke cleared.

CHAPTER SEVENTEEN

Holly was missing Erie. Two different people she loved were in two different towns. Chris was in Erie, and her father was in Salem. How could she spend time with both of them and stay in one place? She couldn't; it was as simple as that.

One of the only pictures she had to remember Chris by was a random snapshot he'd taken of the two of them one time. That picture was helping her cope with her decision to return to her father.

She had called Chris a couple of times, but he was upset with her that she left, and she didn't want to make it worse for him. She was making plans with Josh to come and surprise Chris with a visit, but they hadn't decided on a date yet.

Her solitude was interrupted when her uncle—she was still adjusting to him as a human—knocked on her door to tell her dinner was ready.

Holly wasn't sure if he didn't see her crying or if he simply decided not to point it out. She cried a lot nowadays. Either way, after he left, she wiped her tears, looked in the mirror for any other traces of her sadness, and went downstairs for dinner.

The table seemed much fuller than when she first went to Erie. Now, instead of just dinner for two, they added her Uncle Ken, and occasionally Drew.

Tonight spaghetti was the main meal, but since her father was a chef, the food didn't end there. They started off with a salad, then garlic bread and spaghetti with his homemade sauce, and finished it off with homemade cheesecake.

Even if her father being in Salem wasn't enough to make her the least bit happy, the feast he cooked nearly every day brightened her up. The food in Salem was always better than the food in Erie. When she'd lived in Erie, most of the time dinner was "fend for yourself" or chicken or hamburgers. Sometimes someone would have time to make a better meal, but that had been rare.

As she ate, Holly thought about how she would be able to spend Christmas with her father. She was happy because three months ago her whole situation with her family and Toxanna had seemed like World War III. When she first left Salem, she never would have imagined even seeing her father again, let alone spending the holidays with him in their house as if they didn't have a care in the world.

Despite the happy feast, the room was quiet.

Holly remembered the hustle and bustle of Erie and the

Harper house and missed it terribly. Something was always going on in Erie. Whether it be demonic attacks or just the brothers and Kathy having a loud conversation. Being in a quiet house again made Holly feel like she was missing out on something.

After dinner, Holly was drying the dishes as her father washed them.

"You seem quiet, honey," Holly's father, Simon, ventured. He knew how much she missed Erie, but he was thrilled that they could start a normal life together, something he always tried to offer her. "You want to talk about it?"

She didn't look at him. She carefully dried a plate and put it away in the cupboard.

Simon handed her another dish. "We need to get you re-enrolled in school. But first we need to come up with a way to explain your absence—"

Holly slammed the plate into the sink, sending broken pieces everywhere. "Dad, this is unfair! I just up and left them in Erie without warning! What happens if they die because I wasn't there to help them? How would you live with yourself?"

Holly had never talked to her father like this. She had an uneasy edge that she didn't want to let slip. She knew her father deserved a normal life, but she had unfinished business to take care of.

Simon dried his hands and grabbed Holly's chin with his finger and his thumb and moved her head to face him. "This is your home. I understand that you miss them, but you'll reconnect with your old friends here and forget all about them."

"But I don't want to forget about them!" She was fuming now. How did he expect her to forget about them? When you risk your life to save someone on multiple occasions, you don't just fall into only Christmas-card buddies. You form a bond and a connection that nothing compares to. "Chris won't even talk to me because he thinks that I abandoned him and his family with all of my problems." She put one hand on her hip and the other on the counter, eyes blazing into Simon's.

"A teenage boy hundreds of miles away shouldn't make you feel guilty," Simon said. He reached for her to pull her into a hug, but she shrugged away from him.

"I don't blame him for being angry with me! I ditched them at possibly the worst time!" Holly shouted. "There is some crazy new threat out there, and I just get up and go before I have a target on my back. Most of the allies for this new evil are our enemies!" She stopped, noticing her father's sad look. She was tearing him apart. As much as she blamed him and hated him for dragging her back to Salem, she didn't want to completely crash his hope of a unified family again.

She took his hands and said, "They helped me when I had Toxanna; don't you think I should help them in return?"

Simon nodded and wrapped his arms around her. She let him this time. He rested his chin on the top of her head. "You're a good person. And a good witch. But—"

But. That was it. She wasn't getting her way. She pulled away from him and went upstairs to her room.

THE BLOOD MOON

* * *

After her shower, Holly sat on her bed in a pair of flannel pajama bottoms and one of her dad's old T-shirts. She stared off into space, thinking, as she ran a brush through her wet hair.

She really missed Chris.

And Josh.

And Kathy.

It was so weird to her. She had only known the Harpers for a few months and here she was back in her own room trying to be completely normal and finding it was impossible. It was funny, because six months ago she hadn't even known she was a witch. It was amazing how Simon kept that from her. Or maybe she was just so caught up in herself that she didn't even notice?

Once the beans had been spilled, her whole world turned upside down. Simon hired Drew and her intense witch training started. Despite the extensive knowledge she gained in witchcraft in such a short time, she still wasn't able to stop Toxanna.

Within a month she was running away from the only life she'd ever known. Hopping on a bus in the middle of the night. She left not even knowing if her father was alive. She remembered the long, lonely bus ride too well. Trying to distract herself with some crazy fantasy that this would all work out. Be careful what you wish for. She had reclaimed the life she had before she knew about Toxanna, but now it was the last thing she wanted.

Pins and needles shot up her leg as it fell asleep. She broke out of the trance and looked at herself in the mirror. She had a photo of Chris stuck on the side of the mirror. It was from the weeks leading up to their date when they were practically inseparable. They had gone to one of the overpriced and totally cheesy photo booths in the mall.

She chewed on her bottom lip, thinking of a way she could convince her father to let her go back to Erie. Or maybe he would move there with her? That would be perfect! Then she could live with her dad and see Chris—

Her enthusiasm was cut short by the robotic sound of her cell phone. It was her best friend, Lori. Part of her old life in Salem. Someone she had barely thought about since everything that had happened with Toxanna.

"Hey, Holly! I heard you're back in town!" Lori was too chipper for Holly's mood, but she wasn't about to burst her friend's bubble.

She tried to sound cheerful. "Uh, yeah. Just got back last week."

"That's great! It's been too long. School has been so boring without you," she rattled on, obviously not picking up on Holly's tone over the phone. "I mean, Mr. Jackson in English yesterd—"

"Lori, I'm sorry, I'm not really up to hanging out right now," Holly said. "Still adjusting to the move."

"But you were only gone, like, two months," Lori said. "Why *did* you leave anyway? It was kind of a random time to leave, too. Wasn't it right after that freak snowstorm?"

Holly nodded at first and then said, "Yeah, it was. I really can't talk right now. I'll text you tomorrow, okay?"

Lori paused. "Oh, okay." The strain in her friend's voice almost killed Holly. She had friends in Salem, too. To them, she was going to ditch them for people she'd only known for a few months. For a boy. How cliché. But they didn't understand. It was deeper than that. Much deeper. Something they would never know.

Simon knocked on the door. Holly called out, "Come in!" and continued to brush her hair.

"Can I talk to you, sweetheart?"

"Sure," she said, concentrating on her hair. She hit a few snarls and winced as she brushed them out.

When he sat down next to her, she flipped her hair to the side her father sat on so he couldn't see her face.

"I understand that you want to go back to Erie"—he pushed her hair back so he could see her—"and that you miss everyone, but you need to realize this is your home and I need you here, too."

Holly went to the dresser and grabbed a hair tie. She pulled her hair into a loose bun on top of her head, sensing that the conversation was not going to go the way she wanted it to go. She turned to her father and put a hand on her hip. The same stance she'd had in the kitchen.

"I know you missed me, and believe me, I missed you too, but the Harpers need me more right now," Holly argued. "My enemies just became their enemies, too."

"They're experienced witches just like us, they'll be able to cope," Simon reasoned.

Holly grabbed Chris's picture from her dresser and pointed to it. "What about me and Chris? You just tore me out of Erie without thinking about the friends I made."

"You'll find another boy here," Simon said. "And Drew told me that you practically lived with that boy, too?"

"Oh, please, Dad, you don't think we actually did anything?" Her head was spinning. This was not the conversation she wanted to have. She needed to shift the discussion back to her side.

"I don't know what that boy convinced you to do or not." Simon put up his hands.

"Dad! Chris would never do that! And if you think that I wouldn't be able to handle myself in that kind of situation and make my own decisions, maybe you don't know me at all," Holly said. She was outraged. What did he think she did while she was in Erie? Kick up her feet and hunt for boys? Didn't he give her any credit for killing their family nemesis? Her anger boiled to the top and she shouted, "Get out of my room! Leave me alone!"

Simon obviously wasn't too happy either. "You are not going down there again! I forbid you!" He slammed the door behind him on his way out.

"You forbid me?" Holly mumbled to herself. She couldn't believe he'd just said that. She had almost forgotten about Simon's overprotection and his temper.

She lay on her bed and grabbed her phone. She was going to call Chris. She had his contact information up but couldn't push herself to hit "Send." She cleared it and turned off her phone instead, then rolled on her side and silently cried until she fell asleep.

Chapter Eighteen

"We can't keep this up for too much longer." Josh sighed as he took a seat on the bottom step of the staircase. They had just come back from an unsuccessful attack. It shouldn't have been a big deal, but whoever this new power was must have heard that they were now a witch short and was sending in loads of reinforcements to gang up on the Harpers.

Kathy took a seat next to her nephew. "I know. But we're going to have to adjust without Holly. It's too bad for Mrs. Kors…" They had just lost their elderly neighbor. After she'd been kidnapped, Kathy and Josh had gone to rescue her. Unfortunately, the kidnappers hadn't been friendly with her, and she'd died before Kathy and Josh arrived.

Chris wasn't as helpful nowadays without Holly. Kathy didn't want to push it, but some days they were desperate for his help and forced him to come. Those days never turned out well.

"Do you think she has any family around here?" Josh asked. He couldn't believe the sweet old woman who always wanted to make sure they were okay—to the extent that she was a bit nosey at times—was gone, and it was because of his family.

"I think her daughter lives around here." Kathy wrapped her arms around her knees like a high school student waiting for practice. "But we can't let on that we know anything about it. That would bring up a whole investigation that we can't get involved in."

"This is stupid!" Josh shouted. There was a breeze throughout the house.

"Josh, control your power," Kathy warned. "We're going to figure this out."

"How? We're always two steps behind, and we can't seem to keep our head above water. We need Chris to step up and help, and we need Holly back here," Josh said. "That's how we're going to figure this out!"

Kathy sighed and wrapped her arm around Josh's shoulder. "We've been through a lot in the last few weeks. We're tired. Why don't we call it quits for the day and talk about this again tomorrow after school?"

Josh wasn't going to argue that he would likely have homework to do after school. He wanted a break to be able to sit in front of the TV and fall asleep without having to worry about *something* for a change.

He nodded and walked upstairs.

Kathy sat staring at the floor, worried about the amount of pressure Josh put on himself.

The Blood Moon

* * *

The pancake batter sizzled on the skillet as Kathy poured it on. The relaxing evening the night before had been just what they all needed. Even though the boys were going off to school and she was heading off to a meeting to finalize her divorce—not that it changed her worry that Will still had some sort of power over her—she decided to try and stretch that relaxation out with some chocolate chip pancakes.

When the boys came downstairs, she was just filling their plates.

"Oh, good. I was just going to call you down." She looked up at her nephews with a wide smile before depositing the utensils in the sink. She would get to them later.

"What's this?" Chris asked, slathering a glob of syrup over his plate.

"With everything going on I figured we deserve the right to indulge and savor little things like a hot breakfast." She dribbled some syrup over her own plate. "Also, I think we should have a party on New Year's Eve."

Josh nearly choked. "A party?"

Kathy shrugged. "Yeah. The bad guys don't want attention any more than we do, so having a house full of people will basically ensure that we bring in the new year right. How's that sound?" She took a bite of her breakfast and looked at her nephews. They weren't sure what to think of the idea. Since they'd been born, the house had been almost entirely guest-free. If you didn't count the uninvited guests.

The simple matter was that Kathy missed having parties. Before her sister had gotten married and had kids, she and Samantha would have solstice parties twice a year. New Year's was a little late for the winter solstice, but a party was needed regardless.

"What if there's an attack? What if the new power ignores the blood moon?" Chris asked. The date of the blood moon had a mark on his calendar, and it was a day he was dreading.

"There won't be an attack during the party," Kathy assured. "And besides, I think we need some social interaction. I haven't seen my friends in…" She tried to remember the last time her friends had randomly called her up for lunch. It had been too long, certainly before Samantha had died, maybe even before she'd married Will.

"My point is," she continued, "it'll do us good. Especially you two. Kids your age shouldn't have this much stress." She looked up at the clock. "Oh, we need to get going so I can drop you guys off at school. Hurry up and eat your pancakes!"

* * *

By the time New Year's Eve arrived, the snow was peacefully falling from the sky. As the guests arrived, the boys continued to be tense about the prospect of having a party. Josh especially had a feeling that something bad was going to happen. He didn't voice it because, as a witch, his feelings were usually right.

THE BLOOD MOON

Chris was up in the magic room looking at the magic book. He had lit six candles and placed them in a circle on the floor around him. He had crafted a simple spell—not his best work, but he figured it would still get the job done. He recited from the scrap piece of paper that he used to write the incantation:

Bring my friend from her father,
unless it is a real bother.

In a swirl of white lights, Holly appeared wearing a white robe. Chris's face lit up when he saw her. He moved to hug her before he realized she was transparent. Her could see her, and yet he could also see right through her.

"Holly!" Chris said, then he realized she was crying. "What's the matter?"

She looked down at herself and then back up at Chris. "Isn't it obvious? I'm dead."

His heart began racing. Really, he had known that something had happened to her. Something must've happened to her, she would've called otherwise. "What? How?" He was upset and confused. His mind was flooded with questions he desperately wanted the answers to. Would this have happened if she had stayed in Erie? How was he going to fix this? Why did they kill her? Was it to weaken him and Josh?

Holly looked down at the floor.

"Holly, how did this happen? Who attacked you?"

She shrugged, and her voice was small as she said, "It was

just…a random attack, I don't know."

"Think. This could help us save you. What did they look—"

"Chris, there is no saving me!" she shouted. "I'm *dead*! I have been for a couple weeks. I can't just return to my body without consequences."

Chris could feel his panic overcome him, he didn't know whether he was devastated or furious. Both. He needed more answers. He looked her in the eyes, determined. "When was the attack?"

She shrugged again.

"Damn it, Holly, tell me!" By the look on her face, he could tell that it came out too harsh.

"A week or two ago…I'm not exactly sure," she stammered.

"I'm going to fix this," Chris said. He wanted to take care of Holly, but he was also in over his head.

"How can you be sure that it wasn't my time to die?" Holly asked. "What if this is my fate? How can you be sure that this was a mistake?"

"I can't, but I can't just let them get away with this," Chris replied. "They've killed too many innocent people already." He wanted to find whoever did this to Holly and strangle them.

"Instead of wasting your time saving me, why don't you focus on taking out this new threat," Holly suggested. "I have to go." She looked up and disappeared in a glimmer of white lights.

* * *

The Blood Moon

Chris raced downstairs where the party was just getting started.

"Hey, where were you?" Mark, one of Chris's friends, asked. His had his warm-up jacket from basketball on. His last name, Cooper, was displayed proudly across his back.

"Upstairs. Where are Josh and my aunt?" He craned his neck to look at the people in the next room. The house was packed. He couldn't tell if people came because they were friends with them, or if they were nosey and wanted to know why the house was cut off from the world.

"Josh is in the living room, and I'm not sure where your aunt is," Mark answered. "Why? What's up?"

Ignoring his friend, Chris flashed a quick smile and said, "Thanks. Gotta go," before taking off to the living room.

Josh was playing video games with a couple of his friends. It was one of the few times since school had picked back up in September that he was laughing and having a good time. The two-week break from school was doing wonders for him.

Chris almost felt guilty bringing more stress to his brother. "I need to talk to you and Aunt Kathy. Where is she?"

Distracted by the game, Josh turned his head slightly toward his brother, while keeping his eyes on the TV. "What is it?"

"It's important, let's go!" Chris insisted. He smiled at Josh's friends. He tried to think up an excuse but decided not to say anything. He didn't want to get caught up in lies.

From the tone of Chris's voice, Josh could tell it was serious. He told his friends he'd be right back and gave his controller to one of them. He followed Chris to the kitchen, where Kathy was pulling cookies out of the oven. She was chatting with a couple of her friends. They barely saw each other anymore, and Kathy wasn't up-to-date on the various pregnancies and marriages among them. She was also trying to fend off questions about her own imploding marriage, brushing them off with: "Oh, you know, it was just the typical stuff that led us to divorce…"

"Hey, Aunt Kathy, can I talk to you and Josh in private?" Chris asked, looking over at Kathy's friends.

Kathy smiled and asked her friends, "Could you give us a minute, please?"

After they left, Chris continued, "There's no easy way to say this, so I'm just going to come out and say it. Holly's dead. It's because of this new power. Actually, no, it's because of that jerk Drew, who took her away, and her dad, who probably kept her from contacting us." He was nearly shouting by the end.

Kathy walked to the other side of the counter to console and shush him. "Keep your voice down."

"She's dead?" Josh asked. "How do you know?"

"I tried to summon her for the party, and I ended up summoning her spirit instead," Chris explained.

"You were doing magic while there were mortals downstairs?" Kathy scolded. She started to shout before realizing how loud she was and brought her voice down quickly. "Chris, what were you thinking? What if someone walked in on you? I've been sending people up there for the bathroom all night!"

Chris shrugged. "Sorry, but it's a good thing I did because now I can fix this. I can kill whoever killed her. And I'm going to need your help with that." He turned to his aunt. "We can use your specialty, but we need to go to Holly's father's house and get him to tell us when she died so we know when to go back to."

"What are we supposed to do with our guests?" Kathy asked. "We can't take off with a house full of people."

"Josh can keep them company," Chris suggested.

Josh said, "We can fix the whole Holly thing tomorrow. Besides, how do you know it was actually Holly you summoned? Like you said, there's a powerful new threat that could easily be manipulating you."

"I know what I saw!" Chris was fuming. How did Josh have the audacity to claim that he was being manipulated so easily? He knew a thing or two about tricks by now.

Wanting to prevent an argument, Kathy chimed in, "We might not be able to wait until tomorrow to help Holly. Time travel is different on New Year's Eve."

"How do you figure?" Josh asked.

"Because going back one day would actually be going back a year, and therefore it takes more energy and affects more time," Kathy explained. "But the difficult thing is finding that balance between helping and interfering. We couldn't leave Holly here because this isn't where she belongs, but when she goes home she gets killed."

Chris looked up at Kathy and said, "This is Holly's home."

Kathy looked at her nephew. She could see the pain and confusion in his eyes. "Holly has two homes. We can't be selfish. We'll make sure her death counts for something, but we can't just undo death."

"But we can!" Chris shouted to them. He couldn't believe they weren't going to help him save Holly. Sure they had only known her for a couple of months, but she was basically family now. If they weren't going to help, he was going to have to figure out a way to do it himself. "Fine," he finally said, gritting his teeth.

"Chris…" Kathy started, but he zipped up the stairs.

* * *

Upstairs, he was flipping through the pages of the magic book when he heard screams from downstairs.

He ran to the living room and saw a man with a wrinkly old face throwing fireballs at people. A woman with short black hair, dressed all in black, stood on an end table hurling knives at guests. A few of her attacks made direct contact, and Chris saw several of his neighbors fall to the ground dead.

"Everyone get down!" Chris shouted. When everyone ducked, he tried to blow up the intruders, but nothing happened. His power had no effect on them.

The wrinkly man threw a fireball at Chris, but he was able to blow it up.

"Josh! I need your help," Chris called out into the crowd.

His brother sprinted down the stairs to assist Chris. Stuck into the banister was one of the knives the ninja had thrown at Chris but missed. Josh grabbed it and shot the knife at the ninja, using his magic to direct it. It hit her in the chest, and she collapsed to the ground.

The Blood Moon

"What do we do with him?" Chris asked.

"I just got the spell," Josh said. Then he recited:

You are an evil man.
We use all the magic we can,
to send you back to hell.
And take the terror with you as well.

The man went up in flames before exploding. The brothers looked at the crowd to see their reaction. Most of them were terrified, and some even ran out the door screaming.

When Kathy walked in from the dining room, Chris looked at her with a slight grin. "Looks like we need to clean up the exposure. While we're turning back time, we might as well find out when Holly died so we can do that before midnight tonight." Chris was reveling in the perfect situation he was thrown into.

"Dude, could you always do that?" Doug, another one of Chris's friends, asked. "What are you? That was so cool."

"I'm a witch—" Chris started, but Kathy interrupted.

"Chris!" she yelped.

"They saw it with their own eyes. What's the big deal?" Chris asked.

"It was awesome!" Doug said.

"Can you give us a minute?" Kathy asked Doug. He returned to Chris's other friends. When he was out of earshot, Kathy continued, "We need to clean this up somehow."

"If we go back to save Holly, it'll clean itself up," Chris prodded.

"Chris!" Kathy was sick of his urging.

"Aunt Kathy, we need her!"

There was another scream, and when Kathy and Chris ran in to see what was happening, Josh was being thrown across the room. He smashed into the staircase and tumbled down to the bottom.

Chris couldn't make his way through the crowd to his brother before the woman assassin leaped across the room and stood over Josh.

"Stay away from him!" Chris screamed but knew his efforts were useless. His power had had no effect on her before. He could only hope their friends were brave enough to help. "Stop her!"

The woman pulled her sword out from the sheath on her back and held it above Josh, ready to stab him, but Kathy used her teleportation to appear behind the woman and grab her sword from her hands.

The two fought for the sword. Kathy was eventually shoved down onto the stairs. She swung her leg at the assassin, colliding with her and knocking the woman to the ground.

Josh started to come to and was startled by his aunt and the attacker fighting over him. Kathy grabbed the enemy's arm and flipped her on the stairs.

By now, Chris had squeezed through the throng and put up his hands, ready to attack. The assassin had dived over the banister halfway up the staircase and disappeared into the crowd.

The room went silent as everyone searched for the attacker.

THE BLOOD MOON

Suddenly, the woman popped up at the bottom of the staircase where Josh still lay and drove one of her daggers into his chest.

"No!" Kathy cried.

The assassin kicked Josh in his side. She flashed a sinister smile at Kathy and Chris.

"I thought we killed her?" Chris asked his aunt.

Kathy shrugged. "Maybe she got a power boost?"

"Actually, your witch friend from Salem is the one that gave me the boost," the assassin responded. "Thank her for me when you see her, okay?" She launched two daggers at them, but Kathy froze them in midair.

Chris attempted to blow her up, but the attack was absorbed into her sword, which she swung in defense. He tried again, and this time the blast threw her back into the wall behind her.

"Come on! We need to get out of here!" Kathy grabbed Chris's arm and tried to yank him from the room. She latched on to his arm and disappeared in a flash of red light.

* * *

When Kathy and Chris reappeared, they stood on the street in front of a small, quaint blue house with white trim. Christmas lights still hung from the waist-high white picket fence in the front yard buried in snow. The witches looked around and saw the neighboring houses cooped up for the winter, smoke billowing from a few chimneys down the street. Chris hated to admit that it looked like a nice place to live.

The snow covered the entire town beautifully. It was reminiscent of a tiny little Christmas village setup that Chris's mother used to put up every year. All it needed was a train circling the town.

"Is this where she lives?" asked Chris, shivering in the cold.

Kathy shrugged. "I guess so. Maybe I should've used something of hers to focus on, but I thought the connection we had was enough."

Chris pointed to the mailbox that read Bowen. "We're in the right place." He walked down the driveway to the front door and rang the doorbell. He could see people moving around in the shadows, but nobody answered the door.

"Hey! Open up!" he called to the inside. He started pounding on the door with his fist until Kathy put a hand on his shoulder. In a flash they were inside the house.

The room was dark with only the glow from the light on the street to illuminate it. There was scurrying inside, and it wasn't until Kathy froze the room that she saw who was there.

Drew and another man were hiding behind the doorway. The man had gray hair and was clean-shaven. Pain and terror were very apparent on his old face.

"Is that Holly's dad?" asked Chris.

"I don't know. Let's ask." She waved her hand in front of the men and unfroze them.

"What do you want?" the man asked in a shaky voice. "You've already killed my daughter. Stop taunting us!"

"We're not the bad guys," Kathy said. "We're here to stop

them and fix it."

Simon charged at her with a knife and tackled her to the floor. Kathy reacted just in time to stop the blade from piercing her heart. He had good aim.

"Hey!" Chris and Drew shouted simultaneously.

"Simon, let her go!" Drew was trying to pull Simon off Kathy. "She's not the one who killed Holly! These are the witches from Erie!"

Panting, Simon rose to his knees and tossed the knife on the floor. He wiped his face with his hand. "I'm so sorry. I...I just don't know who to trust anymore. I thought this was all over!"

Chris helped his aunt stand up. She wiped at her chest where the knife had nearly made contact. "It's okay, I understand." She was trying to bring her heart rate down to a normal level, but her adrenaline was running high. "We came here to help."

"How?" Drew asked.

"My specialty is time," Kathy explained. "I can send myself back to the day Holly was killed and change the past."

"The same person who killed Holly also killed my brother," Chris explained.

"So you say," Holly's father replied. "How do we know this isn't all a sham? You could be working for that devil woman!"

"Simon, they're not the bad guys," Drew argued. Chris couldn't help but be grateful for him.

"Look, trust me on this. We can fix it. Make it so Holly never died in the first place," Chris protested.

"Just leave us alone," Simon said, turning toward the kitchen.

Kathy froze Simon and turned to Drew. "I know you trust us. Or at least know that we mean well. I need you to tell me when she died."

"What?" Drew asked. "You expect me to remember an experience I'm trying to forget?"

"Deal with it." Chris was standing with his arms crossed, looking out the window. He refocused to look at Drew. "I am."

"It was about two weeks ago," Drew replied, his voice shaky, uncertain.

"I need an exact date and relative hour, too," Kathy said. She hated to be so intrusive, but it was the information she needed to save Holly.

"Thursday? Like the twelfth?" Drew asked himself. "She was coming home from school, so around two or three."

"So Thursday at two," Kathy repeated. "One last thing…" She was nervous to ask, but she knew Drew was the only one who would have something like this floating around.

"What?"

"Time travel takes a lot of energy. So when a witch—any witch—uses that much magic, it basically drains them. But there is a potion—"

Drew nodded. "Right. You need a power-enhancer."

"If you have it." Kathy looked up at the clock on the wall. They had fifteen minutes until midnight. Not enough time to make a potion from scratch.

Drew disappeared into the kitchen and came back with a black vial. "Only take a sip. This stuff is concentrated."

THE BLOOD MOON

Kathy took the vial and unscrewed the top. She had never taken a potion like this before, although she had heard about it. This was almost like a drug for some witches. They would become engulfed in the rush of power, and soon enough they would need more and more in order to feel the same surge of energy as they did the first time.

Nervously, she brought it to her lips and took a small sip. She felt the warmth spread over her body and handed off the vial to Drew. She bent over, clutching her stomach as the potion took effect.

"Are you okay? What's going on?" Chris worried.

"Give it a minute," Drew said.

Kathy stood upright and felt completely alive. "What is this stuff called? I love it!"

"Careful," Chris warned.

"Vergaritum. It was first created by the Dutch back in the day," Drew said. "That's how witches got the reputation for flying."

Kathy looked at the clock once more. Less than ten minutes until midnight. "I have to go. You said Thursday at two?"

Drew nodded.

She took a deep breath, then closed her eyes.

"Be careful," Chris warned.

Kathy repeated, "Thursday at two. Thursday at two. Thursday at two." In a giant red flash, she was gone.

Chapter Nineteen

Kathy reappeared in the same living room. She looked at the clock and saw that it was two in the afternoon. She had made the trip successfully. She'd had her doubts that it would work. She didn't time travel that often.

Nobody was home. Everything was still. The silence was broken every once in a while by cars driving by the house.

There were banners hanging on the walls welcoming Holly home. Kathy smiled. No matter how much she and her nephews needed Holly for their magical issues, the love Holly's father had for her overpowered it.

She looked outside and saw a school bus go by, so she knew school had let out and Holly was on her way. She hunched down by the window, looking for Holly. Being a small town, Kathy knew the neighbors would pick up on a stranger.

The Blood Moon

Half an hour later, she heard voices in the front yard. Kids were walking home. Holly and a redheaded girl stopped in front of the house, then Holly started to walk up the driveway alone. Her head was turned as she waved good-bye to her friend, and she didn't see that the assassin appeared and was waiting for her behind the garbage cans tucked next to the garage.

In an instant Kathy was outside, yelling for Holly to duck.

Just as Holly dropped to the ground, a dagger flew through the air where Holly had stood moments before. There was no turning back now. Kathy had just changed the past, something she had never done before.

"Damn you, witch!" the woman swore as she leaped toward Kathy. The assassin tackled her and reached for her throat.

Kathy called to Holly, "Run!"

"No," Holly said. She threw her backpack on the ground, produced a switchblade that she had stashed away in her pocket, and threw it at the enemy.

The woman did a flip in the air and landed without a scratch.

Drew appeared in the driveway in a swirl of white smoke. When he saw the attacker, he threw a potion at her that made the woman shrink in size and turn into a toad.

"Kathy!" Holly exclaimed, hugging her. "What's going on? Why are you here? Who was that woman?" Too many questions she wanted answered at once. "I thought witches were the ones who turned people into toads," she joked.

"Holly, you're in danger," Kathy said. "We need to kill that toad and then get you back to our house."

"What? Why?" Drew asked. He reached for Holly protectively.

"Well—" Kathy started to explain, but Drew interrupted her with gibberish. Kathy recognized the spell.

A white glow came over Kathy and soon disappeared.

"Truth spell," Drew explained, "for insurance." He didn't know if this was a shapeshifter or what.

Kathy rolled her eyes and then turned to Holly and explained, "I'm actually the Kathy from two weeks in the future. It's a little confusing. The bottom line is that you were going to die just now. I came back to save you."

Holly was confused. Ten minutes earlier she had been catching up with one of her best friends, and now she was suddenly thrust back into the world of witchcraft. "How did you know I was going to die?"

"I'm having a New Year's party, and Chris tried to summon you, but the only you that was left to summon was your spirit. I came back in time to right now to stop your death." Kathy knew the story was a stretch, but she hoped Holly believed her.

"Wait a minute," Drew said, holding up his hand to stop Kathy. "You expect us to believe that?"

Kathy looked at Drew. "You're the one who cast the truth spell."

Drew was at a loss for words, knowing he was stuck.

"Okay," Holly said slowly. She was staring at the ground, considering her mortality. Even with all the power she possessed, a simple dagger to the heart would have done her in. "So we should kill her, right?" She motioned to the toad, who noticed them turn to it and tried hopping down the driveway. Kathy froze it.

"How do you plan on doing that?" Drew asked.

"Well, Josh did it with her own dagger the first time," Kathy explained. "She came back to life afterwards, but she had Holly's power acting as a second life, so it should work the first time."

"All right," Holly picked up the assassin's dagger. "So we just stab her with this, right?"

"I don't know if it'd work with her in another form," Kathy explained. "We should turn her back before we stab her. But we need to act fast. I'll freeze her and you..." She made a stabbing motion with her fist.

Holly nodded. "Ready when you are."

The women turned to Drew. He produced a potion from his pocket and dribbled it over the toad, instantly returning the assassin to her human state. She sprang to her feet and pulled another dagger from a strap on her leg. She came directly for Holly with a vengeance.

Kathy froze the attacker before she could get to Holly.

"That was too close," Holly said. She moved the blade and set the point against the assassin's chest.

"Just do it quick," Drew advised. "Don't think about it. This woman was going to kill you."

"You're right." Holly nodded. She still didn't like the idea, but with some reluctance she drove the knife straight through the woman's heart.

Kathy's power wore off, and the woman screamed and erupted in flames, leaving a spot on the ground where the snow melted. Once she was gone, the three looked at each other.

"Do you think anyone saw that?" Kathy asked.

Holly shrugged. "When someone starts asking questions, my dad will slip them a little magic to get them off our trail."

"That's handy," Kathy noted. She shivered and wrapped her arms around herself. She was going to get sick from the amount of time she'd been spending outside in the cold. "Let's get inside."

Once they were in and seated around the kitchen table with mugs of hot chocolate, Kathy raised the touchy subject. "You do realize this was only the first of a long line of attacks, right?"

Holly watched the steam rising from her drink. "Wasn't the first. There have been some minor attacks since I came back."

"What!?" Drew nearly spit out his hot chocolate. "You never told me!"

Holly shrugged. "It wasn't a big deal. Almost too easy, like they were feeling me out. I should've seen this attack coming."

"It's the new power," Kathy said. "There's a free-for-all in the demonic community, and everyone is trying to be badder than the next." She sipped some of her cocoa. "They haven't touched us yet, but they've been targeting innocent people within our circles. Strangers, mortals. Making us aware that they're around but not attacking us directly."

"That's scary," Holly said, her eyes now wide with amazement. Usually, if there was a witch around, they were always the bigger target. But to go directly after mortals was unfair, just downright evil. She stared down at her mug again. "So you guys have had your hands full then, huh?"

Kathy sipped. "Pretty much. It's hard without you, but we know this is where you're supposed to be."

"Even Chris?"

Kathy reached for Holly's hand. "It's been hard on him, but he'll get through it. Once we identify this new threat."

"You ever consider Will?" Drew asked.

Kathy smiled. "Of course, first one on our list. But he's actually been showing up to court lately, and his practice has been taking off. He has too much on his plate to add Demon King to his title." She took another sip. "But, just to be sure, we spent a week following him. Nothing seemed suspicious." She shrugged. "He stayed away from evil once, I'm sure he's capable of doing it again."

"You should still keep an eye on him," Drew added.

"Fool me once, shame on you. Fool me twice…" Kathy responded. She turned to Holly. "Part of the reason I'm here is because of this new threat. We're stronger together than we are apart, so I was going to ask you if you'd consider moving back to Erie. Maybe I could—"

Before Kathy could finish, Holly squealed. "Yes! I would love that!"

"I don't think your father would let you," Drew said. "It would destroy him."

"I actually want to talk to him about that," Kathy said. "I'm not talking about just you moving back, I want to see if he would come as well. The more witches, the better."

Holly sighed. "He's not going to go for that. This is our home."

"I'm sure he'd make an exception," Kathy said. "These are extenuating circumstances—"

"No, you don't understand," Holly interrupted. "This is the house he and my mom built. My bedroom is still the same color she painted it before she died. He won't leave that. Besides, his restaurant is here, and it's doing really well. Can't beat a local chef in a small town."

"I would still like to talk with him," Kathy said. "When do you think he's free?"

"Now would probably be best," Holly said, looking at the clock above the stove. "Before the dinner rush."

"All right, then, let's go!" Kathy said. She was determined to get Holly back to their side. They needed her, and the attack she had just prevented proved it.

* * *

"I don't understand why you're all here." Simon looked concerned as he closed the door to his cramped office. He offered Kathy a seat and took his own by his desk.

"Dad, I'm in danger here," Holly stated. "I just got attacked on my way home from school. Right in front of the house! If Kathy wasn't there, I would've died!" She decided to leave out the time-travel part. It wouldn't help her case. He would just argue that Kathy was a shapeshifter or a manipulator or something. "I think we should seriously consider me moving back to Erie with them."

The Blood Moon

"You've been making up excuses to go back there since you came home!" Simon was frustrated. He wasn't sure what to do. After fighting for so long to keep his family safe, he finally thought the focal point of all their misfortune, Toxanna, was dead. But that wasn't enough, it seemed. "You're all I have left since your mother died."

Holly saw that he was on the verge of tears, and she almost hated herself for asking to leave. Toxanna had almost taken everything from him, and here was his own daughter taking the last bit away. "Dad…"

"All emotions aside, the fact is that Holly was going to die today." Kathy tried to be the neutral third party, but she knew that was impossible, so she stuck with the facts instead. "There's a new threat rising, and until we figure out exactly who they are and how to kill them, Holly's life will be in danger."

"The attacks aren't over, I'm sure," Holly added before her father could begin his accusations. "This new power will keep sending more and more people to come and kill me, and staying in Salem will leave me unprotected."

"Not if we have Drew and your Uncle Ken watch you whenever I can't," her father countered. He could see, however, that he was fighting a losing battle.

"That may fend off attacks for the time being, but eventually they're going to succeed." Holly reached for her father's hands. "We don't have the resources here like the Harpers have in Erie. We don't know as much about this new threat as they do. Once I leave, you, Drew, and Uncle Ken will be safer because the danger will follow me."

Her father was turned away and had his eyes closed. He sighed, looked up at his daughter and said, "I'll let you go."

"What!" Drew nearly shrieked in surprise.

"On a few conditions," Simon added. "You take Drew with you. That'll give me some peace of mind."

Holly shrugged. "Okay." She figured he would at least be checking up on her periodically, even if her father hadn't asked.

"I would feel better if he was there," Simon reasoned. "That way he can continue your training."

Kathy smiled, trying to count their blessings while they could. "Of course Drew is welcome. I think that's a great idea. He seems to have a wide knowledge of the craft himself."

"Good," Simon said as he looked up at Drew. He was counting on him.

* * *

The witches appeared in a flash of red light in the midst of a battle in the living room. Josh and Chris were tied up back-to-back to chairs in the middle of the room. The wrinkly old man from the New Year's Eve party in Kathy's alternate time was holding a knife to Josh's throat.

"What the—" Kathy asked as she froze them. She reached for the knife at Josh's throat and cut the rope binding her nephews.

"What are you doing here?" Chris asked Holly with a bright smile. He was rubbing his wrists where the rope had been.

"I'm back." She returned his smile. She lifted her arms in

the air and wrapped them around him tightly. Chris hugged her back and looked up at Drew.

"You brought Drew back too…" He was less than pleased. Drew was a good asset to their team, but Chris didn't like the competition.

"Chris, there'll plenty of time for that later," Kathy said. She pointed to the attacker and looked at Josh. "Who is this guy?"

Josh shrugged. "He just showed up and attacked us. I'm guessing he's under the new power."

Kathy suddenly recognized the man as the one who had killed Josh before her time travel. "A spell…" she muttered to herself, remembering that Josh and Chris had used a spell to kill him before. She ran into the kitchen and grabbed a pen and paper, trying to remember the spell they had used. She wondered if they had found it in the book, but she thought she remembered it pretty well.

Back in the living room, the enemy was slowly breaking out of Kathy's power. She ran up just in time. He unfroze and conjured another dagger, which he hurled at Josh. With a wave of his hand, Josh was able to send the dagger flying in another direction.

"I have the spell." Kathy pulled her nephews in around her.

"Where'd you get this?" Josh asked.

"I'll explain later." She looked up and saw Holly and Drew off to the side, watching. "You guys need to get in here, too. The more power behind this thing the better."

The five of them squished in close to read the paper Kathy had written the spell on. Together they recited:

You are an evil man.
We use all the magic we can,
to send you back to hell,
and take the terror with you as well.

The vanquish was quick and powerful, sending a force so strong throughout the room that the witches took a step back. When they looked up, the enemy was gone without a trace.

"Whoa." Chris smiled. "That was powerful."

Kathy looked around at the group. "This is proof that we're stronger together. We need this much power for the new threat."

Chapter Twenty

It was once again New Year's Eve and Josh, Chris, Holly, and Kathy had been proactive in eliminating any potential threats the week before. Kathy didn't want another attack at her party like she had before.

During the party, everybody was having a great time. Chris was proudly introducing Holly to all of his friends. Kathy was glad to see how much his attitude had changed since Holly had returned. She was the only one that remembered the alternate New Year's Eve party that ended so badly. She wasn't going to elaborate on the details of that night to her nephews. This night was a celebration and a time to relax. With the addition of Holly and Drew, the witches had discovered and triumphed over so many more evils. Kathy thought her time travel was justified by that. If she hadn't gone back to save Holly, many more people would have died, including Mrs. Kors.

Kathy was chatting with her friends in the kitchen. She had to remember to be surprised when she heard the updates on their lives. To her, this was the second time having the conversation.

Kathy's friend Trisha laughed and raised a wine glass to her lips, taking a sip. "Okay, well, I should double check on the kids to make sure they're not getting into anything. I forgot how gorgeous your house is. Wouldn't want them to ruin anything." She set her glass down on the counter and stood.

"I'm sure they're fine," Kathy commented, pulling ice out of the freezer to refill the buckets of refreshments on the table.

"I should go, too," Linda said. She was Kathy's former co-worker from the day care. "I think it might be time to feed the baby."

Kathy smiled, remembering a time when she thought she was going to be following in their footsteps. That was before she knew just how bad for her Will was. And now she had her hands full with everything magic, and she couldn't even imagine bringing a husband or a baby into the mess.

The back door violently swung open, and Kathy jumped and stifled a scream. Devon stepped in from the cold and conjured a fireball. He was about to throw it, but Kathy froze him before he had the chance. She raced to the living room where the party was and scanned the crowd for her nephews. She stopped two people from going in the kitchen. She didn't need to explain a frozen demon in her kitchen. She wished she could get through one party without having an attack.

Finally, she spotted Holly and waved her over. "Find the boys and send them to the kitchen, but don't let anyone else in. Keep people distracted." Holly nodded and disappeared in the throng.

Kathy went back into the kitchen. The wide-open door was sending a chill throughout the house, and she hoped no one would come in to investigate.

Josh and Chris emerged from the party and were about to ask what happened until they saw Devon.

"We'll take care of him," Chris offered. "Aunt Kathy, you stay here and be on the lookout for any of the guests. This new power might want to expose us to distract us." It would be a perfect way to cause a distraction. The media and the neighbors would have them under 24/7 surveillance.

"Wait, where's Holly?" Kathy asked.

"She doing psychic stuff. Palm readings, hypnotism, tarot cards." Josh shrugged. "I didn't realize she knew how to do that stuff."

Kathy smiled. The girl was crafty.

Josh threw Devon out of the house with his power and Chris followed.

No longer under the influence of Kathy's power, Devon hurled attacks at the brothers, who fended them off, pushing Devon farther away from the house until they were at the end of the yard. The snow was coming down heavy, and the wind was bitter. Josh tried to use his manipulation of the wind to stop the breeze, but it didn't work. He wasn't that powerful yet. Neither of the boys were dressed for the weather, so they wanted to make this short.

"What do you want?" Chris asked. He knew he should be taking a better stance for fighting, but he was so cold, so instead he was shivering with his hands buried in his pockets. "Who sent you?"

"The new power," Devon answered. He tried to conjure a fireball, but a huge gust of wind exhausted it. "I'm surprised you haven't heard of it. Everyone's talking about it."

"Who is this new power?" Chris asked. He didn't like Devon's cocky attitude. He was like the annoying bug that you swatted at but couldn't quite get.

"You know him very well. Your aunt especially," Devon explained without giving a name.

"Just tell us who it is!" Chris shouted. The cold was not helping his temper.

"Chris, he's telling us," Josh said. He had his hands buried in his armpits.

"Then who is it?" Chris asked. His teeth were chattering.

Devon flew up in the air, trying to escape, but Chris blew up his wings, and he fell to the ground.

"One of these times…" Chris shook a finger at Devon, who lay in the snow, tending to the loss of his wings once again.

Josh was coming to a realization. He smacked Chris's cold arm and said, "Will!"

"You think it's Will?" Chris asked. "I thought Aunt Kathy ruled him out?"

"Well, he was obviously close to us. Aunt Kathy especially," Josh mumbled, returning his hands to his armpits. They were starting to ache. He could see Chris's lips turning blue. They needed to get inside soon.

"See, we figured it out!" Chris turned to Devon.

Devon gave them a sinister smile that didn't sit well with the brothers. Before they could push him further, flames started to form from the ground, and Devon caught on fire. "No! No! I kept my promise!" the demon shrieked. He eventually burned up, and the only thing left of him was a ring in the snow where the fire had been.

"Guess we won't have to worry about him anymore," Josh said. "But that was weird."

"At least we figured out who the new power is." Chris sniffled. "Let's get inside. I'm freezing!"

They ran back to the house, where Kathy, Drew, and Holly questioned them.

"We'll tell you tomorrow," Chris said. "Nothing else is going to happen tonight, so let's go enjoy the party."

"Are you sure?" Kathy wasn't convinced. She stood behind Josh's chair and rubbed his arms, trying to warm him up.

Chris nodded underneath a fleece blanket. "Devon's dead."

"He's dead?" Drew asked. "You guys killed him?"

Josh shook his head. "Something else. The flames just appeared out of nowhere."

"That's not good." Drew looked worried. "That means that this new threat is really powerful."

"Well, now so are we," Holly said. "We've been kicking butt since we moved back. The five of us make a hell of a team."

"Let's hope that's enough." Kathy patted Josh's shoulders and said, "You boys make sure you get something warm in you soon."

When the others left, Chris asked Josh, "Before, Will was only a Dark Knight, now he can create flames from wherever he was and kill Devon. Should we be worried?"

"We'll figure something out," Josh reassured him. He poured hot water from the tea kettle into two mugs. "Let's just enjoy the night."

"But what if Will comes tonight? Now that he knows that we know he's the new power?" He accepted one of the mugs from Josh and dipped a teabag in.

Josh shook his head. "He won't. He's too smart. He'll take more time to plan something."

Chris added sugar to his tea and said, "I really hope you're right."

* * *

A little after midnight, Holly pulled Chris upstairs by his arm.

"What is it?" he asked with a smile.

"There's a guy here that used to go to my high school," Holly said.

Chris's face dropped. "Oh. So what?"

"He's Zamball in disguise," she said.

"Are you sure?"

Holly waited for some people to pass by in the hall and said, "Yes. He plagued my high school while I was in Salem."

"So why do you think he's here?" Chris asked.

Holly shrugged. "Maybe he's a spy for the new power?"

Chris thought of Devon. If he had been working with Will, then why not Toxanna's son?

"All right, I'll keep my eyes open," Chris said, "and you do the same. Don't go looking for trouble. The party's almost over. We'll ask him to stay awhile."

She nodded and then went back to the dwindling party.

* * *

As the guests were filtering out and saying their good-byes, Kathy asked the man they suspected to be Zamball to stay. When she saw that he was with a woman, she wondered if Holly was remembering wrong.

Kathy froze both him and his friend. Drew, Holly, and the brothers filled the foyer.

"That's definitely him," Holly confirmed.

"Who's she?" Josh asked, pointing to Zamball's companion.

"I don't know," Holly said.

Drew held up a potion. "This will reveal their true selves."

"Wait!" Kathy reached for the wizard's arm. "It won't hurt them if we're wrong, will it?"

Drew shook his head. "It shouldn't."

Kathy let go of his arm and nodded. Drew popped the cork from the potion and shook the contents onto the suspects.

Their skin fell off their bodies and revealed Zamball and a

creature. She had black feathers and wings for arms. Her face was a morphed version of a bird's and human's.

"A harpy!" Kathy shrieked, jumping back a step. She and Samantha had faced a whole nest of them once, and the creatures still haunted her.

"Know a spell to kill one?" Chris asked.

Kathy nodded. "In the book." She turned and raced up the stairs. When she was halfway up, her magic wore off and the enemies unfroze.

Josh reacted quickly and sent them flying back into the front door.

Zamball and the harpy got back to their feet, and he pulled out his wand and pointed it at Chris. Water shot out of the end of it, flinging Chris back into the dining room, soaked. He rolled on the ground, clutching his chest. The force of the water had knocked the air out of his lungs.

Holly kicked the wand out of Zamball's hand, but the harpy tackled her before she could grab it. The bird squawked and scratched at Holly's face. Drew kicked the harpy off and hurled punches in the bird's face.

Kathy ran to Chris to see if he was okay, and Josh tried to deflect Zamball's tiny water balls. Zamball used his wand for the big magic, but he could still do little stuff without it.

After Kathy helped Chris up, she dashed over to help Holly. Chris was soaking wet and still coughing for air, but he stumbled to Josh's side to help him fight.

Chris tried to blow up Zamball's hand, but water came from

his arm and re-formed the appendage. He tried to blow up all of Zamball, but he just turned into a puddle on the ground, and then his body re-formed out of the puddle.

"It's not working!" Chris shouted.

Kathy froze the harpy.

"Repeat after me," Drew instructed and led the witches in a spell:

> *Evil bird, which is a harpy,*
> *I ask you now to hear my plea.*
> *Your face is what I no longer want to see.*

As the spell took effect, Kathy's magic wore off. The harpy's face started to burn up, and she ran around shrieking and squeaking. Kathy and Holly followed her, making sure that it wasn't just an act. Eventually the harpy burst into an explosion of feathers that slowly fell throughout the room.

After she was gone, the ladies joined Josh and Chris. Kathy needed to freeze Josh in the air because Zamball had retrieved his wand and had sent the witch flying across the room in a burst of water.

Chris was thrown into the dining room again, and when Holly moved to attack Zamball, he quickly turned into water and was gone.

"Chris, are you okay?" Holly asked as he sat up from where he had crashed.

"Yeah, I'm just wet," Chris said, pulling his sopping shirt

away from his body. He glanced toward the front door. "Is he gone?"

"Yeah." Holly sank onto the floor next to him, feeling the effects of the long day. Her face was sore from the harpy's scratches.

Suddenly, Zamball reappeared from the puddle that was pooling around Chris. He grabbed Holly by her hair, pulling her head painfully back. She shouted and Chris moved to break the hold Zamball had on her, but the evil wizard was too quick. He cut off a lock of her hair and disappeared into the puddle once again.

"Are you okay?" Chris asked. He gripped her by the shoulders and looked her over.

"I think he just pulled my hair," she said, pulling it around so she could glance at the ends.

Chris looked and shook his head. "No, Holly, there's a chunk missing."

"What! Why would he cut my hair?" She thought of all the spells and potions she knew that involved using someone's hair. None of them were good.

CHAPTER TWENTY-ONE

The sink bubbled as Zamball rose out of the dishwater. Chris and Holly took a fighting stance only to jump as the potted tree in the corner of the room started to uproot, revealing a slender dark woman.

Chris and Holly were supposed to be spending the day together, just the two of them. Josh was at the library studying, and Kathy had a second interview with the literary magazine. The couple had declared a movie day, and Chris had already lit a fire. They had gone in the kitchen to pop some popcorn when the commotion started. It was now the middle of February and had been almost a month and a half since their last encounter with Zamball or anyone in Will's camp. The witches were investigating Will and his rise to power, but their personal lives consumed them, and they let their guards down. Now Holly was clutching a kitchen knife and gritting her teeth at the intruders.

Zamball shot boiling water out of the end of his wand. Chris fell to the ground, pulling Holly with him. The knife she had slid across the floor and under the kitchen table.

Before they had a chance to get to their feet, the woman was pulling Holly up by her hair.

Chris reached for Holly, but Zamball grabbed him from behind, yanking on the witch's T-shirt. The woman cast vines out of her hands that bound Holly. In a last attempt to save her, Chris tried to blast the woman but blew a hole in the wall instead.

"She'll do for now," Zamball said as he pointed his wand at Chris, sending him into the next room with a powerful stream of water. Cold water, luckily. Before Chris could get up, Zamball kicked him in his side and tied his hands up with a cord from a nearby lamp.

Rolling onto his back, Chris witnessed Zamball jumping into the kitchen sink with a splash. Holly screamed in terror as the dark woman dragged her back to the potted tree and disappeared with her.

In an instant everything was silent.

* * *

Chris struggled to get the phone in his hand. His hands were tied behind his back, and the attached lamp seemed to collide with everything he passed, sending shards of glass flying. Once he finally grabbed hold of the phone, he hit the speed dial and called his aunt. Dropping the phone on the counter, he leaned his head down to it to talk.

"Hey, sweetie, I'm just finishing up," she answered.

"Aunt Kathy, they took Holly! She's gone!" Chris felt ridiculous. A table-lamp cord was binding his hands, and he was bent over the counter, shouting into the phone.

"Who did? Will?"

"No, Zamball. He probably took her to Will. But I need you to come home, they tied me up."

Kathy took a deep breath. "Okay, well…Drew said he was going to stop by today. Give him a call and see if he can come now. I want to stop at the herb store and pick up a few things. I saw in the book a recipe for a potion I want to try out on Zamball."

"But she's gone, Aunt Kathy!"

"I know, hon, but we'll get her back. We just need to be smart about this. Will wants us to be impulsive. Do you have Drew's number?"

Drew walked in the front door while Chris was still on the phone with Kathy. "What's going on?"

"I need your help." Chris looked up at Drew, who was a bit taller than Chris because he was older. He turned so Drew could untie him. Once he was free, Chris rubbed his wrists and said, "Holly was captured by Zamball and some other lady. Probably a witch with an earth specialty."

"Did you identify her in your magic book?"

"No, not yet. But I figured that didn't matter because Devon said they're working for Will. Since we can't find him, we won't be able to find her, so we're screwed." Chris ran his fingers through his hair in frustration.

"Let's not give up hope yet," Drew said. "Let's see…we could try the searching ritual?"

Chris leaned on the counter and buried his face in his hands. "She's probably with Will. We haven't been able to find him, so the simple searching ritual won't work."

"We could try my latest potion," Drew suggested. "It hasn't been tested yet, but—"

"What is it?" Chris interrupted. He didn't even know what it did, he was grasping at straws, and this was another outlet to try.

"It's supposed to be somewhat reminiscent of a psychic's vision, or a premonition," he explained. "I think I've got it down. We'll see. It'll help us see where she is and who she's talking to."

Chris slapped his hand on the table. "Good. I'm going to grab the book and see if there's anything in there just in case."

A few minutes later, Chris met Drew downstairs. He was done making the potion and was reciting a spell over it, mumbling words in a language Chris had never heard. As he entered, Drew finished the spell.

They exchanged a look. Chris was cautious of the spell but decided not to push it. Instead, he turned his attention to the potion. It was sitting in a pot on the stove, and then the potion lifted from the pot and materialized to form people. There was no color, and Chris had no idea who they were looking at until the figures began to speak.

"What do you want with me?" a shadow asked. By the sound

of her voice, both boys knew it was Holly. She was tied up to what looked like a chair in the center of the room.

"I want you to get to my beloved," the man in the hooded robe said. He was circling around Holly slowly, "and I know you can do that. Your powers allow you to do that. You have the power of manipulation. Bring her here." He leaned in closer to her face, and Holly turned away. "Quite a powerful witch. Unfortunate, too. You don't even deserve your powers."

"Will? How does he know what her specialty is? She doesn't even know!" Chris looked up at Drew and thought of his mother. Her specialty had been focused on the mind as well.

"Shh!"

"What makes you think I'd help you?" Holly remained calm.

Will got in Holly's face and sneered, "I didn't expect you to agree. I'm going to take your powers from you and do it myself."

Chris looked up at Drew. "He better not stab her." He guessed that Will wasn't going to use the same spell he had a few months ago when he momentarily took their powers. The only other way he knew to steal a witch's powers was to use an enchanted blade, killing the witch in the process.

"He won't. Shh!" Drew pointed to the potion.

Will hurled a potion at Holly, and the liquid Drew and Chris were peering into disintegrated, leaving only a black fluid.

"What happened to the signal?" Chris asked.

Drew sighed and scratched the back of his neck. "I focused the potion on her powers. She must not have them anymore."

"So couldn't you do the same but with a teleportation potion now?" Chris asked.

The phone rang before Drew could respond. Chris answered.

It was Kathy. "Chris, I'm on my way home. Did you find Holly yet? Are you okay?"

"No, we're still figuring that out. And Drew came home and untied me, so I'm fine. Are you driving?" Chris asked.

"Yeah, why?"

"Why aren't you teleporting?"

"Because then what do I do with my car?"

"Isn't there a bigger picture here? We'll pick up your car later." The line went dead. "Aunt Kathy!" Chris called into the phone. He turned to Drew. "Something's wrong with Aunt Kathy, too."

"Seriously, dude," Drew said, "you can't be that dumb."

"Excuse me?" Chris didn't like his tone. It was one thing that he was stuck working with him to find Holly, of all people—the one person they both cared most about—but if anyone expected him to be nice to the guy…

"You already know that your uncle is this big, powerful evil leader," Drew explained, "and you know he still loves your aunt, and he stole Holly's powers—"

"To summon my aunt! Damn it!" Chris slammed his fist on the counter. He felt helpless, and he was running out of resources. He tapped his fingers on the marble counter, thinking. "I don't understand, though. The blood moon isn't until April, right?" He walked to the calendar in the kitchen and flipped the pages to the date they had marked.

"Yeah. Maybe that's when he's at full power?" Drew suggested.

"Wait a minute…" Chris went to Kathy's laptop, which sat

on the kitchen table. He opened the search engine and ran his fingers over the keyboard. "The April blood moon is the second in a series of four. The first one was in October, right around the time you and Holly first came to Erie. Will must've risen to power at that blood moon!"

"Isn't that when your aunt first went to the hospital?"

"I think so." Chris chewed on the inside of his lip as he thought. Had the new power they been fearing really been under their nose and at full power this whole time? He felt like a complete idiot for not noticing it before now. "So Will has been this big, bad evil leader for months and he played it off? Why wouldn't he try to flex his power? And why did Devon make it out like the prophecy was yet to come and not already passed?"

"If you guys knew, you would try to stop him. He needed this time to build his army. Which means he's probably a lot stronger now," Drew reasoned.

Chris tapped his fingers on the side of the counter. He thought back to when Will had aligned himself with Toxanna and Axon and locked them out of the house and tried to steal their powers. Was that his attempt to take them out? After it failed, maybe he regrouped and now he was plotting another surprise attack. "Okay…you need to come up with a spell to either summon Aunt Kathy or take us to her and Holly."

"Why me?" Drew stuck a finger against his chest.

"I'm going to call Josh and tell him what's happening." Chris waved the phone in the air. "Maybe he has some ideas."

* * *

"Josh didn't pick up," Chris announced as he reentered the kitchen.

"Shocker," Drew muttered. He was bottling up a few potions and stuffing them in his pockets.

Chris shot the wizard a look. "What do you have against us?"

"What do you mean?"

"All right, let's cut the crap." Chris was tired of the attitude Drew had had since he and Holly had returned to Erie. "Aunt Kathy told me that you weren't happy Holly's dad let her come back. Why? If her dad could see the reason in it, why can't you?"

Drew clenched his jaw and looked at the witch. "You really wanna know?"

"Let's hear it." Chris crossed his arms.

"When we came here the first time, we were only here until everything in Salem blew over. Once we got home I thought that was it. No more Harpers, no more Erie. Then Kathy shows up and tells us that Holly died in some alternate future, and suddenly we're on our way back to Erie."

Drew had balled his hands into fists and released them. He knew that Simon and the Harpers were right about Holly and her safety. She was a target now—especially now that she had been kidnapped. He needed the help of Chris and the rest of the Harpers to save her.

"I guess I just thought that eventually everything would go back to the way it used to be." Drew thought of the short time between when he'd started training Holly and their escape to Erie.

"I'm sorry to screw up your plans for you and Holly," Chris spat.

Drew bit his bottom lip and took a deep breath. "You guys are right that Holly is safer here than she is in Salem. But right now she's gone, and she needs our help. You and me, we're it. We both just need to shut up and deal with it so we can save her. And Kathy."

Chris relaxed. He hated to admit it, but Drew was right. "All right. When I was upstairs I IDed the witch who kidnapped Holly."

"It was a witch?"

"Yeah. Her name is Terra, and her specialty is obviously related to nature. My guess is that she was recruited because she's able to use nature as a form of a portal. So anything that is rooted in dirt is an access point for her." Chris pointed to the potted tree. "She came and went through that tree."

Drew opened a cupboard and scooped up a couple more potions. "These will turn her magic into rock. Even the most advanced witches have a hard time manipulating rock."

Chris nodded. "We should wait for Josh."

"We have to go now, though," Drew insisted. "Who knows what Will is doing to them."

Chris bit at the nail on his thumb. "Do we have a plan? We don't even know where they are."

"We don't have time. Once we're there we can figure out what we're going to do."

Chris was hesitant. He wasn't keen on diving headfirst into an attack without Josh or Kathy. But he didn't have a choice. "Let's go then."

"All right, let's get this over with." Drew put his hand on Chris's shoulder and recited:

Take us to Holly now.
Her powers are gone somewhere somehow.
It is a dark place we will go.
Where it is, we don't know.

When they reappeared they were in a dark cavern. It was dry and hot. There were fire pits scattered everywhere, and the place had a smoky charcoal smell.

"Where are we?" Chris swatted at the hazy air. "Feels like I just walked into a campfire."

"You don't want to know," Drew responded. Terror was visible across his face as he looked around the dark cavern.

Chris didn't like that. He was afraid Drew was keeping a secret from him, and he almost didn't trust him. But Drew was his only ally, so he had to follow him regardless.

"Chris? Drew?" Holly asked from the shadows. "Where are you?"

"We're over here," Chris called. He couldn't pinpoint where she was in the bleak darkness. "Stay where you are; we'll come get you."

Drew grabbed a torch off the wall and followed Holly's voice down a tunnel.

When they got to the end, there was a hole in the rock where Holly was calling from.

"Holly, stand back!" Drew yelled and Chris blasted the hole open so they could more easily fit through.

"We're here now," Chris announced. "You can come out."

"I'm so glad you're here." When the figure came into the clearing, it was Will in a black robe.

"What the..." Chris muttered, backing up with Drew, who still had the torch in his hand. Chris felt completely fooled for the second time. They had walked right into a trap. He wondered if Holly and Kathy had actually disappeared, or if Will was hexing him. He shook that thought out of his mind. He had seen Holly disappear with his own eyes.

The witch and wizard turned to run back the way they came and stopped short as Zamball and Terra entered the clearing.

"It was a setup." Drew felt responsible for pushing Chris into a trap. He had tunnel vision: getting Holly back.

Chris raised his hands, and in a burst of energy he used his power to blow Terra up. "One down, two to go."

Will shrugged. "Hard to find good help these days. Especially when you and your brother have been killing my best men. But then again, the Queen, Toxanna, Axon, I thought they were strong enough to do my dirty work. Guess it's always better to do it yourself. I needed to send Devon a few times to keep giving you more clues that I was the one you were looking for. Didn't want it to look staged, then you would see it as a trap and I wouldn't be able to lure you witches down here. Where is your brother, by the way?" They could make out Will's white teeth as he pulled his lips back into a grin. "Have you replaced him with this wizard? Drew, is it?"

"You son of a bitch, what are you doing with them?" Chris challenged. He felt stupid for falling right into Will's trap. The Dark Knight was smart, Chris gave him that.

Will waved his hand at Chris, and he flew back into the tunnel again.

"Where is she?" Drew asked, waving the torch in front of him to illuminate the room more.

"Pathetic." Will held out his hand and conjured his sword. "You are the most pathetic wizard I know. What a shame because you had all that potential with the Fire Wizards."

Drew tried a charm, and white smoke swirled around Will and then disappeared even though nothing happened.

"Tried to banish me, did you?" Will dropped his robe and swung his sword. "Where do you think people go when they're banished?"

Drew's heart was pounding in his chest. He was terrified. For once in his life he didn't know what to do. Will attacked and caught the sleeve of Drew's jacket, pinning him to the wall. He slipped his arm out, slicing it along the edge of the blade as he did so. Will moved to attack again, and Drew rolled on the hard, rocky ground until he was closer to the opening. He pushed past Zamball and raced to where Chris lay unconscious.

Drew tried to wake him, but nothing seemed to be working—or at least not fast enough. Will held up his hand and constricted Drew's throat with his magic. He tried to think of a charm or a spell to stop Will's power, but his nerves prevented it. All of his potions were in his jacket, too.

"I told you," Will said, stepping closer and closer to Drew. His power over the wizard increased as he approached, "you are pathetic. Toxanna, Axon, and the others weren't enough to kill you all, so I guess I'm going to have to do it myself. Yet another reason why I'm fit to be the supreme ruler of evil." Will smiled and raised his sword over the wizard, bringing it down hard into his chest. Will watched as the life left the wizard's eyes.

Will stood over Drew's lifeless body and admired his work. He turned his attention to Chris and swung his foot into the witch's side, waking him.

Chris coughed and clutched his ribcage where Will had kicked him. Breathing was difficult for him, and he was worried he had a broken rib. He looked up and saw Will looming over him. He couldn't find the words he wanted, so he held Will's stare. The Dark Knight lost interest and walked over to Zamball.

"I mean no disrespect, sir," Zamball said, "but shouldn't you kill the witch as well?"

"No, I want him and his family to come after me," Will said. He wiped Drew's blood off his blade with the inside of Drew's jacket. "And besides, I have two of the other witches down here. They're separated."

Chris looked over and saw Drew. "What did you do?" he asked, his voice breaking as he realized the answer.

"You're right, it wasn't much fun," Will said. "He didn't put up a fight. I should have dragged it out of him and made him run. Just like the good ol' days."

Chris tried to blow up Will, knowing full well that it wouldn't work. Every time he would blast, Will would heal.

"Poor, poor witch," Will tutted. He made a pitiful clacking noise with his tongue and slowly shook his head. "You don't have your aunt, your brother, or your little girlfriend to help you anymore."

"Where are they?" Chris asked, scrambling back on the hard ground into the darkness.

Will turned to Zamball and laughed.

"I asked you a question!" Chris shouted. He used the wall to help himself up, still clutching his side.

All Will did was look at Chris and smile.

"I swear, Will, if you don't tell me where they are I will—"

"You will what? Kill me? Because I doubt that you can do that without your brother's help. He'll have to find his way down here by himself. And by then"—Will looked at Zamball and shrugged—"it'll be too late."

"Down here?" Chris asked himself. He then turned and started to run back down the tunnel.

"You can't run from me, witch!" Will shouted after him. He made no attempt to chase him.

"Should we follow him?" Zamball asked.

Will held his stare down the corridor. "No. He'll summon his brother, and then we'll have both of them here to kill."

Chapter Twenty-Two

Chris ran in the darkness as fast as he could. He only stopped when he couldn't catch his breath. He fell to the ground, clutching his side, sobbing underneath a burning torch. Drew had never been his favorite person, but he didn't deserve to die like that. No one deserved to die like that. Especially when his killer showed no remorse. Chris hated Will more than ever now.

Trying to control himself, he wiped his eyes. He needed to think of his next move. He was the last hope for Holly and Kathy. Josh was still clueless to the fact that they were royally screwed.

Summoning Josh and the book wouldn't help much. If only there was a way to contact him to do the research prior to coming down here. Wherever here was.

But how long would that take? Chris wasn't sure if he would be able to hide out for that long. Worse, he wasn't sure how long

Holly and Kathy had. And what if Will summoned Josh first? Chris would be all on his own. There was no way he could handle it on his own. He would be fighting a losing battle.

He needed Josh at his side with or without the book. The two of them working together had a better chance at saving Holly and Kathy. But how would he summon him? Were his powers restricted "down here"? What if he was setting Josh up for a trap?

Chris shook his head. He was going to have to risk it.

He stood and muttered a spell. Not his best, but it worked.

In a swirl of white lights that nearly blinded Chris in the darkness, Josh appeared in front of him.

"Where were you!" Josh threw up his hands, "I got your message that you—" The dank light briefly shone across Chris's face, and Josh stopped dead. "What's the matter? Where are we?"

"Will killed him," Chris blurted, his face contorting as he once again was on the brink of tears.

"Who?"

"Drew! And Will took Holly's powers and kidnapped Aunt Kathy. What are we going to do, Josh?" He rubbed his face with both his hands and then ran them through his hair. He crouched on the ground, finding it easier than standing. His side throbbed from the bone-shattering kick Will had delivered.

"Okay, don't panic," Josh said. He knelt on the hard ground in front of Chris. "Where are we?"

"I don't know," Chris said. "But Will just killed Drew. He's dead, Josh. Just like Mom…and probably Holly and Aunt Kathy by now. He's going to kill us next!" He shook as he tried to hold back the tears.

THE BLOOD MOON

Josh grabbed his brother by the shoulders and said, "Listen to me, you need to calm down. Freaking out about it right now is not going to help anyone."

"Do you have any ideas?"

"Well, did Will or anyone say anything that might help us find them or figure out where we are? Anything?"

Chris shook his head. "Not really. He mentioned something about being 'down here.' But two minutes before that, I was unconscious, so I could be imagining that."

Josh shrugged. It was the best they had to go on. Once they figured out where they were, then they could better form a plan. "Let's say you aren't. Describe this place. What's the layout? Anything familiar?"

"No."

Josh slumped his shoulders and looked around. Chris was not much help. He stood and peered around the corner of the tunnel. "Hey, is this thing a maze?"

"What?" Chris was right behind Josh. He didn't want to risk getting separated.

"Here," Josh said, "where we are. Is it like a maze?"

"Yeah, I guess so," answered Chris. "There are a whole bunch of twists and turns and tiny spaces. But how is that—"

"And it's hot in here, with random fire pits." It was more of a statement than a question. Josh contemplated a moment longer, then announced to his brother, "I think we're in the underworld."

"The underworld?" Chris asked in disbelief. "Like from Greek mythology?"

"Well, yeah, why not?" Josh asked. "We've dealt with mythical things before. I mean, this might not be the exact thing the Greeks believed in, but it's the same idea."

"But we've only dealt with mythical beasts and stuff, not an actual place."

"So? Just because the centaurs we met didn't know about the underworld and other mythical things, doesn't mean they don't exist," Josh reasoned.

"Whatever," Chris said. It was the best lead they had yet. "So we're in the underworld. But right now we have worse problems. Holly is alone down here and doesn't have powers, and Aunt Kathy is probably with Will. Or will be soon."

The sand that covered the ground started to swirl in a circle, and a man appeared. His skin was the color of coffee, and he was dressed in black clothing.

"We knew it'd only be a matter of time before you summoned your brother," the man said.

Josh and Chris ran the opposite way, but their speed was slowed as the man shifted the sand under their feet.

As they ran, they could hear the man's voice but couldn't see him in the dimly lit catacombs.

Finally, they came to an open cavern with a rocky ledge. Chris, who was in the lead, hopped up first, but Josh tripped and fell waist deep in the sinking sand. Something was pulling him in from underneath. Lying on his stomach on the rock ledge and bracing himself for the pain in his side, Chris reached for his brother's arms and pulled him out of the sand and onto the ledge.

Once Josh was free and the boys were off the sand, the commotion and taunting voice stopped.

"Is he gone?" Chris wondered, gasping for breath and clutching his aching side.

Josh looked around the empty cavern. "I doubt it."

"Should we come up with a spell or something?"

Josh turned to his brother. "No. He's probably reporting to Will where he cornered us. Which means we have to act fast."

"And do what?"

"In Dante's book he describes the levels of the underworld, or the inferno," Josh explained. "I think I might know my way through it well enough. I just finished reading Dante in English class." Suddenly the question that every teenager groaned to their teachers popped into Josh's head: "When are we ever going to use this?" The relevance of a supposed "fictional" book was amusing in a terrible situation.

"It's a giant maze like the labyrinth; how are we supposed to find our way?" Chris asked.

"We should come up with a spell to guide us through the maze," Josh suggested. The earth began to quake again. "Quickly!"

The ground continued to shake as Chris fumbled for an effective rhyme. The ledge they stood on cracked down the middle, knocking the brothers off their feet.

"Chris!" Josh shouted to his brother as the rock fell, throwing the witches back onto the sand.

Springing to his feet, Chris recited:

DAVID NETH

In this place we call hell,
we need to find Holly's cell.
Let magic be our guide,
so we no longer have to hide.

White lights appeared and moved out of the cavern down a tunnel opposite the one they entered through. Josh and Chris raced after it, happily leaving the chaos behind them. At first, the boys tried to get their bearings as they followed the light, but with the many twists and turns, they eventually gave up.

The light stopped inside a cramped cave and shone over Holly's head, filling the room with light. She was chained to the wall, her head hanging low.

"Holly!" Chris ran to her.

Neither of the boys noticed the bats on the ceiling. The light from the spell woke them, and they left their perches and swarmed over Chris's head.

"Chris! Careful!" Josh warned.

The bats swarmed and rushed to attack Chris, but Josh sent them flying, kicking up sand in the process and creating a small cloud. Chris blew the bats up one by one. The bats' attacks were useless against the brother's teamwork.

After they were all destroyed, Chris ran to Holly.

He stuck a finger under her chin and lifted her head. "Holly, look at me." She was just waking up. He wondered if Will had drugged her. "Holly, come on, stay with me."

"Chris?" she groaned, her eyes barely opening.

"Yes!" Chris cheered. "Josh is here, too. We're going to get you out of here, okay?" He took her hand and looked at the chains cuffed to her wrists. "Don't move, I'm going to get rid of these restraints." Carefully, he focused his energy on breaking the chain that bound her to the wall. He wasn't able to remove the cuffs, but at least she was freed.

"We should move," Josh suggested. They had been in the same spot too long, and he wondered if Will had caught wind of their location. "We still need to find Aunt Kathy."

Chris nodded and helped Holly to her feet. She leaned on Chris for support but was waking up more and more.

"I'm so glad you're here," she said. She hugged Chris and added, "Will took my powers." She buried her face in his chest and repeated, "I'm glad you're here. Both of you."

"Something's up," Josh said. "It wasn't hard to get in here. I don't like it."

"He's probably watching us," Holly agreed.

"How?" Chris asked.

"With onyx crystals," she explained. "I thought it was just a myth, but my dad told me about these crystals that allow whoever holds the receiver to see everything that happens where they've planted the crystals."

"How do we know where they are?" Josh asked.

"Drew taught me a spell to summon all the onyx crystals in a building," Holly said. Chris was struck with the reminder of Drew. How would Holly handle what had happened to him? He felt responsible.

"So we should summon them," Josh considered.

"But after I summon them, Will will know, and he will come looking for us," she warned.

"So we'll just have to move fast," Josh said. "Are you up for it?"

Holly smirked. "Just because Will took my powers doesn't make me useless." She was standing on her own now, and besides a few minor cuts and some dirt, she looked okay.

She held out her hands, palms up, and recited:

Accioire!

In a white flash, five black crystals appeared in Holly's open hand.

"Four of them are what was planted, and the other one is the receiver," Holly explained. "Here, let's each take some so they don't end up in the wrong hands again." They each took a couple, stowing them in their pockets.

The earth began to shake again.

"This way!" Josh took off down the tunnel with Holly and Chris following close behind.

* * *

The trio raced through the maze, zigzagging to avoid the earthquakes. Drew was still lying on the floor, only now his throat had been slit and his blood was splattered all over.

THE BLOOD MOON

Holly screamed and fell to her knees, crying hysterically. Drew was dead. Not only dead, mutilated.

"Holly, I'm sorry." It was Chris. He gently touched her shoulder. "There was nothing I could do."

She shrugged his hand and turned to face him. "You knew about this? What, did you just stand there and watch him die?"

"Of course not! I was unconscious. Will was attacking me." He lifted his shirt and showed his developing bruise. "I ran to save myself. To save you, too."

"I bet you're pretty smug now that he's out of the picture," Holly spat through her tears.

"Holly!" Josh warned. "It wasn't Chris's fault. Yelling at him because you're angry Drew is dead is not going to help any. We need to be looking out for our own lives right now." He wiped the sweat from his forehead. Running was a bad idea in the underworld, but they were desperate. The heat was exhausting.

"I don't think anyone's getting out of this place," Chris said. "We're not leaving until either we die or Will dies."

"We're going to need Aunt Kathy for that, and even that might not be enough," Josh said. "Will has gotten stronger. I don't understand. I thought the blood moon isn't until April? Is this just a glimpse of the power Will will have once the blood moon comes?"

Chris's eyes shot between Holly and Josh. "The one in April is the second blood moon in a series of four. The first one was in October." He shrugged. "That's probably when Will first came to power."

"October!" Holly exclaimed. She thought of the times they taunted Will because they thought he was harmless. He could've easily killed them then, but he didn't. The feeling didn't sit well with her.

Josh was trying to process this new bit of information. They thought they still had time to figure out how to kill Will. "Okay… so do we have any ideas?"

"Why don't we use the spell that Holly used on Toxanna but change it to work for us?" Chris suggested.

"That's different. This isn't a family fight against Will," Josh said. "It won't work."

"Then why don't you come up with the spell rather than rely on me all the time!" Chris snapped.

Josh took a deep breath and bit his tongue. "This is not the time to start turning on each other. We need to work together to take out Will. I'll take care of the spell, and you try to prepare Holly for this. She's not going to be in the mood to fight with the loss of Drew." They looked over at her. She was still cradling Drew's head and crying. Her body shook with each sob, and she was covered in his blood.

Josh paced as he thought. He didn't have any paper, so he was forced to write parts of the spell on his arms and hands. He was grateful he still had the pen from the library in the pocket of his jeans. After about ten minutes, he had a spell that he thought might work.

Chris had talked to Holly, and she was ready to fight. She was still shaken up about Drew, but she was willing to try and channel the pain and anger into killing Will.

In a swirl of flames, Will appeared with Zamball.

"You witches are trickier than I thought you were," Will admitted. "Maybe I should take your powers before I kill you."

"What have you done to Drew?" Holly asked. She was no longer crying. Now she was pissed.

"You took my crystals, so I needed to find another way to keep an eye on you," Will explained. "The blood is a bit messy, though."

"Go to hell," she spat.

Will chuckled. "Don't you know where you are? Now, your powers…" He pulled two potions out of his pocket and threw them at Josh and Chris. Chris blew them up before they hit. "I'm going to love that power," Will said. He stepped closer to Chris and extended his hands toward him. Instead of coming into contact with him, Will's body moved through Chris's and possessed him.

Josh and Holly jumped back.

Zamball moved quickly and grabbed Josh's arms, restraining him. Will forced Chris's body to cut into his own arm with a knife from a table in the center of the room. He dribbled some of Chris's blood into the giant mixer on the table. He exited Chris's body, and Chris fell to the ground.

"Who's next?" Will asked, turning to the other two witches. He walked over to Josh, who was still restrained by Zamball. He took the knife and sliced into Josh's arm but stopped when he was hit with a hard rock. He turned and saw Holly by Chris. She had just hurled one of the onyx crystals at him. He held out his hand and pinned Holly to the wall before turning his attention back to Josh.

Will brought the mixer over to Josh's bleeding arm. He gripped the witch's arm and forced droplets of blood into the giant pot. He brought it back over to the table in the center of the room and muttered over it.

"What are you doing?" Josh asked. He knew there were a number of different curses you could apply to someone with their blood, and he was afraid to find out which one Will was going to use to do them in.

The Dark Knight sprinkled a few more ingredients into the potion and muttered a few more words. "Give it a minute to fester, and then it should be done." He patted his hands clean. "I'm going to steal your powers."

Josh was a little relieved. At least there would be no physical pain. But he wondered just how complete the magic-stealing would be. Would they be able to find a loophole in the midst of this crisis? Would they even survive that long?

Will spoke his dark magic and held out his hands, accepting the boys' powers as they floated out of their bodies and into his open hands. He clapped his hands together and began stirring the air with Josh's power.

The hold on Holly finally lifted, and she fell to the ground. She scrambled to reach Chris, who was just waking up.

Zamball let go of Josh and stood next to Will. "This will be such a good show. A fitting ending, I think."

"Shut up," Will muttered, feeding the growing tornado in the room.

Holly and Chris joined Josh and shielded their eyes as the wind kicked up sand.

"What are we going to do?" Holly asked Josh.

"We need to get to Aunt Kathy to say the spell," Josh said. His mind was racing with how they were going to manage that without their powers. He gripped his arm. The cut was deep, and he needed to apply pressure in order to stop the bleeding.

"We need a spell," Holly said.

The tornado was now self-sufficient, and Will stepped closer to the witches. "You know I could easily kill you with Chris's nice power, but where's the fun in that? See, I thoroughly enjoyed killing the wizard...Drew, was it?"

Holly gritted her teeth.

"Except he didn't really put up a fight. No chase, no attacks, nothing. Now you three"—Will waved his finger at them, stepping closer—"I know you'll put up a fight. So here we are. The ball's in your court. Now, please, entertain me."

Holly raised her second onyx crystal, but Josh grabbed her arm before she could throw it. "No."

"What!" Will faked surprised. "And it was just getting good. She was going to start throwing things!" He held his stomach as he laughed.

Chris closed his eyes, pictured his aunt, and said:

Bring my aunt to this here place.
Hurry now, we have little time to waste.

In a swirl of white lights, Kathy appeared. She had a black eye and a fat lip with scratches and gouges up her arms. Her clothes were torn, and her hair was a mess. She wrapped her arms around Chris and sighed a breath of relief until she saw Will.

"We need your help," Chris said, glancing at Will.

"Sweetheart!" Will said. "So nice of you to join us. Are you excited to watch your nephews die? I know I am!" He created a wind gust that sent Josh, Chris, and Holly back. In a swift move, he gripped Kathy's arm and dragged her next to him. She punched at his arm, trying to get him to let go.

"Easy, love," Will soothed. He created a fireball in his hand and turned to Chris. "Bet you didn't know you could do this, huh? What a shame your power never reached its potential with you." He tossed the burning mass in the air and caught it a couple of times. "Good thing I've got them now." He threw the ball at the witches, but they were able to dive out of the way.

"Where's the spell? We need to hurry," Chris said.

"How is Aunt Kathy going to say it?" Josh asked, dodging an attack from Zamball.

"She'll have to repeat after us!" Chris shouted so Kathy could hear.

"Where's the spell?" Holly asked. She clutched at her arm as a fireball grazed it, giving her a nasty burn.

Josh rolled up his sleeve. His arms were covered in pen marks. He had nowhere else to jot down ideas for the spell. He pointed near his elbow. "Here!"

THE BLOOD MOON

Chris and Holly recited the spell loudly so Kathy could hear. She echoed their chant.

For your evil ways you will be punished.
It's about time that you are finished.
Use the magic from our family.
We erase you now for all eternity.

The wind stopped suddenly, and Kathy freed herself from Will's grip, joining her nephews and Holly.

Thorns shot out of Will's sides, and he started to spin. White sparks encircled him, and he shattered in an enormous blast that sent everyone flying into the walls. Rocks started falling from the ceiling, and the ground shook.

The final earthquake caused some rocky debris to crash down on the witches, burying Chris and Kathy beneath it.

After the shaking stopped, white sparks appeared where Will once stood and entered into the witches.

"We have our powers back," Holly announced happily. She saw Chris and Kathy trapped beneath the rock and tried to move them, but some pieces were too heavy.

Josh used his newly restored powers to help unbury them. The sight wasn't pretty. Both Kathy and Chris had severe injuries. Josh guessed broken bones, if not more. Chris's ribcage would definitely need to be checked out.

Josh looked at Holly. "We need to get them to a hospital."

Chapter Twenty-Three

The witches stood in a loose semicircle watching the pyre burn. They were silent and let the heat from the fire flick across their faces.

"Do you want to say anything?" Kathy asked Holly. She had her broken arm in a sling after she and Chris spent a few weeks in the hospital. The weight of the fallen rocks had caused some internal bleeding for her as well, but she wasn't worried about it now that their biggest enemies were out of the picture.

Holly kept her gaze on the fire, watching her friend burn. It was a ritual of her family's. Burn the body so nothing could possess it and haunt them. She added a bit of rosemary before they placed the body and said a little charm to ensure that she would never forget Drew or his teachings.

She nodded and prepared herself to speak. She didn't know

if she'd even have a voice. She'd been so quiet since he passed, and it pained her but she wanted to wait for Kathy and Chris to get out of the hospital before she set Drew's soul free with the pyre. She had made sure to use a temporary preservation charm to prevent him from decaying any further while they waited.

She cleared her throat. "He was a great wizard, a great teacher, but most importantly a great friend. He taught me everything I know about witchcraft. At this point, all I can say is that I'm glad that we got justice for his death."

Chris reached over and put a hand on her shoulder. He was leaning on a pair of crutches, and his right leg was wrapped in a neon-green cast. His bare toes wiggled out from the end. Holly turned and buried her face in the crook of his neck and let out her tears. She had apologized to Chris for her accusations after finding Drew's body.

"Are we ready?" Josh asked, holding the magic book under his arm.

Holly nodded and Josh and Kathy stepped closer to her and Chris. Josh flipped through the pages in the magic book, past the newly added entry for Drew and all the blank pages that would soon be filled with his many recipes for potions. Once Josh found the correct incantation to conclude the ceremony, the four witches recited aloud:

> *Ashes to ashes, dust to dust,*
> *in our power you must trust.*
> *It's time to let your soul go free.*
> *We send you off for eternity.*

Drew's body became brightly illuminated, and the witches turned their heads from the light. When they turned back, his body was gone and the pyre was dying down.

Holly took a deep breath and broke the silence, voicing the worry that all of them were thinking: "Just because Will's dead doesn't mean that the fight is over."

Keep Reading

Book two, *The Full Moon*, is a prequel to *The Blood Moon* and chronicles Kathy and Will's dark history together. Pick it up and let the story continue!

Leave a Review

If you enjoyed this book please consider leaving a review online. This helps future readers determine whether or not this book is something they might want to immerse themselves in as well. If you really liked this book, feel free to sign up for my mailing list and follow me online. Thank you for your support!

Stay In The Loop

Help out an indie author and subscribe to my newsletter! Subscribers will be the first to receive information on upcoming releases. What are you waiting for? Head over to www.davidnethbooks.com to sign up!

About the Author

David Neth started writing at the age of twelve. The first draft of The Blood Moon was written while he was in high school. Since then he has graduated from Medaille College in Buffalo, New York and Pace University in New York City. He lives in Batavia, New York. This is his first novel.

Follow the Author

www.davidnethbooks.com
www.facebook.com/davidnethbooks
www.twitter.com/davidnethbooks
www.instagram.com/dneth13

Acknowledgements

This novel started when I was very young and had a lot to learn. I still
have a lot to learn, but I've come a long way from the fifteen-year-
old who would rush home from school to type up the next chapter
of this story. These characters have been with me for nearly a decade
and have grown and developed on their own with the help of the
real-world guidance given to me by friends, family, teachers, and now
colleagues. I hope everyone who has been a part of this project knows
how much I appreciate their support.

www.ingramcontent.com/pod-product-compliance
Lightning Source LLC
Chambersburg PA
CBHW031217120726
47905CB00002B/375